Alex T. Smith

MURDER! BY NARWHAL!

A Grimacres Whodunnit!

HODDER

HODDER CHILDREN'S BOOKS

First published in Great Britain in 2024 by Hodder & Stoughton

1 3 5 7 9 10 8 6 4 2

Text and illustrations copyright © Alex T. Smith, 2024

The moral right of the author has been asserted.

A CIP catalogue record for this book
is available from the British Library.

ISBN 978 1 444 97005 0
WTS ISBN 978 1 444 98123 0

Printed and bound by
CPI (UK) Ltd, Croydon CR0 4YY

The paper and board used in this book
are made from wood from responsible sources.

MIX
Paper | Supporting
responsible forestry
FSC® C104740

Hodder Children's Books
An imprint of
Hachette Children's Group
Part of Hodder & Stoughton Limited
Carmelite House
50 Victoria Embankment
London EC4Y 0DZ

An Hachette UK Company
www.hachette.co.uk

www.hachettechildrens.co.uk

THIS BOOK IS FOR SIDNEY R. THOMAS,
WHO LOVED STORIES, SNOW AND
PUZZLING OUT WHODUNNITS.

A. T. S.

CONTENTS

The GRISTLE FAMILY TREE

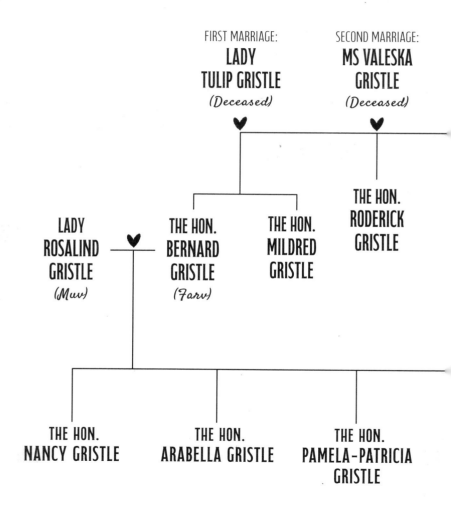

FIRST MARRIAGE:
LADY TULIP GRISTLE
(Deceased)

SECOND MARRIAGE:
MS VALESKA GRISTLE
(Deceased)

THE HON. RODERICK GRISTLE

LADY ROSALIND GRISTLE
(Muv)

THE HON. BERNARD GRISTLE
(Farv)

THE HON. MILDRED GRISTLE

THE HON. NANCY GRISTLE

THE HON. ARABELLA GRISTLE

THE HON. PAMELA-PATRICIA GRISTLE

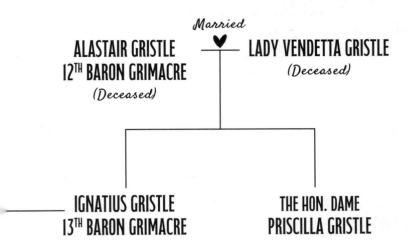

ALASTAIR GRISTLE
12TH BARON GRIMACRE
(Deceased)

Married

LADY VENDETTA GRISTLE
(Deceased)

IGNATIUS GRISTLE
13TH BARON GRIMACRE

THE HON. DAME
PRISCILLA GRISTLE

THE HON.
PERSEPHONE
GRISTLE

THE HON.
AUDREY GRISTLE

THE HON.
EDMUND GRISTLE

THE HON.
EDNA GRISTLE

THE HON. MILDRED GRISTLE

THE HON. RODERICK GRISTLE

THE HON. BERNARD GRISTLE (FARV) & LADY ROSALIND GRISTLE (MUV)

IGNATIUS GRISTLE, 13TH BARON GRIMACRE

MRS DEIRDRE CRUMPET

DR LILLIAN M^cDOUGAL

DETECTIVE BADGER (RETIRED)

THE HON. AUDREY GRISTLE

THE HON. DAME PRISCILLA GRISTLE

MISS GIOVANNA BELLISSIMA

MISS GLORIA BLOUSE

PROLOGUE

I never thought I would be lucky enough to stumble across a dead body because I don't have a dog.

In the newspapers, corpses are always found by people out on bracing morning walks with their spaniel, or whatever. Might be a Labrador, of course. Could even be a chihuahua. Anyway, the walk will begin perfectly normally, but then suddenly the hound will go racing ahead excited by an enticing pong. They dive into a hedge and disappear into the undergrowth, and you can call them until you are blue in the face but they will absolutely not come back. You might as well talk to a rock.

Then, five minutes later, the panting owner (mud-covered now with twigs knotted in their hair and their specs on sideways) comes hoofing through the bracken and discovers their pooch sniffing about at a corpse with an axe in its head. It doesn't have to be an axe in their head. They might have been twanged by a crossbow, for example, or throttled with an old bootlace or something. That's not the point. The point is that some people have dogs and those people have all the luck.

I always hoped that one day one of the corpse-finders would be me. I think I could strike the right balance between being shocked whilst at the same time taking in all the details so I could be terrifically useful to the police. I'd gasp in startled amazement so beautifully because I've been practising for years. But like I say – so far no dog: no dead bodies.

What I *do* have though is a pet tortoise called Charles Darwin. He's marvellous in many ways but as a rule, tortoises aren't the best at finding anything. Well, they are good at finding a bit of cucumber to furiously chomp on, but nothing much else. So really it was *quite* a stroke of luck that Charles Darwin should actually lead me to find my first dead body. It wasn't (as I'd imagined) in a woodland clearing, but you don't always get everything in life and you have to celebrate the successes you do get.

But I'm gabbling ahead of myself. If I am going to tell you about what happened that weekend at Grimacres, I probably need to start from the beginning. But where IS the beginning? The murder wasn't the start of it all, but it was the start of *my* investigation, or as SOME members of my family called it at the time, my 'nose-poking'. Of course the real story started well before then. Well before even the narwhal got involved.

Oh, I forgot to mention that a narwhal, that great tusked, swimming mammal, is involved, but more on that later.

So where DO I begin? I've been sitting here chewing the end of my pencil trying to decide. I suppose, for me at least, it all began on the Friday . . .

GREAT ANCIENT HOUSES OF ENGLAND: ## THE GOOD AND THE DREADFUL.

by Felicity Wattle-Daub.

Without doubt the most foreboding of England's great houses, Grimacres crouches, all blackened brickwork and maliciously glinting windowpanes, like a great, evil toad in a deep valley six miles from the picturesque ancient market town of Much Maudlin.

Set within extensive and sprawling grounds and surrounded by a thick ring of its own privately owned forest, Grimacre Wood, the house is accessed via one thin and winding road which in bad weather regularly, and by design of the Gristle ancestors, cuts the house off from the rest of civilisation.

A residence has stood on the current Grimacres plot since well before medieval times, and the house and grounds have been added to and altered significantly since then by successive members of the Gristle family. The current facade of the house was built by Lord Hades Gristle and looks not unlike a fortress or even a prison.

Due in part to its remote location, but mainly because of the owner's dim view of — to use their phrase — 'sticky-beaked nose-pokers', the exact design and construction of the interior of Grimacres is clothed in myth and mystery. It is unknown how many rooms the vast, sprawling property has, and rumours abound of secret passages, ghostly occurrences and even hidden treasure!

(It ought to be added that the author of this book did write to the owner for verification of these facts and we received our letter back, ripped up with a large note stuck to it that simply said 'NO'.)

It's believed that the current owner, Ignatius Gristle, Baron Grimacre, lives at the property with some members of his extended family as well as an enormous collection of artefacts collected from around the world.

Despite his age, Ignatius Gristle remains the CEO of The Jolly BonBon LTD confectionery company, although the management of the company is handled by his only daughter, the Hon. Mildred Gristle.

More information regarding the family can be found in the book 'A GUIDE TO THE BRITISH ARISTOCRACY' by Sir Henry Fox-Hunt.

WARNING:

Unlike many great country houses that welcome visitors wholeheartedly with a cafe full of buns, the author of this book would advise readers NOT to enter the Grimacres estate under ANY circumstances.

Visitors are NOT welcome and anyone who does call at the property does so at their own tremendous risk.

PART ONE:
A MOVEABLE ZOO

'Little Grey Cells: A Complete Guide to Detection' by Mary Mead. Published by Machette Books. From the personal library of the Hon. Edna Gristle.

CHAPTER 1.
UNSUITABLE BOOKS FOR CHILDREN ABOUT MURDER

We arrived at Grimacres on Friday afternoon just in time for tea, which was good because I was absolutely gasping for a scone.

I was keen to be out of the old Daimler and back in the familiar shadowy walls of my grandpa's house. The journey from London had taken HOURS and every bit of it had been awful because Sid, our chauffeur, has disappeared so Farv was driving us himself. Outside, the snow that had been threatening for days started to fall the minute we set off and it only got worse as we crawled out of the city and travelled up north to Grimacres. By the time we'd squeezed down the narrow lane through the woods into the Grimacres estate, a full blizzard was swirling around us.

The mood inside the car had been just as chilly. Ice cold

and crow black. Everyone (apart from me and Charles Darwin) was in a <u>frightful</u> mood and hadn't uttered a word to each other for the entire journey. Muv was up front, sleek as a she-wolf and hunkered down in her fur collar, livid that she'd had to cancel all her tennis lessons with her very dear friend, Valentino. Farv was growling with temper too about, well, everything. A bad mood had been inflating him like a balloon for weeks, but Grandpa demanding we leave that morning *immediately* seemed to have finally made it burst. Farv crouched over the steering wheel, huffing and puffing like a grampus and driving terribly.

In the back I kept schtum, cursing myself for having eaten the last of my Halloween bonbons before we'd even made it out of our road. After I'd put Charles Darwin into the tea cosy he wears as a jumper on trips to Grandpa's, I realised I had NOTHING to do. As a rule, I don't believe in boredom, but after I'd spent a few nice minutes chewing the end of my plaits, I had to admit that all I *could* do for the rest of the journey was sit quietly with Charles Darwin on my lap and twiddle my thumbs.

What I was panting to do, of course, was get stuck into the book I was reading. It was a terribly good one – all about MURDERS: how they were committed (grisly!) and how the killers were eventually caught (cunning!). REALLY THRILLING STUFF! But Muv (spoilsport) disagrees.

She says my preferred reading matter is *distasteful*. She

wishes I'd read nice books about flower arranging and tittering behind fans and how to seat guests correctly at candlelit suppers. She says these are Useful Subjects for Young Ladies, but honestly who has time for all that sort of nonsense? I don't and neither does Charles Darwin.

The reason I couldn't read my book secretly in the car was because my sister Audrey was sitting beside me and like all siblings she does have a tendency to ruin things. She sat glaring sullenly out of the window, seemingly lost in her own furious thoughts. I knew from experience that didn't mean anything though. All I'd have to do was turn the page too loudly or chortle too uproariously and she'd be tattle-taling on me until the cows came home, and I didn't want to risk another row erupting.

There'd already been a stinker earlier that day when Grandpa's invitation had plopped on the mat. Audrey had immediately started her caterwauling: she <u>COULDN'T</u> leave London this weekend, she <u>HAD</u> to stay. <u>WHY</u> couldn't she be left on her own? URGH, <u>everything</u> was so unfair – NONE of the rest of our other sisters or our brother had to go!

'They don't live here any more,' I said, helpfully, 'and anyway *I'm* one of your sisters and *I* have to go . . .'

Audrey looked at me with one of her narrow-eyed snake looks and spat: 'You don't count!'

There's absolutely no arguing with her when she's in a poisonous mood like this, so I just stumped upstairs to throw some pants in my suitcase. Eventually, after a lot of shouting and door slamming, and Audrey even storming out of the house for a bit, we finally set off. And now, hours later, and almost frozen solid, we had arrived at Grimacres.

As we stumbled, stiff-legged from the car, I took a moment to look up at the house. It loomed over us, big and black against the darkening sky and the white falling snow. I saluted to the two hideous gargoyles that leered down at us from above the porch, but they didn't salute back. They never do. Despite that, I couldn't help but grin. I was delighted to be back at Grimacres, but little did I know then that the countdown to a murder had already begun.

TICK

TOCK . . .

A stuffed deer head, slightly
moth eaten, from the main
hall at Grimacres.

CHAPTER 2.
A SHIVER OF DANGER AT THE BACK OF THE NECK

Aunt Mildred met us at the door, crossing her cardi tightly over her bust and telling us to 'Get in! Get in! Get in!' before we all froze to death.

We got in! Got in! Got in! And she slammed the door firmly behind us.

Aunt M looked like she always did and by that I mean she looked just like Farv. They really could have been twins, except that they aren't. Farv's a bit older, but the likeness is extraordinary. If you cut Aunt M's hair and drew a moustache on her she'd look just like him, or if you shaved Farv, gave him a wig and threw some pearls around his neck he'd look just like her. I might suggest us doing that one day to see if my theory is correct. Now wasn't the time though.

'Goodness, it's absolutely FREEZING out there!' said Aunt

M with a shiver. Her voice sounded tinny and echoey in the cavernous entrance hall.

It was hardly warmer inside. In fact, as I reluctantly wiggled free from my coat, I decided it was definitely colder inside than out. There was an enormous fireplace in the hallway but no fire crackling in it. There never was. Grandpa was a selfish cockroach of a person who only believed in heating the rooms that *he* was currently in. As he left a room he would tip water over the flames. For that reason, the temperature inside Grimacres was always so arctic it would have sent a polar bear reaching for a flask of hot chocolate and a couple of pairs of thick thermal knickers.

As everyone messed about with coats and taking off hats I looked appraisingly around the place. I was glad to see nothing had changed in the hallway since I was last there. That's one of the things I like about Grimacres – it's always exactly the same.

The entrance hall, as big as a ballroom, was panelled with wood stained so dark that it looked black. The vast stone staircase twisted like a broken leg into the gloom above us, and from every wall hundreds of pairs of glass eyes peered at us from the stuffed deer heads mounted on every vertical surface.

I saw Muv and Audrey shudder as they looked at them.

Muv really hates Grimacres. She says the entire place pulsates with a sinister energy. She likes light, bright fussy fabrics with tasselly trims, and vases of pungent flowers. She doesn't like the sorts of houses that have stuffed deer heads staring at you from the walls, or samurai warrior outfits lined up along a landing, or an ancient Egyptian sarcophagus leant up against a chimney breast or an enormous sixteenth-century cannon parked outside the dining room. Grimacres has all of those things.

I don't find it spooky at all. Of course I'd prefer it if the deer weren't dead, but they were dispatched that long ago by Gristles since departed that they're now just like objects in a museum to me. Also, a house as big as Grimacres could make you feel a bit like a lonely little pea rattling about in it, so it's very nice to have a few fluffy snouts sticking out of the walls to pat when you are on your way to the bathroom for a wee for example.

'Right – tea?' said Aunt M briskly. She pointed down the hall. 'We'll take it in the drawing room.' Then she dropped her voice. 'I've got a great big fire lit, but don't tell Daddy.'

I was about to dash off and find Archie, but at the mention of 'tea' my stomach growled angrily and I decided that Archie could wait. If I didn't have a scone immediately, I would simply collapse. I set off at a march down the hall to the drawing room because I don't need telling twice when food is involved, but Farv started to turn the other way.

'Actually, Mil, I . . . er . . . I'll just stick my head in to see the old man – he's in his study, I presume? Just er . . .

need to have a quick word with him about' – he swallowed hard and looked a bit tight about the collar – 'something er . . . important.' He tried to sound jolly, but I could tell he was nervous. He was pulling at his moustache which is a sure sign that he's feeling jumpy. I wondered what the important thing was that he needed to chat to Grandpa about because usually we all try to avoid speaking to him if we don't have to. Grandpa has a horrible habit of being obnoxious and biting your ear off every time he speaks.

Farv was heading for Grandpa's study, but Aunt M stopped him with a hand placed on his arm.

'Oh no, you can't do that I'm afraid, Bernard,' she said quietly, and I noticed for the first time that she too was looking a bit tight and tense about her edges. 'Daddy said that under no circumstances must he be disturbed. He doesn't want to see anyone until dinner this evening. He's very busy this afternoon.'

I strained my ears and sure enough I could hear the distant clack of a typewriter coming from the direction of Grandpa's study.

'Doing what?' said Farv, all crinkle-browed. '*You* run the company!'

'Oh yes,' said Aunt M, doing that thing she does when *she's* a bit unsure of herself which is to fuss with the tissue she keeps shoved up the sleeve of her twinset. 'But he's busy with *separate* business matters at the moment.

With his new secretary . . .'

Muv and Farv's eyebrows hit the ceiling. 'New secretary?' said Farv, tugging at his moustache. 'First I've heard of it.'

'Yes, well,' said Aunt M. 'Hired her whilst he was away in Italy . . .' She pursed her lips after that and said something to Muv and Farv with just her eyes that I didn't quite understand.

I knew enough though to know that the look meant Aunt M had *quite* a lot she wanted to say about this new development but only when my earholes were out of the room.

'Fine,' sighed Farv like a deflating balloon. 'Plenty of time to speak to him later, I suppose.'

'Just you make sure you do,' hissed Muv under her breath, but of course Big Ears (me) heard her all right.

If there was one thing I knew about Grandpa, it was that he hated strangers – loathed them – so this information about a new secretary made my brain twitch. The arrival of a person not just to the grounds of Grimacres, but actually *into* the house and into Grandpa's study – well, that was unheard of and Farv was acting very strangely too. I didn't know why at the time, but it made all the hairs on the back of my neck stand up.

I think it was then that I got my first hint that something unusual, maybe even dangerous, was going to happen that weekend.

China teacup from the Gristle family tea set, decorated with a pattern of poison ivy and toxic mushrooms. Mid 17th century.

CHAPTER 3.
A SUNBURNT FERRET

Aunt M threw open the door to the drawing room and I raced in to find a woman warming her hands in front of the fire. She had short hair and was wearing a pair of flannel slacks and a thick jumper. I beamed when I saw her.

'LIL!' I cried.

She turned round and groaned. 'Oh no! Not YOU!' she sighed in a soft Scottish accent. Then she smiled a twinkle-eyed smile and ruffled my hair.

OOH, I LOVE LIL! It's Doctor Lillian McDougal, actually, but because we are really rather great chums, I call her Lil. She calls me Trouble.

What I like best about her is that she is the only adult who will sit down and have a really good natter with me about infected blisters. Glorious!

'I'll ring for tea now,' said Aunt M, pressing a little button on the wall that ding-dongs down in the kitchen. 'I expect you're all gasping for one after your journey!'

'I certainly am!' said Lil. 'And I've only come up from Much Maudlin. Foul day out there!'

'Look, is everything all right?' asked Farv anxiously as he and Muv sat themselves down on one end of the long sofa. Audrey threw herself sulkily into an armchair and Charles Darwin and I plumped down on the enormous tiger skin rug in front of the fire. 'With Father, I mean?'

'What, medically?' said Lil. She perched on the arm of Aunt M's chair. 'Yes, everything's perfectly OK. I'm here as a guest today.'

She flicked her head in the direction of Grandpa's office. 'He's ticking over fine – not that he ever believes me . . .'

She sighed. 'I can't do right by him at all. Do you know just before he went away to Italy, he said that he actually thought I was poisoning him! Ha! I said, "You can get yourself another doctor, Ignatius!" But he wouldn't, of course. Had me up and down here like a yo-yo demanding medicines for this, tablets for that. I'm telling you – these last few months without him here has been like a holiday for us, hasn't it?'

She gave Aunt M's shoulder a gentle squeeze.

'It's been lovely!' said Aunt M, smiling up at Lil.

As well as being our family doctor, Lil is also Aunt M's special friend. They are always together and Lil is one of the few people Grandpa will allow in the house – although that's for selfish reasons of course. He likes to be checked over daily to make sure nothing is wrong with him. Mum says he's staying alive out of spite.

Aunt M has a nice face, but often – like earlier when we'd been in the hall – it can look rather cloudy and pinched with worry. She runs the family business – The Jolly BonBon Ltd – practically on her own. It's a big job and Grandpa, who is *meant* to be retired, will insist on causing trouble. He's a horrible bully who enjoys sticking his nose in. He MEDDLES and often poor Aunt M has the look of someone who is quietly trying to work out fiendish sums in her head, which I suppose with her job, she often is. But whenever Lil is around, Aunt M brightens, as if the sun has just come out.

'But he's back now,' said Lil, her brow furrowed, 'and worse than ever!'

'Oh . . .' said Farv, wrinkle-browed.

'*I* rather wondered if we'd been called here because he was dying or something?' said Muv hopefully, as she flung one slim leg over another.

Aunt M laughed a rather hollow laugh. 'Oh no, dear. Daddy's too hearty for words!'

'Pity . . .' said Farv darkly.

'Then what's all this about?' huffed Muv. 'Mildred, it's obviously always pleasant to see you both, but really – coming up here for the weekend with no notice is too inconvenient for words! I've had to cancel a weekend FULL of tennis lessons with Valentino and I barely had a chance to let him know – had to leave a message for him. Goodness knows what he'll think . . .'

'I'm sure he'll cope . . .' said Farv dryly.

His eyes flickered to mine and a slight smile twitched under his moustache. I stifled a laugh. Valentino is Muv's very close friend and tennis teacher. She finds him delightful, but Farv and I can't stand him, although I do find him rather fascinating in a scientist-observing-a-specimen sort of way. Valentino really is extraordinary to look at. He must be about seven foot tall and handsome too, I suppose, if you like that sort of thing, which I don't. All year round he's tanned the colour of a polished mahogany table and his arms are so bumpy with muscles that he looks like he's shoved a load of balled-up socks up his sleeves. He's not what I call ha-ha-bonk funny, but Muv titters at everything he says. The pair of them are always off together in their matching pristine tennis whites, her with their expensive rackets and him with the balls. It's a blessing really, because when Muv's off playing tennis, she's not bothering me about standing up straight or brushing my hair or not wiping my mouth on my sleeve.

Muv ignored Farv and ploughed on. 'So go on, Mildred, what's he playing at demanding we come up at such short notice?'

Aunt M shrugged her fluffy shoulders. 'I've no idea! This

morning he just ordered Mrs Crumpet to get the rooms ready and told me you'd all be arriving later today. It was the first we'd heard about it, although obviously we're delighted you're here!'

Farv's forehead was a concertina of frowning wrinkles.

'I wonder if it's something to do with his birthday tomorrow? He'll be ninety . . . Although he usually just ignores birthdays.'

Before anyone could answer, the door creaked open and into the room came not as we'd expected, Mrs Crumpet, the Grimacres housekeeper and cook, but a man. He was carting an enormous tray heaving with toast and butter, scones and jam and teapots and teacups. It looked delicious and made my belly growl like a bear.

The food at home in London had taken rather a nose-dive recently, both in quality AND quantity. Our cook, Mrs Crabb, used to keep us well fed with all sorts of lovely things. You couldn't move for jam jars at breakfast for example, all different varieties. But that's changed recently and for the past few months we'd been rationed to one pot of blackcurrant jam (the worst flavour) and the bread's been like cardboard. The sight of Mrs Crumpet's glorious tea tray filled me with bursting confetti cannons of joy.

The man carrying the tray advanced at a snail's pace all hunched over, the tray shaking and the cups jangling in his jittering hands.

'You . . . rang for tea, m'lady,' he said in a quavering voice as he placed the tray on the table. Then in a flash he straightened up and grinned round at everyone and in his normal, drawling voice said, 'I make an excellent elderly butler, don't I?'

Well, no actually, he didn't, because he'd sloshed hot tea over half the tray. Also he couldn't have looked less like a butler if he'd tried. It was my Uncle Roderick, and he looked, I thought, like a very sunburnt ferret.

Uncle Roderick is Farv and Aunt M's younger brother. Half-brother, actually. He was born much later when Grandpa remarried after my granny died yonks before I was born. He's very tall and slim with a pencil-thin moustache and hangs about with the type of people that Farv sniffs at and Muv calls 'Most Unsuitable'. He lives abroad in roasting hot places and swans about there in pastel linen slacks and open neck shirts. He was wearing that now which looked completely out of place in the dark, arctic gloom of Grimacres.

'Oh Roderick, you are silly!' said Aunt M. 'Now, when did you get here?'

'Just now,' said Uncle Roderick. 'Flew in this morning, got a car and came straight up. Filthy weather as per! People are abandoning their cars out there – one's wedged in a snow drift just up the road, but I battled valiantly through!' He puffed out his chest. 'Couldn't deprive you of seeing your dearest baby brother, could I?'

Farv snorted. He doesn't like Uncle Roderick.

'Oh! I didn't hear the front door go . . .' said Aunt M.

'It was unlocked anyway, but I met dear Mrs Crumpet in the hall and she saw me in. I said I'd bring the tray in for her. Told her it would give me a chance to slip some poison into the pot first!'

He grinned a devilishly devious grin. I laughed loudly – I rather like Uncle Roderick when he is in this sort of mood – but no one else did so I piped down pretty quickly and stroked Charles Darwin on the tea cosy.

'Well, that was very kind of you,' said Aunt M, vaguely. 'Well, sit yourself down and have some tea and – oh! Who's this?'

We all turned to look.

Uncle Roderick had thrown himself on to the sofa allowing us all to notice for the first time that behind him, in the darkness beyond the flickering light of the fire and the dim, little table lamps, someone was lurking.

Fang (slightly chipped) from a
tiger skin rug. Early 18th century.
Originally from India.

CHAPTER 4.
AN UNSUITABLY DRESSED MOUSE

It was a woman.

'Hello,' she squeaked in a little mouse voice as she stepped forward nervously.

'Oh yes,' said Uncle Roderick, shoving a whole slice of toast into his gob and talking with his mouth full. 'Family: this is my girlfriend, Gloria Blouse. Gloria: my family.'

A look fluttered between Muv and Farv and I knew exactly what that one meant. It meant, 'Oh . . . here we go – another one!' because every time we see Uncle Roderick, he has a different person on his arm and they always, without fail, look exactly the same.

Gloria Blouse was no different. Small and glamorous with big blonde hair and great blinking blue eyes like a startled bushbaby. She was, like Uncle R, completely unsuitably dressed for a winter weekend in an English country house. Poking out from under her sundress I saw that her stockingless knees had turned mint green with cold and she was shivering all over like she'd just clambered out of the North Sea.

'I meant to check if it was OK for her to come,' continued Uncle Roderick. 'But well . . . you know how it is.'

'Oh yes, you are always very busy, aren't you, Rod?' said Farv. 'Just wish we knew what it is you exactly do.'

Farv and Uncle Roderick locked poison-dart eyes with each other before Uncle Roderick turned to Aunt M instead.

'Be all right, won't it, Mil?' he said.

More flustered tissue fussing from Aunt M. I knew what she was thinking – that Grandpa wouldn't like an unexpected stranger in the house – but after a moment she smiled a tight smile and said of course it was fine and told Gloria she <u>MUST</u> come and get herself nice and warm by the fire.

Gloria smiled nervously and settled herself down next to Uncle Roderick, politely thanking Farv, who placed a hot cup of tea into her shaking hand. Me and Charles Darwin were quite toasty by now so I thrust the tiger skin rug at her to put over her knees, but all she did was scream as its large fangs clonked against her hand.

I tutted. *Another one frightened of everything in this house*, I thought, rolling my eyes at Charles Darwin. He looked at me as if he agreed.

'Where is Father anyway? The old reptile not joining us?'

said Uncle Roderick, slapping my hand away from the scone I was about to help myself to and taking it himself. 'Need to see if he might like to help his little boy out . . .'

Farv snorted again. 'What mess do you need him to get you out of this time?' he growled. Uncle Roderick ignored him, but was annoyed when Aunt M said Grandpa was busy until after dinner.

'Busy?' cried Uncle Roderick, 'Oh I like that! Orders me back urgently from abroad – AT MY EXPENSE, I MIGHT ADD – only to be too busy to see his darling baby son! A fine welcome, that is!' Roderick chomped furiously on the scone. 'What is this sudden, urgent house party for anyway?' he said, spraying crumbs everywhere.

'That's exactly what we were all wondering,' said Muv. 'He's definitely up to something. If he's got us here to celebrate his birthday, I must say that's a bit rich. He's never been a bit bothered about birthdays before, his or anyone else's. Never a card for his own children or grandchildren – the nasty, mean old snake!'

'Ros!' said Farv, but only half-heartedly. None of us could disagree with Muv on this point.

'All I know,' said Aunt M, in a soothing voice, 'is that Daddy wants us all together this weekend. I expect we'll all find out why soon enough. It must be rather important . . .'

We all pondered this in almost-silence, punctuated only by the sound of me chewing. The grown-ups seemed tense which made my nerves feel unexpectedly jangly. Audrey wasn't eating so I slid the slice of toast off her plate and started on that to distract me.

'Who else is coming this weekend?' said Uncle Roderick, trying to lighten the mood. 'Just a cosy, little family get-together I take it?'

'Yes, just us,' said Aunt M, dusting cake crumbs off her bosom. 'Well, and George is coming, of course, and also—'

Everyone groaned.

'Not BADGER!' cried Uncle Roderick. 'Why does HE have to come?'

'Because he's an old and very dear friend of the family,' said Aunt M, firmly, 'and he's been very helpful keeping Daddy entertained . . .'

'Only person dull enough to find Father interesting,' mumbled Uncle Roderick.

'And besides,' continued Aunt M, talking over Roderick's low grumble, 'he was SUCH a help to us all back in February with . . . you know, *The Incident.*'

I'll admit that my earwigging on the conversation had been flagging a bit up to this point. Grown-ups can't half go on, but with those two little words – *The Incident* – I sat bolt upright.

Black velvet eyepatch, embroidered with a skull and crossbones motif, personal property of the Hon. Edna Gristle.

CHAPTER 5.
SECRET WINKS AND MYSTERIOUS PACKAGES

Here we go! I thought, mentally rubbing my hands together. At last I was going to find out what had actually happened here last February. Charles Darwin and I got ourselves ready to listen *very* carefully indeed.

For months now I'd heard whispers about *The Incident*. Something had happened here at Grimacres just before Grandpa went off on his long holiday, but no one will tell me what it is. I hadn't been here since, so I hadn't had a chance to ask Archie yet. Audrey seems to know, but I haven't been able to wheedle it out of her yet either. And there was nothing in her secret diary about it when I checked. That's one of the several annoying things about Audrey: unless it's twirling about in a tutu, she simply isn't interested. Now, however, with this fresh mention of *The Incident*, my ears were practically on stalks with the effort of listening. I was determined to find out what the mysterious event was, but unfortunately, Aunt M just breezed on.

'And of course Daddy's new secretary is here too,' she said, 'and will be joining us for dinner.'

BLAST!

'What?' said Uncle Roderick.

Lil whistled a low whistle.

'Oh yes!' she said, grinning. 'None of you have met the marvellous Miss Bellissima yet, have you?' Her eyes were sparkling with glee now. 'I think Ignatius has taken QUITE a shine to her! SMITTEN I'd say . . .'

Everyone shuffled closer to Lil (even Charles Darwin) but before she could continue, Aunt M coughed a polite little cough and her eyes darted in my direction.

'Go on,' I said to Lil encouragingly, ignoring the look.

'Edna, dear,' said Aunt M, 'I wonder if you'd like to go and see Mrs Crumpet in the kitchen. Take Charles Darwin down for a lettuce leaf or something? I'm sure she has lots of nice nibbly things for him.'

'Oh, he's all right thanks, Aunt M!' I said, brightly. 'He's just been eating the fringing on the bottom of the sofa.'

'Edna, do as you're told!' growled Muv.

She wanted me out of the room too, I knew it. They all did. Just when things were getting interesting!

They think when you are eleven you don't know anything,

but you know when grown-ups want to have a chinwag behind your back.

I tutted, got up and walked slug-slow towards the door. I've got a slight limp on account of one of my legs currently being a bit shorter than the other, so I played that up a bit too. I was hoping they'd all feel sorry for me and beg me to stay.

Suddenly, a hand shot out and grabbed my wrist.

'Just a moment!' said Lil, and I brightened. Good old Lil! She'd never chuck me out of the room!

'Come here, Long John Silver!' she said. 'Let me check your eye!'

I've got a case of Floating Iris too, hence the eye patch. I should have explained that earlier, I think. It's not painful or anything, and apparently it'll get better on its own as long as I keep it covered. Lil likes to keep an eye (ha ha!) on it for me. She's the one that sorted me out with my snazzy eyepatch. It's black with a secret skull embroidered on it that you can only see when it catches the light. Muv *loathes* me wearing it. She said it isn't ladylike at all. I just snorted because on the subject of many things, dear Muv is useless. How she can't see that it lends me a dashing, piratical look that a lot of people my age are sadly lacking, I do not know.

Lil gave my eye the once over. 'Looking good!' she said. 'Keep the patch on though, won't you?'

I nodded. Lil's the only person I do as I'm told for.

'Now,' she said, pulling a parcel wrapped in brown paper out of her doctor's bag, 'if you're going downstairs, I wonder if you might be able to pass this to Mrs Crumpet for me. It's some, er . . . vitamins she asked for.'

I looked down at the package and saw quite clearly that instead of Mrs Crumpet's name, my name was scrawled across it in Lil's awful, spidery handwriting.

FOR THE ATTENTION OF MISS EDNA GRISTLE.
TOP SECRET!

I grinned and Lil gave me a secret wink. Then I practically skedaddled out of the room.

I paused with my hand on the doorknob for a moment just to give the grown-ups the opportunity to invite me to stay, but no chance. Muv was glaring at me, but Lil had turned back and started talking again.

'So, Miss Bellissima!' Lil was saying. 'She must be the most efficient woman in all of Italy. Practically running the joint here at Grimacres! Thick as thieves, she and old Ignatius are!'

'Italy?' said a squeaky high-pitched voice. The sound made us all jump.

It was Gloria and this was the first thing she'd said apart from hello and thank you to Farv for the tea. She'd melted into the sofa cushions after that. Now, however, she was sitting bolt upright on the sofa, eyes as wide as tea plates.

'Yes, Sicily, I think,' said Aunt M.

'Sicily?' said Uncle Roderick, exchanging a quick look with Gloria.

'Yes,' grinned Lil. 'Where all the gangsters come from in films!'

'Stop dawdling, Edna, please!' snapped Muv.

I sighed, but as I gave the room one last look I noticed a very worried expression on Gloria's slow loris face. Uncle Roderick, who has been lounging languidly, had suddenly sat up straight too, the ferrety nose on him twitching with Intense Interest.

Now what's all that *about*, I wondered . . .

Ornate, late 17th century door lock fitted to the drawing room door at Grimacres. Key missing. Lock bunged up with Unknown Matter.

CHAPTER 6.
A TORTOISE IN MY CARDIGAN

The drawing room door blocked out the warmth of the fire and in the hallway I shivered. Then I felt the glassy eyes of the mounted deer heads looking at me from the walls and I shivered some more. What was wrong with me? Usually I delighted in the foreboding sense of doom that radiated from the walls of Grimacres, but something this weekend made me feel . . .

What did I feel?

Prickly. That was it. Prickly.

Like an anxious hedgehog . . .

Everyone was acting strangely. Of course, Grimacres is full of mysteries and I'm well used to them. There's supposed to be a secret passage, and even buried treasure hidden somewhere within the Grimacres estate, and ghosts are meant to stalk the corridors, moaning and groaning. The only moaning I've heard when I'm here is from Muv complaining about how long we have to stay. And as for buried treasure – I'm yet to find it. Not that I haven't tried. Last summer, me and Archie dug up every inch of the overgrown flowerbeds in what used to be the ornamental garden, and we've looked in every likely hidey-hole in the house, but nothing. It is my one disappointment with Grimacres.

But my prickly feeling wasn't caused by any of that. *That* was all exciting. It was the way the grown-ups were behaving that was making me feel funny. They were all on edge.

What is Grandpa up to? I wondered. I glanced down at Charles Darwin. He blinked vaguely.

'You're right,' I said to him. 'We'll find out soon enough.'

I shook the prickles off, gave the deer on the walls a stern look and busied myself with my parcel. Now that WAS something jolly to distract me! I wedged Charles Darwin under my armpit and tore off the wrapping paper. It was a book, as I guessed it would be, but the title nearly made me collapse on to the floor with joy.

What's Your Poison?
A Complete Guide to Deadly Toxins
by Dr Ivy Foxglove

GOOD OLD LIL! I thought, grinning so broadly my eyepatch momentarily flipped up and smacked me on the forehead. She always comes up with the good stuff! She was the one that gave me the book about murders and, upstairs in my Grimacres bedroom, in my secret hidey-hole beneath a loose floorboard, there was a book she'd given me last time all about diseases of the human body. The illustrations were DISGUSTING. You really couldn't ask for a better book to get your nose into before bedtime.

I dithered for a moment. Half of me wanted to find Archie and hoof it immediately to the airing cupboard for a good old chinwag, perhaps get our noses stuck into this poison book with some snacks pilfered from the kitchen. But that would mean giving up on eavesdropping on whatever it was that the grown-ups were talking about and I wasn't going to let a closed door stop me from earwigging. I suspected the main topic would be this new secretary person who I was keen to know more about, but might that slide into a discussion about *The Incident*? Or gangsters? Or buried treasure?

When I'd asked Farv before about the supposed secret things at Grimacres, he'd said it was all stories. He told me that when he was growing up here, he'd looked all over and had found nothing – no secret passage, no ghosts, and definitely no treasure. Hmm . . . _I'll_ see about that!

I made a decision – my poison book could wait. I jammed

my ear up against the keyhole of the drawing room and listened carefully for a moment, but besides a low murmur, I could hear nothing. I peered into the keyhole and discovered that the lock was blocked up.

Hmph.

I'm not one to leave things alone. If there was something stuck in that hole, I was going to prise it out. I cast about for something to use. A hairpin? Too small. An antler from one of the stuffed deer heads? Too big.

What I needed was a screwdriver. None could be found in the drawers of an old sideboard in the hallway, but it then occurred to me that there'd probably be one in the collection of junk stuffed into the cupboard under the stairs with all the old coats and scarves and boots that no one ever uses any more. So I popped Charles Darwin down my cardi, shoved the poison book into the waistband of my skirt and headed there right away.

I pulled open the door and walked into the cramped dusty darkness. It's an awful tip in there. A real mess. But I ferreted about a bit and soon found what I needed.

Just as I was about to leave, I noticed a slightly pongy, moth-eaten fur coat and popped it on to keep warm. (Of COURSE I checked the pockets for any forgotten-about money but sadly they were empty.)

JINGLE JANGLE.

I suddenly straightened up, listening closely.

The front door had opened and closed. A blast of icy air had blown in, and now there were footsteps and the jingle-jangle sound of things jostling about in the pockets of someone coming down the hall.

I stuck my head out of the cupboard and saw George Badger walking towards me taking his gloves off and using them to dust the snow from the shoulders of his jacket.

HECK IT! I thought. My chance to unblock the keyhole was done for now, but I shoved the screwdriver down my sock anyway and clambered out to greet him.

'Hello, Mr Badger!' I said heartily whilst saluting him. 'Don't suppose you've been brought out of retirement to solve any crimes since I last saw you?'

'Oh hullo, er . . .' said Badger, squinting at me to work out which sister I was. 'Edna,' he said eventually. 'No, no . . . Just been working on my book and harvesting my cabbages. The only criminals I've had to apprehend recently were the slugs in my veg patch!' He chuckled to himself.

'Well, I suppose that's something,' I said, disappointed. He wasn't looking at me – too busy unwinding his scarf and folding it over his arm, but I shut the cupboard door quickly with my bottom and looked casual all the same. 'I wasn't up to anything I shouldn't have been,' I said. I thought I'd better get that clear from the start.

'Good, good,' he said vaguely, as the snow on his shoes left puddles on the floor. 'Everyone in there?' he continued, pointing down the hall to the drawing room. I nodded. He nodded back and jingle-jangled in to see the grown-ups.

I sighed. Badger is *such* a disappointment to me. His parents were the gardeners here a long time ago and when he grew up, he went off to be a policeman first, then a detective, THEN a private investigator. An extremely successful one too, actually. As such you'd think he'd be all neat, twirly moustaches (his is even bigger and bushier than Farv's), trench coats and fingerprint kits, but he's not. He's retired now, and back living in the cottage across the courtyard, and all he's interested in is quietly growing vegetables and writing what sounds like an astoundingly boring book about the history of Grimacres. It has four whole chapters about the roof tiles and six just about the toilets.

If he'd now joined the grown-ups, I could bet my front teeth that there would no longer be anything worth me earwigging. They all get a bit jumpy around Badger because he used to be a policeman. Especially Uncle Roderick. All natter about *The Incident* would cease and they'd be on their best behaviour, and there is nothing more boring than people on their best behaviour. So I decided it was time to go and find Archie.

There was also a delightful whiff coming from the kitchens

downstairs, and if Charles Darwin and I couldn't jam our lugholes up against a door, we might as well go and find a biscuit.

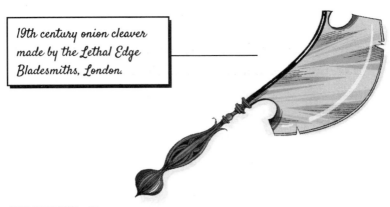

CHAPTER 7.
A SNEAK IN THE HOUSE

'Sure, wasn't I just wondering when you would make an appearance down here!' cried a voice when Charles Darwin and I entered the kitchen. It was Mrs Crumpet. She's Irish and as tiny as a blue tit. She was standing on an old iron diving helmet to reach the table where she was up to her elbows in a mixing bowl.

'Hello, Mrs C,' I cried. 'Where's Archie?'

Archie is Mrs Crumpet's great nephew. He's the same age as me and apart from my tortoise, he is my best friend. My only human friend really, I suppose.

Mrs Crumpet made the sound of a goose. 'Well, now isn't that a nice way to greet me – asking immediately where himself is, and me here after not seeing you for what seems like an age!'

She looked me all over with her beady currant eyes. 'Well, you're looking healthy at least,' she said, 'but you've been cutting your fringe again, haven't you? With blunt scissors.'

'No!' I fibbed. Mrs C laughed.

'Archie'll be back in a minute,' she said. 'He's bringing the chickens up from the henhouse. If this blizzard carries on, they'd freeze to their perches out there. Now listen, why hasn't your mother brought any of her staff from London with her? I was counting on the help this weekend.'

'Oh, she doesn't have any any more,' I said. 'And Sid the chauffeur's disappeared too. That's why Farv drove us down himself.'

'Disappeared?' said Mrs Crumpet with her eyebrows on the ceiling.

'Not properly disappeared,' I explained. If he'd *really* vanished that would have been very exciting. I could have set about detecting where he was and I'd have tracked him down. The truth was less thrilling. 'He just went off to get another job. Said something about regular pay or something . . .'

I sighed. I'd always liked Sid. Sometimes when I was at a loose end back home, I'd wander down to the garage and he'd let me wear his chauffeur's hat and help him change the oil in the Daimler. He said one day he'd teach me how to hotwire a car in case I ever needed to get one going quickly in a getaway situation.

See, that's a proper skill for a young lady in my eyes. Not embroidery or fan tittering.

Mrs Crumpet looked at me hard. 'Oh. I see,' she said eventually. 'It's like that, is it . . . Very interesting. Well, I suppose it's not like I'm not used to running this place single-handed!'

When Grandpa was my age, Grimacres was teeming with a bustling staff. Then, by the time he was an adult, his dad, my great-grandfather, got rid of nearly all of them and they've never been replaced.

'Too mean to pay the wages' is what Muv has to say about it all, but she hasn't said that for a while.

Mrs Crumpet returned to her mixing. 'Now, if you're to be down here you needn't think you're to be sitting in front of that oven roasting the toes off yourself! I'm up to the eyebrows with things to do with you all here! A great dinner tonight and another one tomorrow. And a cake! A *three-tiered cake!* Bit much for afternoon tea if you ask me, and your grandfather usually so tight with the purse strings! Certainly too tight to pay for the full staff a house this big needs. So you can put that animal down, wash your hands and help!'

I was going to tell Mrs C that Charles Darwin is a reptile, specifically of the Testudinidae family but I didn't. She was flushed in the face and surrounded by a three-course meal in various stages of being ready and I could tell she didn't have a moment spare for my tortoise talk.

I looked around for somewhere to put him and Mrs Crumpet pointed to a cardboard box lined with newspapers and leaves near the range oven.

When I saw it, I grinned. 'Did Archie make that?'

Mrs Crumpet nodded.

'Oh, good old Archie!' I said, then, with an anxious glance I asked quietly:

'How is he?'

'Sure, you'll see yourself soon enough.'

I nodded and left it at that, and after Charles Darwin was settled and gnawing his way through half a Savoy cabbage, I gave my hands a quick swill and got helping. Mrs C gave me a biscuit and had me chopping veg.

'Been chucked out from up there?' she said, nodding her head to the ceiling.

'Yes,' I said. 'Lil started talking about Grandpa's new secretary and then Aunt Mildred told me to come and see you.'

Mrs C stifled a laugh. 'I bet she did. Wanted to have a good old gas about the woman without your ears working overtime.'

I let a moment pass wondering what I should start with. I always like to pump Mrs Crumpet for info about things because as well as being a good cook, my goodness can she talk! Now, I wondered, should I start with *The Incident* or the strange appearance of this mysterious new secretary? I plumped for the latter, so I said all casual, 'I heard Miss Bellissima is from Italy and Grandpa is very keen on her?'

'Edna Gristle, if you've come down here thinking you can dig out secrets from me, you've another think coming!' said Mrs C. There was a moment's silence. Then she added, 'All I'll say is that Miss Bellissima seems very good at her job. There. That's it.'

She mimed zipping her lips and carried on with the mixing bowl.

I concentrated on my chopping, and waited patiently. Then, Mrs C said, 'Now . . . what I WILL say, and you know I'm not one to gossip AT ALL, is that although Miss Bellissima has only been here a week, she and Lord Ignatius have been as thick as thieves. In that study of his day and night and the typewriter clattering non-stop. Busy! Busy! Busy! Even had me and the milkman in to sign something the other day, but what it was don't ask me because I don't know. I'd dropped my specs in some cake batter and had to wait until the thing cooled down before I could dig them out. It was something official and important looking – that's all I know.'

She was quiet again for a moment, but I knew she hadn't finished.

'I think your aunt feels Miss Bellissima is taking over, you know. Put Mildred's nose out of joint, if you ask me. Although I wouldn't be surprised if she was also a bit relieved not to have your grandfather bullying her about the business at all hours.'

'Aunt M doesn't know what they are busy doing?' I asked, surprised. If it was anything to do with The Jolly BonBon business, surely Aunt M should be included?

Mrs C shrugged and walloped an onion in half with a great, shiny cleaver.

'But other than that,' she continued, 'like I say, Miss Bellissima seems very nice. Quiet. But . . .'

My eyebrows wiggled and I leant in closer.

'But what?' I said. I was playing a risky game, because you never know when Mrs C will clam up. Luckily, though, she didn't.

'Well . . .' she said, dropping her voice to a whisper, 'I can't help feeling like she's . . . taking stock of the place. I came back from Much Maudlin market the other day to find her searching in my cupboards! "Can I help you?" says I, and she jumps up, red-cheeked. Knocked one of my knives off the counter, she did. "Oh!" she says, picking it up and putting it back. "I was just looking at all the English food . . ." And then she scarpered pretty sharpish. Well, I might have believed that, because she probably hasn't seen tinned custard powder before being Italian and that,' – Mrs C said 'Italian' like 'Eye-talian' – 'but then, when I was getting the rooms ready for you all, she slipped into the library. I was dusting in there and in she snuck, and had a good nose around. She didn't see me because I was crouched behind the armchairs giving the skirting boards the damp cloth, but I saw *her*! Little notebook she had, tucked down her cardi. She'd look around and then out came the book and a pencil and she'd start making notes!'

Now *this* is the sort of thing I love to hear – a mysterious guest up to no good! I got a bit goose-pimply and my brain had started to twitch again in the same way it had earlier.

But before I could ask Mrs C any more, the back door opened and in came Archie looking like a snowman and with his arms full to the brim with clucking chickens. He grinned when he saw me and waved a bedraggled hen in my direction. I raced over to help him, glad to get him on his own.

We put the chickens into one of the old larder rooms.

'Cor, am I glad to see you!' I said, helping to scrunch old newspapers around the hens to keep them cosy. 'I've got lots to tell you!'

Archie's eyebrows jumped inquisitively and he pointed with a chicken to the ceiling which I supposed meant, 'About that lot upstairs?'

I grinned and nodded excitedly. 'Yes, they're all behaving very strangely.'

I guessed he knew about the new secretary already, but I wondered what he knew about Grandpa's urgent invitation, and I wanted to tell him about the grown-ups being all jumpy and tense. And that cheeky little mention of *The Incident* earlier had got me all of a quiver.

I needed to natter it through, because combined, it was making me feel like I'd just listened to someone play a bum note on a violin – sort of ear-scrunchy and twisty-faced.

I also, VERY IMPORTANTLY, needed to ask him if he was OK. Mrs Crumpet had written to me back in February to let me know that Archie had stopped talking. He'd just shut up like a clam one day and no one knew why. She had wanted to see if I could find out, but as I hadn't been back to Grimacres since, I'd not had the chance.

I'd written to him a few times, but Archie's not much of a one for writing letters. He finds words a bit tricky because they jump around the page when he reads or writes. All I'd had from him in the post since was the most beautiful drawing of his favourite chicken. It was as if since February, all words had deserted him.

Just then the little alarm clock Mrs C keeps on the windowsill above the sink started to trill loudly.

'Edna!' came Mrs Crumpet's voice. 'You'd better fetch this animal and get yourself upstairs and ready for dinner!'

HECK IT! No time to chat with Archie now.

'I'd better run, but as soon as we can, let's meet in our cubbyhole for a good chinwag, OK?'

Archie nodded and gave me a double thumbs up.

'Good! Oh – and keep your peepers open!' I said. 'Something strange is happening here at Grimacres, I'm sure of it. I'll tell you more later!' Then reluctantly, I dashed out, scooping up Charles Darwin and my poison book on the way.

As I hoofed it up the stairs, I thought about Miss Bellissima snooping about the house. Was she just looking at things in the Gristle collection, or was she searching for something in particular? The Gristle Buried Treasure for instance? And why exactly *had* Grandpa brought us here, and why were my whole family acting so strangely? I narrowed my eyes suspiciously and looked at Charles Darwin. I'm not sure if he was thinking the same things as me, but he narrowed his eyes too.

'Seems to me, Charles Darwin, like we're going to have to do a little bit of snooping ourselves,' I said, stepping into the great hall.

But before we could start, the collection of grandfather clocks struck six and it was at that point that quite a lot of shouting started from the floor above.

CHAPTER 8.
THE SURREPTITIOUS REMOVAL OF A STUFFED MONGOOSE

For a moment, I thought that someone had been murdered, but actually that would come later. We were, without knowing it, building up to *that* dramatic moment. It was only when my brain kicked into gear that I realised that the shouting right now was coming from Muv and Audrey, and I knew exactly what it was about, so I hoofed it up the stairs sharpish.

Whenever we are at Grandpa's, he always insists that before the dinner gong goes, everyone goes upstairs and gets washed and changed into fancy evening wear. I can't understand it really. Why get all gussied up only to splash gravy down yourself ten minutes later?

Anyway, that's what was happening at this point. The grown-ups had all gone up to their rooms to get ready and the shouting was for me to remove the zoo.

If you think there are a lot of dead things downstairs at Grimacres, just wait until you see the bedrooms. From each gloomy corner, a whole menagerie of dusty old and often moth-eaten beasts stare out. Of course, Muv and my sister hate them (hence their caterwauling), so I have to move them all into my room. I start with the ancient stuffed polar bear (my favourite because he has an eyepatch like me from when Grandpa pinged him with a bow and arrow when he was a boy and the glass eye got lost) and then I work my way down in size to the voles.

It occurred to me this time though, as I lugged the polar bear into my tiny bedroom at the end of the corridor, that this bit of taxidermy removal might allow me to partake in some light snooping. It's amazing how little attention a person will pay to you when you are quietly removing a stuffed beaver from their bedroom.

I could maybe even get a sneaky peek into Miss Bellissima's room, which would be a bonus.

I left Charles Darwin getting himself comfortable on my pillows and made my way back down the corridor with my sleeves pushed up and my eyes and ears on full alert.

First, I went into Muv and Farv's room and as I suspected, they didn't notice me slipping in the door.

Their bedroom is painted the colour of drying blood and there's a huge four poster bed in the middle. A great number of antique masks grin grimly down from the walls. On a low lacquered cupboard stood the sleek shape of a wolf, prowling. Above the mantelpiece was a very raggedy-looking bear's head mounted mid-roar and on the table by the bed, a mongoose was throttling a snake. As slowly as I could (to increase my listening in time), I started to gather up the animals, but I needn't have worried. Muv and Farv were too busy getting ready and talking in Hushed Tones to pay me any attention.

'You'll have to see your father the *minute* dinner is over, Bernard,' Muv was saying. She was sitting at the dressing table redoing her make-up. 'Roderick is obviously after some money from him and you need to get in there first. We need it more than him. Since those investments you made failed, the doormat has been littered with red-stamped envelopes every morning. The embarrassment, Bernard! The shame!'

Well, that was very revealing. Since our butler left, I'd been the one to collect the post and it was true: envelope after envelope arrived, each one stamped with big red letters saying 'URGENT!' and 'FINAL REMINDER' and 'OH BOY DO WE MEAN IT THIS TIME!' I hadn't known what to make of them, but now it all became clear. I gulped.

Muv glared at Farv, who was standing over by the window, doing up his dickie bow.

'I know,' he sighed, 'but you know what Father's like. I really think he loathes me. And if I have to tell him I'm practically penniless, he'll just laugh at me, Ros, like he has done my whole life.'

Muv wasn't listening. She just ploughed on with her own train of thought.

'You know Mrs Crabb is only staying on because I paid her with a pair of my chandelier pearl-drop earrings? At this rate we'll have to sell the car!'

'Or stop your tennis lessons . . .' said Farv.

Muv turned and gasped, hand clasped to bosom.

'Never!' she said, and it came out a bit strangled. 'It would simply destroy Valentino! I'm the highlight of his week!'

Farv made a grumbly noise and picked up his cufflinks from the dresser. They were his good ones – solid gold with his initial B engraved on one and G on the other, each letter accompanied by a little diamond. I knew they'd been very expensive and now he'd probably have to sell them.

Muv turned back to the looking glass and with a shaky hand applied some blood red lipstick.

'And then there's Audrey's eighteenth birthday party in three months!' she continued. 'Three months, Bernard! And we've no way to pay for it! Her dress, the venue, the caterers . . .'

'It'll have to be cancelled,' said Farv flatly.

Muv gasped again, outraged. 'It can't be! The invitations went out months ago! It's the social event of the year! If we have to cancel it, I'll never recover from the embarrassment. I've managed to get SIX dukes AND a prince to come. If she marries any one of them she'll be rich which is <u>absolutely</u> the most important thing!'

'Well, I'd rather she was happy really,' Farv said quietly. Muv gave him a look and he deflated like a sad, limp balloon.

'All right, I'll talk to Father tonight,' he sighed as he fiddled with his left cufflink which, because he's left-handed like me, was proving rather tricky to fasten. Poor Farv.

There was a dainty clatter and Farv let out a roar of frustration. 'These RUDDY cufflinks! Can't get the blighters to click! This one keeps popping off!'

Muv got up in a swish of satin evening frock and fixed the cufflinks in place. Then she squeezed Farv's hand very tightly and looked him right in the eyes with a wolf-like glare. 'I mean it, Bernard. If *you* don't sort this money situation with your father tonight, *I* will.' And two pink patches of fiery anger bloomed on her cheeks beneath her white powder.

Just then one of the animals I was carrying slipped from my grip with a clatter alerting Muv to my presence.

'What are you doing in here?' she said, sharply. 'Why aren't you dressed for dinner?'

'I'm doing what you asked!' I said innocently. 'Removing the animals.' My arms were a bit encumbered, but I managed to jauntily wave the mongoose at her. She shuddered.

'Well, hurry up then,' she said, 'and for goodness' sake tidy yourself up a bit!'

I nodded, but as I slipped through the door, I heard Muv

say the words that strike fear into any eleven-year-old's heart.

'And we need to get Edna a governess, Bernard. A really strict one, because that child is out of control.'

At the word 'governess', I scarpered.

Tiny key which opens a drawer
in a Louis XVI dressing table.

CHAPTER 9.
A SWAN WITH WONKY LEGS

After I'd dropped off the mongoose and his pals, next I slipped into Audrey's room to fetch the stuffed swan with the wonky leg.

I stopped for a moment in the doorway to look at my sister. She's an awful pain in my rump a lot of the time, but I have to say she really is a vision. All she was doing was sitting at the bureau looking at something, but she was just like someone in a painting. Straight-backed and elegant with her glossy dark hair swept back and held in place with a glittering pin in a way that if I'd done it on my hair would make me look like I was wearing a bird's nest. She looked lovely sitting there in the evening gloom. She had a blanket draped around her shoulders against the Grimacres chill and was fiddling with something in her lap.

Audrey suddenly looked up sharply and caught sight of me in her looking glass. Instantly the soft expression on her face vanished as her snake eyes glared in my direction.

'What?' she snapped, and I noticed that a red flush was blooming at the base of her throat and working its way at speed up to her face. She covered whatever it was she'd been gawping at with her hands, hiding it from view.

I pointed at the dead swan on the chimney piece.

'Just take it and scram!' she snarled.

There was an old, mottled mirror above the fireplace in Audrey's room, and as I fetched the bird, I used it to have a little peeky-pie at what my sister was doing when she thought my back was turned. Furtively, she squirrelled a sheet of paper away in her dressing table drawer. It was a letter, I realised, and if I wasn't mistaken (and I rarely am) it was the same one I'd handed her that morning at breakfast when I'd given Farv the invitation from Grandpa. And there was something else in the drawer too. I saw a flash of something pale blue before she shut the drawer again and locked it with a tiny key. Then she made a show of tidying her perfectly coiffed hair in the mirror.

'Urgh, this house!' she grumbled.

'I like it,' I said, balancing the swan on my hip.

'**You** would!' said Audrey crossly. 'But it's just a beastly prison full of beastly people, and Grandpa's the worst.'

'Are you OK?' I asked. It occurred to me that the redness

on her cheeks that I had thought was embarrassment might actually have been anger instead.

Audrey let out a little laugh. Not a ha-ha-bonk laugh; more of an angry snort.

'*You* wouldn't understand,' she said, turning back to the mirror, 'but all I'll say is, there'd better be a good reason for Grandpa making us come here this weekend, or else . . .'

She clenched her delicate fists so tightly that all her knuckles cracked like snapped bones. Then she glared at me angrily.

'Just get rid of those revolting animals and leave me alone!'

So I did as she said. She's absolutely wretched when she's in that sort of mood, so I ambled out of the room, but not before seeing my sister's hand flutter up to her neck where something I hadn't noticed before glittered.

I stood on the landing then for a moment with the swan under my arm wondering what to do next. I wanted to jam my eye up against the keyhole in Audrey's bedroom door, so intrigued was I by the contents of the bureau, but there were still animals to remove and, more importantly, other people to snoop on.

Uncle Roderick and Gloria Blouse hadn't specifically shouted for me to remove the animals from their rooms, but perhaps I should anyway?

Gloria seemed a jumpy sort and I knew that in her room were a couple of baboons being quite free and easy about flashing their bright red bums – quite alarming for the unprepared on a midnight trip to the loo. Her door was locked, but I could hear voices coming from inside. I put my ear to the door and listened.

'Look! I said I'd deal with it!' Uncle Roderick was saying. 'I'll get the cash from Dad after dinner and we'll leave!'

Then I heard Gloria's squeaky voice. 'But . . . but this new secretary,' she stammered. 'Miss Bellissima . . . We were just in Sicily! You don't think she can be' – there was a long pause – 'one of them?'

'Keep cool,' Uncle Rockerick replied. 'I'll sort it. I'll get the goods and we'll scarper. We can go in the middle of the night. Now come on – and for goodness' sake, stay CALM.'

Then I heard my uncle's heavy footsteps coming towards the door. Quickly me and the swan melted behind a large statue and watched as my uncle and Miss Blouse scurried downstairs like two startled mice.

Rather battered leather doctor's bag containing a variety of medicines. Property of Dr L. McDougal.

CHAPTER 10.
CLAMMY PALMS AND WEAK ANKLES

Back in my room, I exchanged Significant Glances with Charles Darwin.

'Just like I thought earlier . . .' I whispered to him. 'All the grown-ups are behaving oddly. They all seemed to have nerves jingling like sleigh bells.'

Uncle Roderick and Gloria seemed particularly tense, and I realised that I too was far from relaxed – my palms were clammy and I'd been holding my breath.

I plonked the swan down and straightened up.

'We're just being silly,' I hissed to Charles Darwin. 'Grown-ups are ALWAYS weird. Perhaps we're just hungry and it's making us a bit jittery?'

Charles Darwin looked at me sternly. He was, of course, right – I MUST pull myself together.

I cracked my knuckles and had a think. I still needed to tidy myself up before dinner, but the gong hadn't gone yet so perhaps I had just a little more time for snooping?

Earlier in the drawing room, before I was ordered out Lil had been ready to spill the beans on Miss Bellissima. I wondered now if maybe Lil and Aunt M were having a good gossip about the new secretary as they got ready for dinner. If they were, my ears were ready to listen.

I slipped out of my room and tiptoed down the landing to the last two doors near the stairs.

As luck would have it, I noticed the door of the room that Lil usually stayed in was ajar.

Now, Lil is a sensible sort who doesn't cock an eyebrow at the flock of stuffed vultures dangling from the ceiling and the snarling badger in her room, but I thought if she weren't chatting to Aunt M this might be a nice chance for us to have a chat. Perhaps I could ask her about how exactly one would go about cutting off a leg if it got crushed under a steam roller, for example. The thought cheered me greatly, so I knocked on the door.

There was no answer, so I just slipped inside anyway.

Lil wasn't there, but her doctor's bag was. It was open on the end of the bed. I was just considering a little look-see inside when I heard voices.

Lil's room connects to Aunt M's next door with a door hidden behind a faded tapestry of a lion engaged in fisticuffs with a unicorn. The voices were coming from the other side, so I ducked under the cloth and peeked through the gap in the adjoining door. It was Lil talking. Like me, Lil won't tolerate a dress so she'd changed into a smart tuxedo. I could see her pacing up and down on the hearth rug in an agitated manner, fiddling with her cuffs. It was strange to see her like that. Usually, Lil is as cool as a cucumber sandwich.

'I'll speak to Ignatius tonight,' she said. 'There's no need for you to be stuck here in . . . in this ice palace any longer!'

'Oh, it's not that bad . . .' said Aunt M quietly. She was drawing the curtains and looking nice and well upholstered in an arsenic green frock.

Lil snorted. 'It is and you know it! The past few months without him here have been wonderful, but he's back causing trouble and making you miserable! We ought to be living happily in our own house! You could run The Jolly BonBon perfectly well from my place in Much Maudlin.'

Aunt Mildred sighed. 'I know that – of course I do – but . . . oh, you know Daddy wouldn't like it. He says the office has to be here.'

'Where he can interfere and be a lousy, malicious, old bully!' said Lil, angrily.

'Well, yes . . . that too,' said Aunt M.

There was silence for a moment then Lil said:

'It would be better if he were dead, then we could live here together!'

Aunt M chuckled, but like Audrey's laugh earlier, it wasn't a real laugh.

'You know when Daddy dies Grimacres goes to Bernard – he's the eldest child.'

My eyebrows shot up. This was very interesting indeed. One day Grimacres would be Farv's? Blimey. As hard as I tried, I just couldn't imagine Muv living here.

'Oh, him and Rosalind won't want this place!' said Lil, echoing my thoughts exactly.

Aunt M sighed and sat down on the bed with a soft flump and it was at this point the dust from the tapestry got up my nose and before I could stop it, I sneezed. LOUDLY. It sounded like a hippo roaring. The two women in the other room looked over in my direction. They couldn't see me, but I heard them get up and come towards the connecting door.

I scarpered back into Lil's room, picked up the stuffed badger and tried to look casual.

'Everything OK, Edna?' asked Aunt M. She found me, casually studying a painting of a bowl of decaying fruit on the wall VERY closely indeed.

I floundered for a minute, but thankfully Archie came unknowingly to my rescue downstairs walloping the dinner gong loudly.

'Oh!' I said, suddenly inspired. 'Oh yes, I was just coming to say . . . it's dinner time! In case you didn't hear . . . the gong.'

Aunt M smiled vaguely. She seemed quite distracted. 'Too sweet of you,' she said, heading towards the door. 'We'd better go down. Lillian?'

She looked over her shoulder at Lil, but Lil didn't reply. She was standing at the window, looking out at the night. She clenched her fists then followed Aunt M out of the room and down the stairs. Her face was like thunder.

I started to follow them, but remembered I hadn't changed for dinner.

BLAST IT! I'd never hear the end of it from Muv if I didn't at least try to tidy myself up. I raced back to my room where I wiped my mouth on my sleeve and wiggled into the old suit jacket and bow tie I keep in the wardrobe at Grimacres for dinnertimes. I refuse to wear the frilly dresses Muv wants me to put on so this moth-eaten jacket is my compromise. I threw the old fur coat I'd been wearing back on top for warmth and admired myself in the looking glass. *Gorgeous*, I thought. *An absolute VISION.*

My stomach growled as I picked up Charles Darwin and together we set off at a run down the corridor.

At the top of the stairs, I paused briefly by the small window there and peeked out. The weather outside was slightly less frightful than it had been, but the whole world beyond the glass was thickly covered in a pale blue glittering blanket of snow. In the distance, the dark gloom of Grimacre Woods sat black against the night sky.

As I stood there, something caught my eye.

A flash of light in the woods, like the beam from a torch.

Surely there isn't someone out in the woods in this weather?

Then the next moment it was gone.

Hmmm . . . I thought, as I stumped down the stairs to dinner. *Must have imagined it.*

A GUIDE TO
THE BRITISH
ARISTOCRACY

by Sir Henry Fox-Hunt.

—Ignatius GRISTLE, 13th Baron Grimacres—

Father:
see entry for **Alastair Gristle, 12th Baron Grimacres** *(deceased)*

Mother:
see entry for **Lady Vendetta Gristle (nee Venom)** *(deceased)*

IGNATIUS GRISTLE is the semi-retired CEO of the world-famous confectionary company The Jolly BonBon LTD, and the patriarch of the Gristle Family.

A spoilt and rebellious child, Ignatius grew up on the family estate, Grimacres, outside the town of Much Maudlin where he was regularly in trouble both at home and with the local police for causing, well, we'll call it Mischief, but it was often worse than that ...

As a young man, tensions flared with his father and, aged twenty, Ignatius fled England and spent a number of years travelling around the world. It was during this time that he added to the already sizeable Gristle collection of rare and unique objects, which he had shipped back home at enormous expense (charged to his father) and are now believed to fill Grimacres almost to bursting point.

Following the death of his father, Ignatius returned home in his late twenties having inherited both the family business and the estate.

He married his first wife Lady Tulip Gristle *(see entry)* and had the first of his three children – the Hon. Bernard Gristle *(see entry)* and the Hon. Mildred Gristle *(see entry)*.

Later, in middle age and following the death of Lady Tulip, Ignatius married his second wife, Miss Valeska Gristle *(see entry)*.

This marriage was short-lived, as was Valeska, who died only days after their one and only child, the Hon. Roderick Gristle *(see entry)* was born.

When asked to speculate on the value of both the business and the Gristle collection at Grimacres, a financial expert said the figure would be 'staggeringly immense'.

Ignatius is infamous for not only being an unpleasant man, but also very mysterious and secretive.

He leaves Grimacres only when absolutely necessary. People who have made his acquaintance have described him variously as 'mean', 'bullying', 'sly', 'cunning' and 'a real stinker of a person'.

For more information on the Gristle home, Grimacres,
I would recommend reading the entry on the estate in

**GREAT ANCIENT HOUSES OF ENGLAND:
THE GOOD AND THE DREADFUL**

by Felicity Wattle-Daub

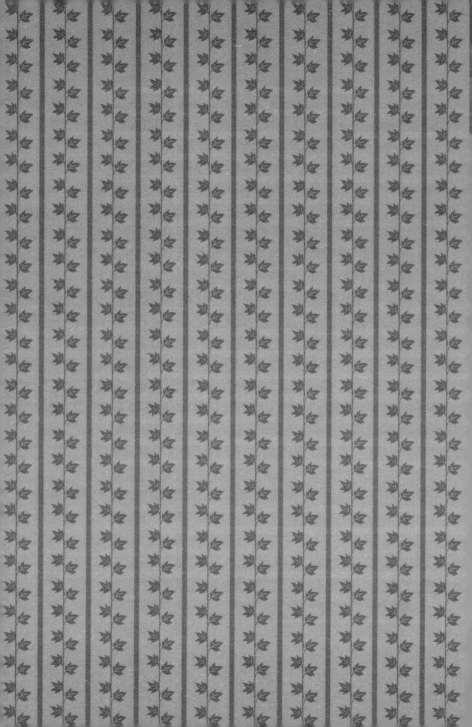

PART TWO:
AT LEAST THERE ARE ROAST POTATOES

A Late Victorian teaspoon
(for tea, not scooping out brains).

CHAPTER 11.
APPETISER:
A MOUTHFUL OF SPITE

Most of my family were already sitting around the enormous table in the centre of the dark, cavernous dining room when Charles Darwin and I slipped in. There was only Grandpa and Miss Bellissima still to come. Everyone was waiting in stony silence. They looked like marble statues in the flickering candlelight. The only thing that told me they were alive was the little clouds of warm breath freezing in the arctic air around their noses. There was a glittering of frost on the inside of the mullioned windows, and it wouldn't have surprised me to have found icicles dangling from the unlit chandeliers.

As I settled Charles Darwin down in front of the very weak fire, I felt a shiver go down my spine. The dining room seemed to be vibrating with a tension that made my teeth itch, and I knew then that this dinner was not going to be the jolly sort of birthday meal I'd hoped it might be. There certainly weren't any balloons, and unless Farv was going to put on a red nose and a curly wig, there wasn't going to be a clown either.

The reason for the tension was, of course, that my whole family was braced for my grandpa's arrival. At that moment, I really wished my grandfather was the sort of grandpa you read about in books. Cheerful and kind, always with caramel sweets in his pocket to share, and fun to be around. Warm-hearted and be-cardiganned. A good whistler, that sort of thing. My grandpa had never been like that – to his own children nor any of his grandchildren. He was foul to us all. My oldest sister Nancy told me that when I was born, Grandpa took one look at me in my cot and said (as he had about all my siblings too) 'REVOLTING' and walked away blowing his nose before throwing the tissue in beside me, like my cot was a wastepaper bin.

I took my seat next to Badger and wondered if I should talk to him. I wanted to ask him about where I'd be able to get some handcuffs for the emergency kit I was thinking of putting together for myself, but the room seemed too frosty and quiet for conversation.

All the rest of the adults were zip-lipped and fidgety, so I buried myself deeper into my too-big-for-me fur coat and snaked my hand across the table for a bread roll. Muv caught me and gave me One Of Her Looks. I quickly abandoned the bread roll and concentrated on drumming my fingers on the starched white tablecloth instead.

Somewhere in the dark room, a clock was ticking.

TICK

TOCK . . .

With every move of the invisible hands, the tension grew. Muv smoothed her napkin. Audrey fiddled with something on a thin chain around her neck. Farv moved his knife a fraction to the left and Lil moved her fork fractionally to the right. Beside me, Badger calmly jingle-jangled the coins in his pocket.

All of a sudden the dining room door flew open and in came Grandpa, alone and hunched over like a banana. His pale skin was stretched over his knobbly bones, and his face, twisted with fury as usual, looked to me like that of an angry Halloween skeleton.

'Where's that useless idiot boy?' he snapped. 'Having to open doors for myself in my own house – OUTRAGEOUS!' His voice was harsh like someone taking a cheese-grater to a boulder.

One second later, Archie came tearing in, his face tomato red. I could feel myself getting cross already because Grandpa is always so horrid to Archie for no reason whatsoever.

'Too late!' snapped Grandpa, as Archie dithered beside him. 'I'm here now. Pull that chair out for me.'

(There's never a please nor thank you in my grandpa's mouth.)

Archie ran to do so, tripping over his own feet making his red face darken to a beetroot purple.

'Honestly, it's like he's had any brain he might have possessed scooped out with a teaspoon!' said Grandpa. 'I'd have been better off hiring a gibbon. Would have been cheaper too . . .'

He swept a watery eye over all of us, disappointment plastered over his face.

'What on Earth have you come dressed as?' he said, when he got to me. 'Take that fur coat off immediately!'

'But it's keeping me warm!' I protested.

'I don't care!' snapped Grandpa. 'It looks like it's full of fleas and I won't have it at the table. Take it out of the room. Now!'

He glared at me then stared at Farv.

'That child needs something to do to keep her out of mischief. Get her up cleaning chimneys or digging graves or something. Hard work would do her some good. I should have done that with you three.'

He glared at Farv, Aunt M and Uncle Roderick. They looked down at their plates.

Farv said gently: 'Just do as your grandpa says please, Edna.'

I tutted and hopped down from my seat, rolling my eyes at Archie as I went. In the hall, I was just opening the door to the cupboard under the stairs and grumpily removing my coat when I heard a swishing sound from somewhere above. I peered out and watched as someone began to descend the staircase.

It was Miss Bellissima.

CHAPTER 12.
FIRST COURSE: COCK-A-LEEKIE
A CHICKEN SOUP SERVED WITH BREAD ROLLS THAT CAN BE USED AS A WEAPON

All of my older sisters are what most people find nice to look at. Like I said earlier, Audrey is like something from a painting or a fashion magazine. But Miss Bellissima was different. She was GLAMOUROUS.

She was tall and wore a sweeping velvet gown the colour of blood, with lipstick and perfectly manicured nails to match. Her long, chestnut hair gleamed and her dark eyes, framed by long, dark lashes, shone. She looked like a film star. You could almost hear the projector whirring and the music swelling as the camera zoomed in for a soft-focus close-up on her striking face.

At the door, she placed a delicate hand on the door handle and briefly closed her eyes. She took a deep breath, tossed her hair back and put her chin up, determined. She made me think of an actor about to go on stage, or a boxer heading into the ring for a fight.

Then she pushed open the door and swept into the room. I quickly stashed the fur coat under the stairs and followed her in, scurrying back to my seat just in time to see everyone swizzle around to gawp. Eyes popped. Jaws hit the floor. Even Aunt M and Lil looked bamboozled and they'd met her before. She surveyed everyone serenely from under her thinly arched brows and gracefully walked towards the empty seat at the table next to Grandpa.

Archie stepped forward to pull her chair out and she thanked him politely as she seated herself quietly.

'Ah, Giovanna,' said Grandpa in what was probably to him a nice tone of voice, 'meet my useless family . . .'

He waved a dismissive, skeletal hand at the stunned faces around the table.

'Allow me to introduce everyone. You've met Badger already, so my children then – all of them a terrific disappointment. Not a single backbone between them. I'd have been better off bringing up slime from a drain really, but anyway . . . My eldest, Bernard the bore. Middle-child Mildred, who won't let me run my own business any more . . .'

'Now, hang on a moment!' said Lil, hotly, but Grandpa swept on.

'And my youngest, Roderick, who seems only to exist to

beg me for money. All three of them are just waiting for me to slip into my grave so they can get their mitts on my money, no doubt.'

Around the table, knuckles gripped napkins and knives tightly.

'Next,' continued Grandpa, 'we have Lillian, who is *apparently* a doctor but I'm yet to see any good that she does. Then there's Ros, Bernard's wife: sly as a fox and a monumental gold digger. Then we have two of my many revolting grandchildren, Audrey: gormless, and Edna: feral.'

Grandpa sat back in his seat. His face twisted into a malicious and very satisfied smile.

Miss Bellissima looked around at us all and smiled a slightly nervous smile.

'Buona sera,' she said, which I looked up afterwards and it means 'good evening' in Italian.

Everyone murmured a glum greeting of some kind whilst still staring at the newcomer. I felt that we needed to be more welcoming so I leant forward and said '*spaghetti*' because that was the only Italian word I knew at the time, and gave her a hearty wink. I think Giovanna liked that because I got a nice, not nervous, smile back from her and she seemed to relax a little.

Grandpa clicked his fingers and Archie started serving the soup. It was *cock-a-leekie* for everyone else and tomato for me because I won't eat anything with a face. As Archie served, his hands shook dreadfully especially after he splashed a dollop over the tablecloth near Grandpa's dish.

'Stupid boy!' growled Grandpa, and I ground my teeth.

In the meantime, Aunt M was valiantly trying to get a conversation going. She said:

'I was telling everyone earlier, Miss Bellissima, that you've recently joined us from Sicily . . .'

There was a clang from Gloria, who dropped her entire spoon into her dish and I saw Uncle Roderick give her a knife-sharp glare.

Miss Bellissima swallowed a mouthful of soup and smiled.

'Yes, I was working for my father's business there,' she said, 'which of course was where I met Lord Ignatius.' Her accent was lovely. It made me think of stretching out in the summer sunshine and bright blue skies.

'I think you were in Sicily recently, weren't you, Roderick?' said Aunt M, her voice strained. Gloria dropped her spoon again.

'Oh,' said Uncle Roderick, 'only er, very, very briefly, you know.'

At the head of the table Grandpa laughed one of his hollow, fairground ghost-train laughs.

'Didn't bother to come and see me, did you?' he snarled. 'You knew I was there and you just didn't bother. Came back here quickly enough, though. Probably thought I was about to croak it and so hurried back to get your hands on the

Gristle cash. How much do you want from me this time?'

Uncle Roderick tried to laugh casually but it came out a bit like a malfunctioning whoopee cushion.

'Hey, come on, Dad!' he said in a shadow version of his usual jokey manner. 'We've come to celebrate your birthday!'

Grandpa cackled horribly. 'Ha! Birthday, indeed! What do I care about birthdays? I've had enough of them. I know why you are all here, of course. It's written on all your faces. Can't wait for me to pop my clogs, can you? Well, sorry to disappoint you all but I'm going nowhere, am I, Lillian? She'll tell you.'

All eyes slid to Lillian, who didn't say anything, but the stormy expression on her face spoke volumes.

There was silence after that. The only sounds in the room were the ticking clock and me slurping my soup.

Grandpa looked at each of us with his tiny, spiteful eyes.

'Waste of space the ruddy lot of you,' he growled. 'Well – not you, Badger, and of course not you, Giovanna, my dear, but the rest of you – HUH! I'm surrounded by idiots.'

At this point, Archie, who was trying very hard to clear the soup dishes as quietly as possible, dropped two of them on to the floor with a clatter.

'See!' said Grandpa, pointing a gnarled finger at my friend. 'No bigger idiot in this house than that boy! An absolute dunderhead! Did you all know that this boy is so stupid he's forgotten how to talk?'

Now, there are two things I absolutely can't bear: onions and bullying, and Grandpa was being a great, big bully.

It made me tremble like an infuriated jelly to hear him call Archie stupid. Archie isn't even remotely stupid. Quite the opposite, in fact. He's clever in so many ways – fixing things, building things, caring for things – you just had to spend some time with him until he felt safe enough to show you what he could do.

As Grandpa shouted at Archie, and Archie stood there shaking, I felt a red-hot burst of temper tremble up from my toes.

'HEY!' I shouted, and I lobbed a bread roll down the table where it struck Grandpa right on the nose. 'ARCHIE ISN'T STUPID. HE'S JUST QUIET. MAYBE IF YOU STOPPED TALKING QUITE SO MUCH YOU'D REALISE THAT, SO LEAVE MY FRIEND ALONE, YOU TOAD.'

I paused for a moment.

'ACTUALLY TOADS ARE NICE AND YOU AREN'T SO FORGET I CALLED YOU A TOAD.'

There was a collective gasp from everyone around the table. Everyone was looking at me, eyes a-bogglin'.

Grandpa glared at me. A vein was throbbing on his forehead.

Oh cripes, you've done it now, Edna, I thought with a gulp.

'Would you look at that!' he snickered. 'Seems like there

IS a member of this family who has a *bit* of backbone . . .
unlike the rest of you!'

At this point, Muv piped up.

'Listen, Ignatius,' she said in the voice of Audrey (when
she's in a jolly mood) which I call her Duchess Voice, 'you
invited us all down here this weekend . . .'

'And you all came running – ready for me to empty the
bank vault into your grubby little hands . . .'

Muv ignored him. 'Why don't you just tell us why you've
brought us here. Then we can go and leave you alone.'

For a moment Grandpa didn't say anything.

The clock ticked.

Then something very disturbing happened. His face broke
into a wide, wild grin. He looked like a tiger just before it
leapt at a wounded antelope.

'Well, I do have a little surprise for you all,' he said slowly.

We leaned in.

The air was soupy with anticipation.

'Tomorrow,' he said, 'I am getting married.'

Antique carving knife. Very sharp. Made by the 致命的な鋭い Blade Company, Japan.

CHAPTER 13.
MAIN COURSE: ROAST GROUSE
(BUT NO ONE IS HUNGRY)

'WHAT?' my family shouted all at once.

'I said, I'm getting married,' Grandpa repeated. 'Tomorrow.'

I could tell he was having terrific fun, his skull-like face was almost cracking in half with malicious glee.

The door opened then and in rattled Mrs Crumpet with the main course on her hostess trolley, her timing impeccable as ever.

'MARRIED?' cried Muv. 'TO WHOM?'

In the candlelight, the large knife Mrs Crumpet was using to carve the roast grouse glinted.

Grandpa turned and smiled indulgently at Giovanna, who looked sheepishly into her lap.

'Her?' cried Farv.

'She has a name!' snapped Grandpa. 'And you will show

your new stepmother some respect!'

Farv's nostrils flared. 'I'm sorry, Miss Bellissima, it's nothing personal,' he said in a voice trembling with the exertion of staying polite, 'but Father, this is *ridiculous* – you hardly know her!'

As I heaped roast potatoes on my plate next to my omelette and got started on them, eating them like fairground toffee apples, my mind cogs turned. Mrs Crumpet said that since his return, Grandpa had been busy. *Probably organising this wedding*, I thought. And of course that elaborate, three-tiered cake in the kitchen had been a stonking great big clue. It was a wedding cake!

'Did you know about this?' I asked Mrs Crumpet quietly as she stood beside me with the gravy jug.

She shook her head. 'I did think that cake was a bit odd – especially the bride and groom decorations on the top, but . . .' she trailed off. I knew she wasn't fibbing. She never fibs. Fussing with her apron, Mrs Crumpet quickly left the room. I waggled a message with my eyebrows at Archie. He waggled his back. He hadn't known either.

'What about you?' said Farv, turning to Badger, then Aunt M and Lil. 'Did you know?'

They all shook their heads. This wedding was obviously news to them too – they were gobsmacked.

In the fuss, I noticed that no one was eating their dinner so I took the opportunity to pinch some more potatoes. Under my eyelashes I had a sneaky look at Giovanna. What was *she* making of all of this? Was she really going to be my new step-grandmother? All the focus was on Grandpa and everyone seemed to be ignoring her. She was looking studiously down at her uneaten food and I saw her swallow nervously.

Aunt M pulled herself together and decided to try a different approach.

'Daddy,' she said, 'I'm sure you are fond of Miss Bellissima, and Miss Bellissima, you seem a terribly nice person, but this is all *very* sudden. Might you want to take a *little* time to think about it a bit more before making any big decisions?'

'And let's be honest,' said Muv, 'Miss Giovanna is a lot younger than you.' This was true. Miss Bellissima couldn't have been much older than my sister Arabella, who is twenty-five.

Grandpa slammed his cutlery down on the table.

'I don't care!!' he snarled. 'I want to marry Miss Bellissima and I <u>always</u> do what *I* want.'

The tension in the room popped like a balloon then. An enormous row erupted with my family all shouting over each other all at once. Grandpa was behaving outrageously, they said. The wedding MUST be postponed, he needed to be *sensible*, take more time over such important decisions.

After a few minutes of this, Grandpa stood up, beating a fist on the table and knocking over a glass of wine. The red liquid oozed across the snowy white tablecloth like blood from a terrible cut.

'Shut your nasty little faces, the lot of you!' he bellowed, and to my surprise everyone did.

'I will do whatever *I* want to do,' he said in a low, dangerous voice, 'and it's about time this family learned that lesson once and for all.'

His malicious grin spread across his face again and his eyes flashed dangerously in the flickering gloom. He was really enjoying himself. He loved causing trouble on purpose.

'And if any of you are worrying about the Gristle fortune, well **don't**. From tomorrow, it won't be your problem any more.'

'What do you mean, Ignatius?' said Muv, weakly.

Grandpa cackled. 'Let's just say that the new Lady Gristle will be *very* comfortable indeed . . .'

I didn't catch on to what he meant at first. I thought perhaps he would be using the family money to buy Miss Bellissima some new cushions, but apparently I was wrong.

Farv leapt to his feet. He looked ill.

'You CAN'T do that!' he cried.

Grandpa reached for his cane.

'I can. And I have. As soon as I marry Miss Bellissima tomorrow morning at ten, my new will leaves *everything* to her.'

There was a sharp intake of breath from everyone around the table (apart from me because I was still crunching spuds).

We all (even Charles Darwin) watched as Grandpa hobbled towards the door. He turned, his wrinkled walnut face creased up with another awful, jack-o-lantern grin.

'That is, of course, unless one of you murders me in the night!' he said with a cackle.

Just then, Mrs Crumpet burst back into the room carrying a silver tray with a large pavlova heaped with cherries and a row of lit birthday candles flickering on the top. She started to sing, 'Happy Birthday to—' but stopped abruptly, when she found herself face to face with Grandpa in the doorway.

He took one look at the dessert and then deliberately knocked the tray from her hands. The pudding fell to the floor and landed with a horrible wet *splat*.

Grandpa stepped over the mess and a moment later we heard his study door slam.

And all we were left with was the sound of the clock.

TICK

TOCK . . .

Crystal brandy decanter with silver skull stopper. Originally from Transylvania, late 1800s.

CHAPTER 14.
DESSERT: PAVLOVA
SERVED À LA THE DINING ROOM FLOOR

Miss Bellissima leapt from her seat to help clean up the dropped dessert, but Archie and I were already on it. We dolloped it back on to its plate and put some napkins on the sticky red mess on the floor.

'Sorry about earlier,' I said to Archie in the tiniest whisper I could manage. 'He's such a horrible old goblin.' Archie managed a little smile. He was very pale. He hates shouting. I patted him on the hand.

Miss Bellissima stood awkwardly for a moment at the end of the table, straightening her frock. My whole family were staring at her and an embarrassed glow was creeping up her neck.

'I . . . I have a headache,' she said, rather weakly, 'I think I will go to bed . . . please excuse me,' and with the rest of my family glaring at her with red-hot eyes, she made to leave the room.

I felt sorry for her, and as I opened the door to let her out, I gave her what I hoped was an encouraging smile. She gave me a little sad one back and disappeared into the hall.

With the pavlova tidied up, I slipped back to my seat just as Badger beside me stood up, tugged at the ends of his moustache and placed his napkin on the table.

'I think I'd better leave you all to it . . .' he said, shifting uncomfortably. 'I expect you'll all want to talk this . . . er . . . news through in private. I suppose I'll see you tomorrow for this . . . um . . . wedding.'

He rose from his chair but Aunt M told him to sit. 'You're practically family, George,' she said.

'At least stay for a brandy,' said Farv, which I thought was quite kind of him.

Archie brought over a bottle and some glasses and Farv dished them out as Badger sat down again.

I made myself very still so that I wasn't sent out of the room. The grown-ups were obviously livid about Grandpa's news and I wanted to stay and find out more. If Grandpa wanted to get married again, why shouldn't he? I wondered. Personally, I liked the look of Miss Giovanna Bellissima and I wondered if she might make Grandpa a nicer person.

I saw Muv's eyes slide in my direction and I braced myself to be dismissed from the room, but salvation came suddenly from Audrey, who had decided to speak. As I looked at her, I wondered again where the necklace she was wearing had come from. I hadn't seen it before.

'How will the vicar get through this snow for the wedding tomorrow?' she said, and do you know, it was the first sensible thing I'd heard her say in a long time.

We turned as one to look at the great mullioned windows of the dining room. The curtains were still open and we could see the dark world outside. The pitiful fire had fizzled out so frost was now etching itself on to the inside of the glass in swirling patterns, but beyond it the snow had stopped. However, we could see that what had already fallen was incredibly deep and banked up very high against the walls of the house. It was impossible to think how Reverend Steeple would ever get his rickety old bicycle through it all to conduct the wedding. He'd be wet through to his sock garters.

At the other end of the table, Lil knocked back her drink. 'Oh don't worry,' she said, 'if Ignatius wants something badly enough, he'll find a way.'

'Yes, if it isn't tomorrow, he'll still do it another day and soon, the rotter!' said Uncle Roderick. He turned to Aunt M and Lil and Badger. 'Truthfully, neither of you knew about this?'

They shook their heads.

'I'm telling you, Rod, none of us knew. I'm bewildered by it all! BEWILDERED!' Aunt M said. She was twisting her napkin around in her hands like she was throttling it. 'I know that she's been in the study with Daddy all hours with her typewriter clattering away non-stop and post flying out the door every day but . . . a wedding?'

She frowned then. 'But didn't it look to you all like even Miss Bellissima was a bit embarrassed by the engagement?'

YES! I thought, that's what I'd felt too. Hardly an excited bride. When one of my sisters had got married a few years ago, she hadn't shut up about it. It was veils this and rings that, all with a terrifyingly excited gleam in her eye. Miss Bellissima hadn't glinted at all.

Farv snorted like an angry bull. 'I don't think so. This will have been her plan all along, you mark my words. Sneak into the family and then steal all this from us!' He waved his hands around at the dining room. A cufflink fell off and clinked against Badger's glass and bounced along the table.

'Cursed cufflink!' he shouted.

Gloria handed it back to Farv, who continued talking.

'All of it,' he said, discombobulated. 'She'll have all of it!'

I considered this for a moment but it didn't seem very likely. Giovanna seemed quite shy beneath her film star glamour. She didn't strike me as a sneaky plotter, but maybe, like a film star, she was acting the whole time?

Muv was tapping her long, scarlet nails on the table.

'And a new will already made . . .' she mused, narrow-eyed.

'What IS a will?' I asked. I couldn't help myself.

'It's a good for nothing piece of paper that legally tells everyone exactly who gets to keep what when you croak it,' said Uncle Roderick between clenched teeth.

'It has to be signed by two people though,' said Aunt M, 'and it can't be one of the family. You haven't signed anything have you, Lillian?'

Lil shook her head.

'Neither have I,' said Badger.

There was a collective sigh of relief from the older members of my family.

'Perhaps he *hasn't* made the new one then,' said Muv, her brow uncrinkling a little. 'You know how he likes his cruel little games.'

But something in my brain clicked.

'Earlier, Mrs Crumpet said that she and the milkman had to sign something for Grandpa the other day,' I said, 'but she doesn't know what it was because her glasses were in a cake at that moment.'

The grown-ups darted looks at each other. I felt maybe I had said the wrong thing.

'So he wasn't lying . . .' said Muv, gravely. 'That's it then – the minute that wedding takes place tomorrow *she* gets everything – all of the Gristle money, this house. EVERYTHING!'

I glanced around at my family, at their tight expressions.

I tried to cheer them up a bit.

'I'm sure that won't happen!' I said. 'Grandpa's not dead yet and Miss Bellissima seems very nice. I'm sure she'd let us all have some money and we'll still be able to come and visit Grimacres.'

There then followed some not very nice laughter around the table. The sort grown-ups do when they think you are being silly, and I wondered if I was being a bit silly after all.

'She . . . she wouldn't stop us visiting, would she?' I said.

Panic twisted my stomach. I loved Grimacres. I loved all the things in it too and if I couldn't come here again then I'd never be able to find the buried Gristle treasure.

Aunt M smiled sadly at me. 'You're young, Edna, dear – you don't understand,' she said. Then she straightened up and I knew what was coming.

'Actually,' she continued, 'why don't you hop along and see if Mrs Crumpet and Archie need any help in the kitchen or . . .' She stopped suddenly, stricken. 'Oh!' she cried. 'Aunt Priscilla! No one's taken a tray up to her! Be a good girl, Edna, and take your great aunt her dinner, will you? The grown-ups have a lot to talk about and you'd be doing me an enormous favour.' She smiled at me nicely.

I sighed. I didn't want to go. I wanted to stop to find out how worried I should be about Grimacres, but I knew I wouldn't win any arguments to stay. Then I brightened. If Grimacres might not be ours much longer, I would have to get a shift on and find the buried treasure sharpish. Great Aunt Priscilla had lived in Grimacres all her life and I wondered then if she might be able to help me work out where it was?

I stood, bowed graciously like a butler to my family, and set off. Archie was clearing the plates from the table. On my way past, I gave him a look. It meant, *I'm up to something. You stay here and keep your eyes and ears open.* He nodded, gave a tiny salute and I slipped out the door.

As it closed behind me, I heard Farv slam his fist down on the table making the glassware rattle like broken teeth.

'We have to stop this wedding!' he growled, and I had to admit, he sounded very determined indeed.

CHAPTER 15.
A DISGRUNTLED OWL IN THE ATTIC

Five minutes later, I was trotting merrily upstairs with a tray for my Great Aunt Priscilla. It had some hot soup and bread on it and a large glass of something that smelt like whiskey.

Great Aunt P (or Gappy as we call her) lives in the attic at Grimacres. It used to be a load of little bedrooms for the maids, but when they weren't needed any more, the rooms were turned into a suite for Grandpa's sister instead. Gappy is only a smidge younger than Grandpa, and I always think it's a shame that she wasn't born first, then Grimacres would've belonged to her. She's lived here all her life, unlike Grandpa, who went travelling around the world for a bit when he was a young man (probably annoying everyone he met). She's the only other person who really loves the place like I do.

A few years ago, Gappy's memory started to go a bit funny. It's all there still, but it gets all knotted and tangled. You can be talking to her quite happily one minute and then suddenly her brain will fill with fog and she's travelled back in time and thinks she's five years old, or twenty, or that she's the banished empress of a faraway land. I think Gappy should be allowed to come downstairs and join in with us all. She'd like that, but Grandpa won't have it. Her memory fogs drive him up the wall because he has no patience with her (or anyone), which is why he's shut her up in the attic. He'd lock her in if he could, but Aunt M and Lillian have been very firm about not letting him do that so far. Like me, they know she can't help having a wobbly sort of memory and think it would be jolly for her to join the rest of us. She'd enjoy that immensely, but Grandpa's stubbornly put his foot down.

I find Gappy interesting. The way her memory flits about, it's like having lots of nice aunts in one person.

She was sitting, as always, in her tented bed, wrapped in fur stoles with her wispy white hair encased in a glittering turban. There were heaps of sparkling costume jewellery all over her and she was busy applying a thick coat of lilac lipstick.

'Oh!' she said, looking at me over her hand mirror. 'Are you new, dear?'

'Huh?' I said.

'How long have you been with us?' said Gappy, clearly.

'I hope Mrs Irongirdle is treating you well?'

'Mrs Irongirdle?' I asked.

'Our housekeeper,' said Gappy, very loudly. She is quite hard of hearing and thinks everyone else is too. 'I was just chatting to her yesterday – or was it the day before . . . ?'

She trailed off, her brow wrinkling. I realised that Gappy was in a foggy moment and she thought I was a new maid, because of the tray. I also remembered vaguely that Mrs Irongirdle *had* been the housekeeper at Grimacres, but yonks ago when there'd been a full staff. I'd seen a picture of her in one of the fading photographs on the wall in the kitchen. She'd been a large, grim woman who looked like she'd been riveted into her uniform by a team of shipbuilders.

Gappy put her mirror and lipstick down, got comfortable against her pillows and had a good look at me through her enormous spectacles.

'She needs to keep her staff in check – some of them can be quite impertinent – but you look rather a nice girl,' she continued. 'Are you the replacement for whatshername? You're terribly young for a maid though, I must say . . .'

When Gappy is like this, you have two options: you can either play along until she finds herself again, or you can attempt to lasso her brain and bring her back to the present. I decided on that approach. I placed the tray on her lap and sat down on the eiderdown at the end of the bed.

'I'm afraid I'm none of those things,' I said, gently. 'I'm

Edna, you remember – your nephew Bernard's youngest daughter.'

'IMPOSSIBLE!' boomed Gappy. 'Why Bernard's only a boy! Always running about the place, getting in the way. Found all of them last week creeping about the house with the biscuit tin looking for secret passages! Bernard and er . . . Mildred and oh – who's the other one?'

'Uncle Roderick?' I said. I could imagine him doing that, but the thought of Farv and Aunt M larking about made my mind boggle. They'd always been so sensible.

'WHOOOO?' said Gappy, both looking and sounding like a disgruntled owl.

'Uncle Roderick,' I repeated.

'NEVER HEARD OF A ROGER!' said Gappy, dismissively. 'Knew a Rupert once but I couldn't BEAR him . . .'

Now, I was, of course, very interested in hearing more about this Rupert, but it was time for me to try and get control of things again. 'I'm your great niece, Aunt Priscilla, and I've brought you up some dinner.' I pointed at the tray.

Gappy looked at the tray, then immediately fell asleep. She does that sometimes. I waited, wondering how to get the conversation around to asking her where she thought the Gristle treasure might be buried when suddenly a few minutes later, her eyes pinged open again.

'Edna, darling!' she cried, recognising me immediately and

grinning. 'How lovely to see you! Love the eyepatch. Very dashing! And you've brought me a tray – too sweet of you! Are you here for the weekend? What's going on down there? Tell me everything.' She started to slurp the soup.

I wasn't sure what to say really. 'Well, everyone was having dinner and now they are arguing,' I said.

Gappy laughed. 'I bet my brother caused that!' she said, and I nodded. 'What's he done now? Swapped the sugar for the salt? Filled a bath full of spiders again? Flirted with the maids? Stolen a horse?'

I began filling her in on some of what had gone on. 'No one seems happy about Grandpa's new secretary Miss Bellissima, Giovanna, but I think she's rather nice. Now they are all arguing about a will.'

'WHOOOO? said Gappy again. 'Will? Who is Will? Some rapscallion coming here to pilfer the silver?'

Her memory was starting to fog again. It was clear I wasn't going to get a chance to ask about the buried treasure tonight, so I just smiled and said, 'Something like that.'

Gappy yawned and suddenly looked very tired. 'Well, I'm sure it will all be OK in the morning, dear,' she said. 'Wonderful what a bit of summer sunshine will do for everyone's mood . . .'

I looked out of the little slanted window on to the snow-covered roof, and smiled. 'That's very true, Aunt P.'

'I think I'm done with this tray now, dear,' said Gappy,

settling herself back into her pillows.

'Would you like anything else?' I asked. 'There's no pudding because it ended up smushed on the dining room floor . . .'

'No, thank you, I think it's time for my beauty sleep,' she said with another yawn, this time so wide her entire face nearly disappeared into it. 'Just send . . . er . . . thingie up . . . whatshername . . . Georgina?'

'Giovanna?' I said, surprised. What could Gappy want with Miss Bellissima?

'WHOOO?' shouted Gappy, cupping a hand around one of her little ears. 'My father?' she said, mishearing me again. 'Oh, you can't send him up to me, dear – would be frightfully difficult – he's dead!'

I laughed. 'I'll send Mrs Crumpet up,' I said. I knew Mrs C would sort Gappy out.

'Ooh yes, do!' said Gappy, sleepily. 'I'd like a crumpet! Very hot with lots of butter, please.'

'And jam?' I said.

'Oh no, I wouldn't have ham on a crumpet, dear.' said Gappy and with that she fell asleep. Her great, rumbling snores rattling the bed frame.

I picked up the tray and tiptoed from the room. I was just about to step down from the attic stairs on to the landing where all our bedrooms were when I stopped suddenly.

My ears twitched like a hare's.

I'd heard something.

The twist of a doorhandle.

The squeak of a hinge.

The creak of a floorboard.

There was no doubt about it: someone nearby was creeping about.

Helmet belonging to a suit of armour, 'CLIVE'. Medieval.

CHAPTER 16.
CREEPING MOUSE-LIKE IN OSTRICH FEATHERS

I craned my neck like a giraffe so that I could have a sneaky little peeky-pie around the corner. There's an old, rusted suit of armour (Clive, to his friends) stationed on the landing near the attic stairs, which provided me with a rather useful bit of cover. Tucked behind Clive, *I* could see down the landing, but whoever was creeping about couldn't see me.

I raised my eyebrows in surprise.

It was Miss Bellissima.

'Now, what's *she* up to?' I whispered to myself, but also to Clive.

Her bedroom was the next one to mine but on the other side of the long corridor. I watched as Grandpa's secretary crept, mouselike, from her room and closed the door as quietly as possible behind her. She glanced about, then began slinking down the landing. She paused every so often, cocking her head to the side. I recognised that behaviour very well because I do it myself – it's the work of a master earwigger. She was listening very carefully. Below us was the distant rumble of loud voices. The tremendous row from earlier had started up again.

Satisfied that no one was coming upstairs, Miss Bellissima carried on slinking. She stopped again, this time outside another door, and pressed one of her ears against the wood. More earwigging.

From my vantage point, I couldn't see exactly whose room it was. Gloria's, I thought, or maybe Uncle Roderick's? Either way, the room didn't belong to her, so what was she doing? I leant further out to get a better view.

CLANK!

Gappy's soup spoon fell from the tray and clanged loudly against Clive's metal shoe. Miss Bellissima nearly jumped out of her skin.

'HECK IT!' I said to myself. 'You'll have to style this out, Ed.'

And so I did. I pretended to stumble and appeared at the end of the corridor.

'AHOY!' I said, in a loud, slightly breathless voice as if I'd jogged down the attic stairs. 'Just –' *Puff! Pant!* – 'bringing this down from Great Aunt P!'

Miss Bellissima looked wide-eyed at me and that red flush

started creeping up her neck again. I could tell she was embarrassed to be caught sneaking. I decided now to approach the situation like I was an explorer who'd stumbled across another like-minded pal deep in a jungle.

'I say!' I said, heartily. 'Not lost are you, old chum?' I saw her visibly relax. I was just Grandpa's little granddaughter, what harm could I be? Sometimes it's very wise to pretend to be as stupid as some grown-ups think children are.

I walked towards her. She'd changed out of her evening frock, I noticed, and was now in a silk nightie under a billowing sheer robe with a thick border of ostrich feathers at the cuffs and hem. It was completely unsuitable for the cold of Grimacres, of course. You really need to wear pyjamas so you can wedge a hot water bottle into the waistband to avoid getting frostbite on your bum, but she did look rather wonderful. She smelt wonderful too. Something floral . . . Rose and Geranium face cream, I deduced.

'Oh,' she said, quietly, 'no, I'm not lost, I was just . . . er . . . looking for . . . a book.'

I looked at the door we were standing beside.

'In Uncle Roderick's bedroom?' I said.

Again that crimson creeping flush.

'Ah!' Miss Bellissima said. 'Then perhaps I am a *little* lost. I meant to go to the library. But that's on the floor below . . . silly me.'

Hmmm . . . I thought. Something about all of this was

making me suspicious.

Beside me, Miss Bellissima suddenly sighed and seemed to deflate.

'This evening has been very . . . trying,' she said softly and looked confused.

Below us, there was another roar of raised voices and I heard someone (Farv perhaps?) slam the door of Grandpa's study. Both Miss Bellissima and I winced at the bang.

'Actually, I think I'll leave the book,' she said, turning back down the corridor to her room. I realised then, as her shoulders drooped under her extravagant dressing gown, that she seemed sad. I decided to try and cheer her up.

'Are you sure?' I said. 'If you want a nice bit of bedtime reading, I've got a cracking book about dreadful diseases in my room you can borrow?'

Miss Bellissima smiled. 'That's very kind of you,' she said, 'but I think I'll just go to bed.'

I nodded. 'It's a big day tomorrow, isn't it?' I said. 'Are you excited for the wedding?'

Miss Bellissima sighed. 'Oh . . . I'm sure it'll be fine,' she said in a voice which sounded the opposite of fine. 'Your grandpa's been kind to me, but . . .'

'Yes?' I said encouragingly.

She sighed again and I realised that she wasn't really talking to me but rather thinking aloud. 'It's just I never really . . .'

Never what? I wondered, but then to my utter dismay,

just at that very moment there was another deafening shout from downstairs (maybe Uncle Roderick this time?) and the study door slammed again. The noise shook Miss Bellissima from her thoughts. She looked at me, as if only just noticing I was there.

'I must go to bed,' she said, and she touched me lightly on the shoulder and started to return to her own bedroom.

'Goodnight, Miss Bellissima,' I said.

'Oh, please,' she said, 'call me Giovanna.' Then she disappeared up the corridor and into her room.

I watched her go, thinking.

If Grandpa had his way, by lunchtime tomorrow I'd be calling her Granny.

CHAPTER 17.
BLACK AIR AND BLUE LANGUAGE

Furiously disappointed not to have wheedled more from Giovanna, I hoofed it down the stairs to the kitchen to return Gappy's tray, screeching briefly to a halt outside Grandpa's study door. I could hear raised voices from behind it. Grandpa was telling someone to leave before he kicked their backsides out the door.

The drawing room door was shut too, and a heated discussion was clearly going on in there as well, but if I went in, there was a very real possibility of me being sent to bed, so I kept on heading down to the kitchen.

Mrs Crumpet was up to her armpits in soap suds, washing up.

'What's going on?' I said, jerking a thumb to the ceiling. Mrs Crumpet's face was flushed pink with excitement and she was bursting to talk.

'Now, you know I'm not one to gossip at all,' she said, furiously scrubbing a roasting tin, 'but the air in that room is black and the language blue! Sure, I've never seen the lot of them that angry! And poor Miss Blouse and Badger sitting there in the middle of it not knowing where to put their faces.'

She shook her head and banged the tray down and started on another. I grabbed a dishcloth and got drying.

'All of this over a will?' I asked.

She nodded. 'I'd not have signed the thing if I'd have known, but my specs, you know, in the fruitcake . . .'

'It's not your fault,' I said. 'You didn't know what you were signing, and anyway, I'm not sure what the problem is. Giovanna seems quite nice, really.'

Mrs Crumpet flared her nostrils like a horse.

'I'm sure she is, but this time tomorrow she'll be the new Lady Gristle, and the minute your grandfather drops dead *everything is hers*. It's no wonder your family are raging. Your father being the eldest child would have got the house and everything in it *and* half of the fortune of course, and the rest of the money – a smaller amount but still a huge sum no doubt – would have gone to Mildred and Roderick. Now, they're all not after getting a penny of it!'

She held a soapy finger aloft and said very dramatically: 'This is the end of Grimacres!'

My stomach crocheted itself into a knot.

'Giovanna will still share it with us though, won't she?' I said.

Mrs Crumpet snorted. 'She'll be one of the richest people in England, and if there's one thing I know about most very rich people it's that they soon forget what sharing means.'

Just then Archie arrived with his hands piled high with more things to wash from the dining room. I helped him with them but nearly jumped out of my skin when a sudden trilling noise filled the room.

We all turned to look at the bell board, where the bell labelled 'Study' was ringing its head off. Mrs Crumpet groaned and wiped her hands dry on her pinny.

'Lord Ignatius wanting his bedtime whiskey, no doubt.'

She shuddered. 'And him just sat smugly at his desk, surrounded by all those revolting objects of his. Shark jaw bones, and snakes preserved in goodness knows what, and that dirty, great big stuffed fish above the fireplace, with its evil-looking tusk or whatever it is . . .'

'The narwhal?' I said. 'Oh, I quite like that. It's a mammal actually . . . The unicorn of the sea, they call it . . .' I pictured it there above the mantelpiece, a tiny whale with an enormous pointy spear jutting out of its head.

Mrs Crumpet snorted. 'Unicorn, my eye,' she said. 'Mark my words, he'll be sitting there, face the colour of a beetroot, polishing those arrows of his. It's a wonder he hasn't fired one of them at his children!'

Beside me, Archie gasped and went very pale. When I looked at Mrs Crumpet, she looked stricken. A strange silence fell on the room which I didn't understand . . . but I guessed Archie didn't much fancy delivering Grandpa his whiskey. Poor Archie.

Mrs Crumpet gathered herself quickly and poured the whiskey into a crystal glass then put it on a little tray. 'I'll take it!' I said, brightly. I gave Archie a little smile. 'Save you a job.'

I picked up the tray, and with my spare hand I urged him to follow me into the dining room.

Once we were on our own, I put the tray down and turned to Archie. 'Are you all right?' I asked.

He nodded, unconvincingly.

'Hmm . . .' I said. 'You don't look all right. What was all that about?' But Archie didn't answer. He looked frightened. He shook his head and I didn't push it. Archie would talk when he wanted to, I knew that, and when he did my ears would be waggling and ready to listen.

'Well don't worry,' I said, picking up the tray again and headed for the door. 'I'll deliver this to the old troll!'

As I opened the door, the rumble of voices got louder. I could hear Grandpa roaring at someone.

'Awful, isn't he?' I said turning back to Archie. 'A real stinkin' ogre!'

Archie nodded with a nervous little smile. He put two fingers either side of his head like devil horns and pulled a horrific face. I laughed as I slipped out the door, but I had to admit, I was a bit worried about him.

Stepping into the hall, the shouting became very loud. I'd just got to the study door when it flew open and Lil burst out from it, stormy-faced, her bowtie hanging limply around her neck.

'You'll regret this, Ignatius!' she said as she strode right past me and disappeared into the drawing room.

I slipped into the study as bravely as I could and presented myself in front of my grandfather.

'What do you want?' he snapped.

'I've brought you your bedtime drink,' I said. Then I shuddered. He looked so alarming, sneering at me from behind the desk. Frightening almost. The lamp beside him was casting an eerie green glow on his skin and making strange, dark shadows dance across his puckered face. His bushy eyebrows stuck up like horns, and in his hands, the lamplight flashed across a razor-sharp arrowhead clutched in his claw-like fingers.

Above him, the narwhal hung on the wall above the roaring fire, its horn glinting in the flickering light, and the glass eye seemed to glare right at me. The whole scene was like something from a horror film and was enough to give a different sort of person the willies.

I put the glass down on the table and waited.

'You *can* say thank you,' I said after a moment, but of course he didn't. He just continued to sit there, holding a dangerously pointed arrowhead up to the light.

'Not got poison in it, has it?' said Grandpa, gesturing towards the whiskey.

'Of course not!' I said.

'Pity!' said Grandpa, with a crocodile smile. 'I could have slipped it into the coffee pot for that lot in there. Got rid of all of them in one swoop!' He pointed with the arrow in the direction of my family in the drawing room.

'That's a horrible thing to say!' I said, but he just cackled like a goblin.

'None of them are any use anyway! It would be doing the world a favour really . . .' He glared at me across his desk. 'Why are you still here?'

I didn't move.

'Why ARE you so horrible to everyone all the time?' I said, ignoring my nervously knocking knees.

'Because I <u>like</u> it,' he said, grinning devilishly again. 'There's nothing more fun to me than cruelty. Needless cruelty – it's MARVELLOUS! Now, I'm tired of my foul family polluting my study. So, GET OUT!'

The unexpected shout made me jump. I picked up the tray and wondered how much trouble I'd get in if I walloped him over the head with it. I decided not to risk it this time. As I got to the door, it once again swung open before me, and there was Farv.

Beyond him, in the gloom of the hall, I saw a crowd had assembled. Lil and Audrey were halfway up the stairs, Muv had a hand on the newel post and next to her, looking grim, was Uncle Roderick, with Gloria Blouse peeking nervously out from behind him. Badger was loitering just inside the drawing room, looking embarrassed with his coat on, and Aunt M was floating in the hall, one hand fussing with her pearls. Mrs Crumpet was standing by the door down to the kitchens and Archie, holding Charles Darwin, was standing frozen by the telephone table, eyes darting about anxiously. I scurried over to stand beside him.

It was Farv who spoke up. He's a tall man, but in that moment he looked shrunken and exhausted. I felt sorry for him. He took a deep breath.

'Father,' he said in a very calm, very polite voice, 'things have gotten out of hand this evening. And we are all terribly sorry about that. It was just a big shock to us to hear about this wedding tomorrow, and your . . . er . . . plans for Grimacres, but look: we just want to make sure you know what you're doing. We're . . . well, we're begging you – all of us – to reconsider. Have a think about things before you make any big decisions. Put the wedding off for a bit. We're worried about you.'

Grandpa didn't say anything. He just turned the arrowhead in his hand over and over.

'Father?' said Farv eventually.

'Worried?' Grandpa snarled. 'WORRIED?'

Then he laughed his horrible goblin laugh again.

'YOU'RE ALL JUST WORRIED ABOUT THE MONEY!' he roared, then with a whoosh, he threw the arrowhead like a dart across the room, where it landed with a crunch and a vibrating twang in the doorframe just above Farv's head.

We all gasped. Farv staggered from the room, blinking dazedly.

'Oh, leave it, Bernard,' snapped Muv, starting up the stairs. 'There's no talking to him at all. Come up to bed. You too, Edna!'

In front of her, Gloria Blouse, Audrey and Lil scuttled upstairs and disappeared into the gloom of the landing. Muv stalked up behind them followed by Uncle Roderick and Farv, both their faces looking like tropical storms.

All the excitement over, Mrs Crumpet vanished back to the kitchen again telling Archie to hurry up and follow her. It was time for bed. He handed me Charles Darwin with shaking hands before disappearing down the stairs.

'I'll be off now,' said Badger, quietly. He bravely stuck his head into Grandpa's study to say a few words and goodnight to Grandpa before returning to the hall.

'Thanks awfully for dinner,' he said to Aunt M as he put on his scarf.

Aunt M sighed, 'I'm so sorry about it all. Really too dreadful! Are you sure you won't stop here tonight? It's frightful out.'

Badger shook his head, pulling on his gloves. 'Thank you, Mildred, but I'm only across the courtyard. Now you try and rest, OK? Let me know if you need anything.'

Just then the clocks in the hall chimed eleven o'clock, clanging right by my earhole.

'Oh!' said Aunt M, flustered. 'Daddy's medication – I'm late with it!'

'I'll see myself out,' said Badger. 'You sort Ignatius. I'll see you in the morning for this er . . . wedding.'

Then he jingle-jangled his way out of the front door and into the freezing night.

I dawdled a bit, hidden in the doorway of the drawing room, and watched as Aunt M took Grandpa in a small capful of something, which he snatched and swallowed with a grimace, then she slipped upstairs too, her forehead as wrinkled as a pug's.

I was the last one up to bed that night.

On my way I snuck a final peek through the banister at Grandpa. He was sat in the lamplight, looking like a spider in the centre of his web, surrounded by his prized objects and the tusk of the narwhal glinting in the light. I noticed he was toying with another arrowhead turning it over and over in his hands and looking grimly thoughtful. Then he got up and shuffled to his study door. I withdrew into the shadows, afraid he would see me and give me an earful, but he didn't. He simply glanced into the hallway, then slammed the door tight.

'Edna! Bed. NOW!' Muv cried from upstairs, and with Charles Darwin tucked under my arm I hurried up into my room.

PART THREE:
MURDER
AFTER
MIDNIGHT

CHAPTER 18.
THE USEFULNESS OF KEEPING A SCREWDRIVER IN YOUR PYJAMA TROUSERS

Sometimes my ears are a curse to me.

Even when I'm conked out, they are working overtime, earwigging like mad.

I was woken by them just a few hours after going to sleep. A knife-thin blade of moonlight was slicing into my room from a gap in the curtains and for a few moments I just lay in its eerie half-glow, listening. My first assumption was that the noises were just Grimacres, creaking and groaning, as rickety old houses tend to do, but I was wrong.

I soon realised two things:

1. Someone was wandering about on the landing.
2. Charles Darwin had disappeared.

He wasn't in bed beside me and a quick glance around my tiny bedroom told me he wasn't anywhere else in the room either.

That's when I realised a third thing:

3. My door was open.

It wasn't *wide* open, but it was open enough for a very determined tortoise to escape through. I obviously hadn't shut it properly before I went to bed.

People think tortoises are slow creatures but when they put their minds to it, they can be as quick as a whippet. Well, Charles Darwin can . . .

HECK IT! I thought. I'd have to go and find him. He should, of course, at that time of year, have been hibernating, but you try telling *him* that. Charles Darwin does exactly what he wants at all times.

The floor was icy when my bare feet touched it. I crouched down and groped around beneath the loose floorboard by my bedside cabinet to retrieve my hand torch from my secret hidey-hole. (This is where I stash all the things I don't want people to find – sweets, torch, screwdriver, inappropriate books, anything I've stolen from the pantry etc.)

I was just about to embark on my tortoise hunt when I suddenly stopped. I wasn't sure why, but something – probably that same strange, prickling feeling I'd been feeling since I arrived at Grimacres – made me grab the screwdriver too. I slipped it into the waistband of my pyjama slacks and set off.

Charles Darwin wasn't outside my room, or on the landing.

After a moment of consideration, I decided that he would have definitely made his way downstairs towards the kitchen. There'd been a half-eaten tomato in his cardboard box earlier and if I knew Charles Darwin, he'd be wanting to finish it.

I began creeping towards the stairs but swiftly had to back myself into the shadows and switch the torch off. I wasn't the only person awake and wandering about. There were voices and footsteps coming from further down the corridor.

I held my breath, but when, after a moment, no one appeared, I slowly continued down the landing. The door to Giovanna's room was closed. I gently tried the handle and found it locked.

I carried on. Gloria Blouse's door was closed too but across the hall, whispered sounds were coming from Uncle Roderick's bedroom. I jammed my lughole right up to the keyhole. It was a bit tricky to hear, but I could just make out Uncle Roderick saying, 'Look, don't worry about it. We'll go first thing in the morning before anyone can find out!'

I wanted to linger a while longer to find out what *that* could mean, but there was the sound of footsteps again. I squished myself back into the shadows, just in time to see a figure, bulky in a thick dressing gown, step on to the landing from the top of the stairs.

Who this figure was I couldn't tell. In the darkness it could quite easily have been Aunt M *or* Farv. Aunt M sleeps with her hair up in a hairnet so their likeness is made more confusing. The figure slipped into a room, but as a soft light was leaking out from under both Farv and Aunt M's bedroom doors and they were next to each other, from my hiding place I was none the wiser.

I prowled at speed after that to the top of the stairs, noting that there was no sign of Charles Darwin anywhere. I was just about to descend when from behind me I heard the sound of running water coming from the bathroom. I disappeared into the inky blackness of the stairwell, peeking out just in time to see Lil come out of the bathroom, wiping her hands on her pyjama trousers. A gurgling noise told me that she'd just washed them.

I held my breath as she walked straight past me, heading for her room at the top of the stairs. Once she was back inside, I raced downstairs.

It was pitch black in the hall and absolutely freezing, and like a right donkey I'd not thought to put my travelling coat on. It was in my room and I wasn't going to run back up and get it. I stood for a moment, shivering in the dark. Then inspiration struck – the fur coat! Keeping hawk eyes on the hall for sneaky creepers, I reached into the cupboard under the stairs and retrieved it, thankful for its warmth as I chucked it on, even though it smelt of old raccoons.

I raced down to the kitchens. Once there I switched my torch on and had a snoop around, but Charles Darwin wasn't anywhere. I thought he might have been turbo-chomping his way through the vegetable drawer, but no luck there.

Mrs Crumpet was out for the count (her deep, grumbling snores were rattling the jam jars in the room next door) and a quick peek into Archie's room told me that Charles Darwin wasn't there either and that Archie was curled up like a field mouse, completely zonked.

So where was Charles Darwin?

I chewed one of my plaits thinking hard. *He must be in one of the rooms on the ground floor*, I thought. Back up I raced, desperate to find him so I could return to the relative warmth of my bed. But Charles Darwin, the slippery crook, eluded me. He wasn't in the drawing room, or the dining room, or Aunt M's little office, or the morning room, or the library.

I did notice something odd in the library though – a whiff of flowers. This was strange because I knew there weren't any there. Grandpa never saw the point of them. Why have a vase of flowers when you could have glass cases displaying stuffed poisonous frogs? But there are only so many mysteries one person can juggle and for me, at present, a missing tortoise was the most pressing.

I went back to the hall, hands on my hips. I called softly for Charles Darwin but no answer. Where *could* he be? Then my eyes slid to the only room I hadn't tried – Grandpa's study. I shuddered but decided I'd have to have a look. The door was closed and, when I tried it, I found it was locked.

Not in there then, I mused, but just as I was about to walk away there came a soft sound from inside the study. It was the padding of little feet and the quiet bump of a small head against woodwork. *Surely not?* I thought. I bent down to the small gap under the door and gasped. There, unmistakably, were Charles Darwin's scaly feet, covered in a ragged mess of dust and spider silk.

'What on earth are you doing in there, you clown?' I whispered.

No reply.

How he had found himself inside a locked room I had no idea. *I'll have to puzzle that out later*, I thought. The main thing for now was, how to get him out? Grandpa had been in such a foul mood earlier I didn't want his temper to worsen by finding tortoise wee all over his office. I knew that would be *just* the sort of thing Charles Darwin would do in this situation.

I tried the door handle again, but it wouldn't budge. I eyeballed the lock, but it was jammed up with something from the inside.

HECK!

Brain whirring, I ran my hand over the surface of the door. It was made from thick, dark wood inlaid with panels. It was in the corner of one of the lower panels that I found my solution. There was a very small woodworm hole in it.

Remembering my screwdriver, I whipped it out from my trousers, plunged it in the gap and started wiggling. It was tricky work, but in a few minutes I'd worked the panel loose. I knew Grandpa would be furious with me in the morning for damaging his door, but I'd have to deal with that problem when I came to it. I reached into the gap for Charles Darwin only to see that he had run away – back into the dark depths of Grandpa's study.

'Charles Darwin!' I hissed. 'Now is not the time for you to be playing silly beggars!'

HECK IT! I realised I'd have to go in. There was, I thought, just about enough space for me to wiggle through the gap if I really sucked my tummy in and didn't mind a few splinters.

I crawled through and was soon in the room.

I was standing there, flashing my torchlight around, when I spotted it.

Not Charles Darwin, but something else.

Something awful.

I slowly raised the torch light, and all the air in my lungs left me.

There, sitting in his chair, was Grandpa.

And he had the narwhal tusk sticking out of his chest.

Victorian taxidermy narwhal, complete with tusk.
WARNING: TIP OF TUSK IS DANGEROUSLY SHARP.

CHAPTER 19.
CLUES BY TORCHLIGHT

My hand that was holding the torch started to shake, the weak light from it bouncing around the room, making macabre shadows dance on the walls behind Grandpa.

Hold it together, Ed! I told myself firmly. *This is your first corpse, the moment you've been waiting for so just STAY. CALM.*

I took a deep breath and reached out to touch Grandpa's hand. It was unnaturally still, but warm. Well, as warm as a hand can be in Grimacres. I thought back to my murder book upstairs and I realised that if he wasn't marble-statue cold, then he couldn't have been dead very long at all. A nasty idea crashed into my brain. Was the person who stuck the narwhal tusk into him still in the room?

Frantically, I shone my torch around the study, but there

was no one else there. The room looked exactly as it had earlier in the evening – Grandpa's desk, a smaller desk by the window which I took to be Miss Bellissima's as it had a neat little typewriter on it. On the other side of the room was a large table piled high with boxes and a mess of papers. What they were, I didn't know and I had no time to investigate. I checked under Grandpa's desk in case the culprit was hiding, but there wasn't anything or anyone there.

I was alone. No, not alone. Charles Darwin was there, crawling on to my foot, and Grandpa was at his desk.

Dead.

MURDERED!

What else could it be?

'Grandpa couldn't have done this to himself, and he couldn't have fallen on the tusk either,' I whispered to Charles Darwin. 'It was on the wall behind him when I went up to bed – I saw it. So without a doubt someone had taken it off the wall and . . . and done him in!'

My breathing was shallow. I knew in a minute I'd have to call for someone – everyone, probably – but the main person I needed was Lil. As a doctor, she'd know exactly what to do for sure. But before I woke her, I wanted to take a good look for clues. I knew (again because of my murder book) how important it is to take in as many details as you can when you find someone murdered. These first clues are usually the most important.

I forced myself to inspect the scene.

A quick peek confirmed that the tusk had gone right through Grandpa, pinning him to the seat. His head was flopped down on to his chest and his hands – hang on a second – what was that? One of Grandpa's arms was dangling limply over the arm rest but the other one was on the desk, resting on his blotting pad. It was this that interested me. Carefully using the tip of the screwdriver to avoid disturbing any fingerprints (good old murder book teaching me that little trick) I nudged his hand and shone the torch. The tip of his index finger was black and wet. It was covered in ink from an upturned bottle nearby and drawn on the sheet in front of him was a strange mark.

I looked at it one way, then another, then I realised: it was the number 13. The other fingers on that hand were clean so I knew it had to have been drawn deliberately.

13 . . .

Was this a message? Had Grandpa, realising a narwhal tusk was pinning him to his chair and that he didn't have long left, tried to give whoever found his body a clue? Some important piece of information? What could it mean? 13 . . . what? I couldn't think.

Once again, I flashed the torch over the whole grisly scene in front of me and suddenly I felt my knees begin to tremble. I'd held myself together so far, but now my body was tensing up like a startled snail as the enormity of the situation I was in hit me.

Someone had murdered Grandpa!

Right here!

In Grimacres!

And I was standing in a room with a dead body!

I knew *it* couldn't hurt me, but the person who'd done it could still be somewhere in the house. We could all be in danger!

A chill came shivering over me, like I was standing in a draught, but the doors and windows were closed.

My heart was racing.

My mouth was dry. A strange tingling sensation pricked my arms and legs.

The room began to spin.

Then the torch fell from my hand, clattering on the floor, and before I could stop myself, I screamed.

Antique wrought iron key belonging to the study door, Grimacres. c.17th century.

CHAPTER 20.
PANDEMONIUM IN PYJAMAS

The next hour passed in a complete blur.

I remember hearing the sound of my own scream echoing around the study before my brain seemed to stand abruptly to attention. *Quit your caterwauling, Ed, and look sharp!* it demanded, and I pulled myself together. My heart was still racing, but at least I'd shut my gob.

Next, I remember a great thundering of feet on the floor above me followed by the sound of them cascading down the stairs. It was like a herd of stampeding wildebeests, and then voices – shouts, questions, more shouts, then eventually, 'IT'S EDNA! SHE'S IN HERE!'

Fists hammering on the study door.

'It's locked! We'll have to smash our way in!' came a voice. I think it was Uncle Roderick.

The sound of several pairs of feet taking paces back ready to charge.

My brain jolted awake again.

'No, wait!' I cried, almost back to myself again. 'The key's in the lock!'

Oh! I thought – my mind sharpening for a moment. The key's in the lock? Then how did the murderer leave, for cripes' sake? That was important!

I ran over and turned the key. I barely had time to leap out of the way before the door swung open and everyone piled in, practically falling over themselves on to the rug.

'Edna, dear! Whatever's the—' started Aunt M, but she stopped suddenly. Farv had clicked on the light switch and the room flickered into a revolting, yellow glow. I remember briefly thinking how funny everyone looked in their nightclothes: Farv and Aunt M in nearly matching tartan robes; Muv and Audrey enveloped in silk; Lil in flannel pyjamas; Uncle Roderick in boxer shorts and a vest and Gloria, shivering behind him in a thin cotton nightie. Mrs Crumpet of course had her thick, knitted bed jacket on, and Archie was, as always, neat as a pin even though his pyjamas were a half size too small, the trouser legs halfway up his skinny calves. I briefly registered that Giovanna wasn't there but then everyone spotted Grandpa.

The room erupted into shouts and cries. Swear words

hissed on exhaled breaths, like leaky gas pipes. Lil, naturally, leapt into doctor mode and was over to Grandpa in a flash, pressing her fingers to his neck, looking for a pulse, then shaking her head.

Mrs Crumpet was the first to speak, practical as always. 'Burglars!' she said. 'It'll have been burglars!'

Uncle Roderick bounded to the windows. I noticed his face had a horrible green tinge to it. I think he was glad of something to do.

The curtains were open and yellow light from the room was spilling out on to the snow beyond.

'Locked!' he said, rattling the window, then he ran his fingers over the edges of the panes. 'Not just locked. Painted over. Sealed shut! These haven't been opened for years!'

'Then how did . . . ?' Muv started but her voice petered out. 'Edna, are you sure that door was locked?'

I nodded. I was definitely sure. The mechanisms had clunk-clicked as I'd turned the key.

'I'll phone the police!' said Aunt M, and she dashed from the room into the hall. The telephone lived on a small table near the front door beside a full-sized cannon and next to an almost complete salamander's skeleton.

'Oh!' came her voice. 'The line's dead.'

Farv was standing stock still in the centre of the room, his brows a thick, grim line across his forehead. He was just staring and staring at Grandpa's body.

'It'll be the weather, Mil,' he said, mechanically. 'The lines will be down.'

'No,' said Mildred returning to the room, looking shaken. She held up the telephone receiver from which dangled a short length of frayed cord. 'Someone's cut the line!'

My eyes found Archie's. We looked at each other, goggle-eyed. We both knew what that meant: whoever had cut the cable had also cut Grimacres off from the entire world beyond the Grimacre Woods. The narrow road to Much Maudlin would be impassable now because of the snow and without the telephone we couldn't ring anyone to tell them what had happened, or to come and dig us out.

'See . . .' said Mrs Crumpet. 'Burglars!'

Suddenly I felt all eyes on me.

Lil came and crouched down until she was on my level. She looked at me firmly, but kindly. 'Listen, Edna, I know this has been a shock, but you *must* tell us exactly what's happened. Start from the beginning.'

And so I did.

I left out the bit about hearing and seeing everyone moving about upstairs, and also the bit about the number '13'. Just as I was about to mention that, I stopped. Something – and I don't know what, maybe a look from Charles Darwin? – made me keep that little bit of info up my PJ sleeves for now. Instead, I started with Charles Darwin disappearing and then finding him in the room. I pointed to the missing panel I'd removed from the study door and then just told them about discovering the body. After I'd finished, my words seemed to hang in the air like the dust left after a bomb explosion. Everyone looked wide-eyed and worried.

'Absurd!' said Muv.

'What are we going to do?' said Aunt M.

Before anyone could offer any suggestions, there was the sound of footsteps in the hall and a minute later, through the study door came Giovanna, wafting in in a cloud of ostrich feathers and scented face cream.

She stopped when she saw us all.

'What's happening?' she said. 'I was sleeping and then I heard noises.' She glanced around and seemed to realise for the first time that she was standing in the study. I saw her brain working.

'Is it Ignatius?' she stammered. 'Is he OK?'

'Not really,' I said, cocking a thumb over my shoulder in the direction of the desk. 'He's dead.'

As one we shuffled apart so that Giovanna could see Grandpa for the first time. She was still for a moment, then she screamed like a banshee and fainted, crumpling like a dropped dress on to the floor.

Everyone sprang into action then. Lil and Aunt M leapt to help her.

'We need to get her out of here!' commanded Lil. 'Take her to the drawing room sofa!'

Farv and Uncle Roderick manhandled the collapsed figure between then and started for the door but found Badger standing there. He was dishevelled in hastily put on clothes – shoes but no socks, coat, gloves and scarf, a vest hanging out of his trousers and his sparse hair all tousled. It would have been quite funny if there hadn't been a corpse in the room.

'Got up for a glass of water then heard a scream – thought it was a fox or something – then saw the light on and . . .' he said, looking wildly at all of us, trying to work out what was going on, then he cried, 'GOOD HEAVENS!' as he saw Grandpa's body for the first time, the tusk sticking out from it.

He stared at it hard for a couple of seconds, then a complete transformation came over him. His face hardened, his eyes sharpened, and for the first time, I saw a glimpse of the detective he must have once been years before.

'Right,' he said in a firm voice. 'Has anyone touched anything?'

We all shook our heads.

I kept schtum.

Badger nodded decisively then said: 'OK, everyone out of here immediately! Go to the drawing room and wait. No one is to come in here again without my permission.'

Then I felt a fizzing thrill of excitement as he said the words I'd always longed to hear:

'This is now a crime scene.'

CHAPTER 21.
SEARCHING IN THE MIDDLE OF THE NIGHT

In the drawing room, Giovanna was still collapsed on one of the sofas.

Mrs Crumpet disappeared downstairs, then came running back a moment later with a bottle of brandy, a damp flannel for Giovanna's head and a cast iron frying pan 'for protection'.

Archie and I plumped down on the rug by the unlit fire, Farv in front of us, pacing and tugging at his moustache.

'I don't understand how this could have happened?' he said.

'He must have disturbed the burglars,' twittered Aunt M. 'They must have slipped in there looking for things to steal, the study is awfully close to the front door so they probably nipped in there first, and found him . . .'

'Ignatius is – WAS – always falling asleep at his desk . . .'

mused Lil from beside Giovanna. 'And you know the fuss he would have caused if he'd discovered anyone trying to take his things.'

Everyone nodded. Grandpa was very selfish. He hated anyone touching his treasures.

'Yes,' said Farv, 'then after they . . . did what they did with the narwhal tusk – to silence him, I suppose? – they must have scarpered out the front door . . .'

Badger came in then, catching the end of what Farv had said. He shook his head.

'No sign of anyone,' he said. 'I've just checked outside the front door – nothing.'

A confused silence.

A slight whimper from Giovanna, who was having a drop of brandy sloshed down her by Lil.

'The thing is . . .' I said. 'How did the burglars leave the room? The doors and windows were locked. I had to break in and squeeze through that tiny door panel.'

I looked around the room. 'No one else could have done that!' I continued. 'Not even Archie – his legs are too gangly.'

Archie looked down at his legs and then nodded in agreement.

Before anyone could answer, Muv suddenly clasped her chest.

'You . . . you don't think they're still in the house, do you?' she gasped. Her face was the colour of sour milk.

'Oh cripes!' said Uncle Roderick. 'You might be right! We'd . . . we'd better check, eh Badger?'

Badger nodded grimly, and the search party left immediately, practically falling over themselves to collect iron fire pokers and heavy objects to use as makeshift weapons. I was meant to stay in the drawing room with Muv and Audrey and Aunt M and Gloria (and Giovanna, who was still coming to), but there was no way I was going to miss out on the excitement, so leaving Charles Darwin on a nice comfy cushion, I gave them all the slip and scampered to catch up with the searchers.

I grabbed Archie and took the opportunity to get him on his own properly for the first time since I'd arrived at the house.

'A murder, Archie!' I said, steering him away from the rest of the search party. 'HERE! In Grimacres. And us two right in the middle of it all! It's quite exciting, isn't it?'

His eyes were wide when they returned my gaze. He didn't seem too sure.

'Where shall we look first?' I said. 'We've got to think like a criminal . . .'

Archie pondered for a moment then pointed to the morning room. We opened the door and ran in. I flicked the lights on and had a good look around. Several marble busts of long dead Gristles leered at us, but there wasn't a culprit anywhere to be found, which was very disappointing. There were no clues either like bloody footprints or a dropped sack with

'SWAG' printed on it or anything.

'Where next?' I said.

Archie tugged my sleeve over to the green baize door and downstairs. The rest of the grown-ups had split up: Farv and Uncle Roderick were searching the ground floor, Lil and Badger had bounded upstairs. No one had thought to search the kitchens.

'Oh, good idea!' I said, as we descended the steps.

'You didn't hear anything, did you?' I asked. I knew Archie was a good earwigger like me. When you don't say much like Archie, your ears don't half work well. And since these days Archie wasn't talking at all, I thought this might be doubly so.

But Archie shook his head and did a funny little mime of himself sleeping soundly, then waking up to a scream. It was a first-class performance.

We were in the kitchens now. I was concerned about whether the potential intruder had been helping themselves to any of the very sharp, very dangerous objects that Mrs Crumpet kept in her drawers, but I pushed that thought from my mind. The kitchen, at least, seemed to be empty.

Then Archie pointed down the long, dark corridor and mimed a door opening.

'Of course! Badger has checked the front of the house,' I said. 'But what about the *back* door. The murderer could have slipped out there – easy!'

Archie shook his head and pulled out a heavy iron key from the chest pocket of his pyjamas. He mimed locking a door with it.

'Right, you locked it yourself?' I said.

Then he mimed someone sneakily hitting something.

'Oh!' I cried. 'But it might have been bashed in!'

Archie nodded to confirm this was exactly what he meant, and we raced down the kitchen corridor to check. Sure enough, the door was locked tight and, to our disappointment, thoroughly untampered with.

Archie unlocked it anyway and pulled the door open. A blast of freezing air hit us straight in our faces and we realised very quickly that no one at all had been near the back door for hours. The snow beyond it was banked up practically to our waists so even if someone HAD battled through it AND bashed the door in without being heard, they would have left a deep track through the snow AND great wet splodges of melted ice from their boots everywhere. But the snow was pristine and the corridor was bone dry.

'The mystery thickens . . .' I said, and Archie waggled his eyebrows in a way which I knew meant he felt the same. Despite his nervous disposition, I could tell he was getting excited about the case too.

Quickly, we checked the kitchens and the other rooms in the basement of Grimacres. The chickens were all fine in their newspaper beds, neither the larder, the scullery nor any of the kitchen cupboards were hiding any criminals. No windows were broken either and nothing seemed to have been stolen.

Archie pulled a face which meant, 'Odd?'

'I agree,' I said, and we both scratched our heads. Then, slightly dejected, we climbed back up to the ground floor arriving just as the rest of the search party re-entered the drawing room.

'No bandits anywhere!' said Uncle Roderick, trying to be his usual jovial self, but his jolliness sounded hollow and flat. 'No sign of a break in, nor any robbery.'

'Nothing at all?' asked Aunt M. 'How extraordinary . . . Then it seems someone broke into the house with the sole intention of . . .' She trailed off, fussing with the frilly collar of her winceyette nightie.

Lil finished her sentence: '. . . Of murdering Ignatius!'

There was silence as everyone took this in. My mind, however, was taking me in a slightly different direction. A seed of a thought that had planted itself in my head downstairs in the kitchen was now starting to bloom. I looked at my idea from all sides and then nodded.

Yes, I thought. That's the only explanation there *could* be, as horrible as it was to think it.

I had to say something.

'Of course,' I said, 'the other possibility is that someone in this house murdered Grandpa.'

There were sharp intakes of breath and Muv cried, 'EDNA!

144

You mustn't say such awful things!'

'No,' I said, firmly. 'There aren't ANY signs of someone breaking in, or entering from outside – front or back – so the killer _has_ to have been in the house already. We've looked all over and there isn't anyone hiding anywhere. I know _I_ didn't kill Grandpa – I couldn't have reached the narwhal tusk on the wall for a start, so . . .'

Everyone was glaring at me, but I wasn't going to be put off.

I _knew_ I was right.

'So . . .' I continued, matter of factly, 'the murderer _has_ to be one of you lot.'

A pencil (slightly chewed) belonging to the Hon. Edna Gristle.

CHAPTER 22.
AN ITCH AT THE
BACK OF THE BRAIN

Of course, I was sent to bed after that.

I wasn't even allowed to go with Mrs Crumpet and Archie to make tea for everyone, and I was dying to run over my theory with Archie.

I protested, but Muv had a vein popping on her forehead, so I knew it was no use. I retrieved Charles Darwin from his cushion and stomped angrily up to my room.

As I went, I heard Muv's fluttering anxious voice behind me.

'Over excited!' she said in a pretending-to-be-cheerful way. 'I expect it was a bit of a shock for her finding Ignatius like that . . .'

But I *knew* I was right, and what's more, someone else did too. I'd caught Badger's eye as I was skulking out of the room and he looked at me, approvingly.

In my room I was too jittery to sleep. It dawned on me really for the first time that evening that my grandpa was dead. It was a strange thought. Only a few hours ago he'd been roaring like a dragon. *Well, he won't be doing <u>that</u> again . . .* I thought.

Of course, I should have been feeling very sad, but I wasn't. Grandpa hadn't been a nice man or very loveable so it was rather tricky to feel upset. What I could do, I realised, is be USEFUL. I could find out who had stuck him that narwhal tusk.

I decided to set to work immediately.

I knew if I was going to be any help at all in this case (and OH BOY was I determined to be) I needed to make sure I remembered absolutely everything I could about the events of the evening.

I found a pencil, grabbed my murder book and flipped right to the back where there was a good handful of useful blank pages, for situations just like this no doubt. Then I opened the curtains, settled myself on the window seat and, by moonlight, I started to write.

THE MURDER OF IGNATIUS GRISTLE, BARON GRIMACRE (GRANDPA)

Body discovered by: EDNA GRISTLE (ME)

Cause of death: MURDER (by narwhal)

WHEN?
Sometime between: Just after 11 p.m. when I went to bed
(after all the grown-ups had gone up before me)
and 12.30 a.m. – 1 a.m. (ish), when I found him.
Probably closer to 1 a.m. because Grandpa's hand was
still warm.
(Check with Lil.)

IMPORTANT INFORMATION:
Door to the study: LOCKED (from the inside. Key in lock)
Study windows: LOCKED (PAINTED SHUT)
NO signs of BURGLARS or a break in
No burglars in the house (we looked)
NOTHING STOLEN

ANY CLUES?
Nothing in Grandpa's study EXCEPT:
The number 13 drawn by Grandpa with an inky finger
before he croaked it

I cursed myself for not thinking to remove the sheet of
blotting paper with the writing on it. I'm not sure what it
could have told me but I could have looked at it very closely
and considered it carefully. As it was I'd just have to ponder

on the meaning of '13'. *Unlucky for some . . .* I mused, and certainly so for Grandpa.

I then chewed the end of my pencil for a moment, trying to think of other useful things before flicking to the front of the murder book. There was a section near the beginning that said that for a murder to be committed there had to be something called A MOTIVE. This meant a reason for the murderer to do it. Usually, the book said, the main motives were love (yuck!), revenge, or money.

Money.

I circled the word. There's been a lot of talk about that earlier. Especially about that new will . . .

I flipped to the back of the book again and wrote:

NEW WILL.

Then I made a list of everyone who had been in the house at the time of the murder:

ME (EDNA GRISTLE)
CHARLES DARWIN
ARCHIE
MUV
FARV

AUNT M
LIL
UNCLE R
GLORIA BLOUSE
AUDREY
GIOVANNA BELLISSIMA
MRS CRUMPET
GREAT AUNT P
SOME CHICKENS

I then crossed off everyone who I knew couldn't have done the murder and why:

ME (EDNA GRISTLE) — because I didn't.
CHARLES DARWIN — because he is a tortoise.
MUV
FARV
AUNT M
LIL
UNCLE R
GLORIA BLOUSE
AUDREY — snoring.
GIOVANNA BELLISSIMA
MRS CRUMPET — snoring.
ARCHIE — fast asleep.
GREAT AUNT P — couldn't leave the attic without help.

~~SOME CHICKENS.~~ – Sleeping (also, they are chickens).

I couldn't as yet see a motive for Gloria Blouse to murder Grandpa – she'd only met him at dinner, and didn't stand to gain anything from his death – but I decided to keep her name uncrossed-out all the same.

As for most of the others, well, money WAS a good motive. With Grandpa dead, they'd be rolling in it, especially as Grandpa had died *before* he married Miss Bellissima. The new will only came into effect AFTER the wedding which wouldn't happen now because you can't marry dead people.

And as for Lil and Miss Bellissima, they might not get any money *now,* BUT Grandpa's death might be good for them. Lil would, I supposed, be able to move into Grimacres and live with Aunt M, or if not then Aunt M would at least be able to go and live with her. And when I spoke to Miss Bellissima earlier on the landing, she certainly didn't seem to be very excited at the thought of the matrimony. With Grandpa dead, the wedding was off.

I wrote all of that down too.

There was certainly a lot for me to think about.

I turned on to a fresh page. The whole day leading up to the murder had been odd and something in my head told me to write down everything I thought *might* be important. There had been so many things that it made my brain itch trying to remember them, but I tried my best.

- Muv and Farv worried about money
- The mysterious contents of Audrey's drawer and her (new?) necklace
- A new secretary at Grimacres. (Miss Bellissima) — who likes snooping around
- Uncle R needing Grandpa to give him money
- Farv needing Grandpa to give him money
- Lil very angry. (Unusual)
- Grandpa's new will
- Gloria & Uncle R being nervous about Miss B
- ITALY
- The Incident (What is it?)
- Flowery smell in the library
- A lot of people being awake around the time Grandpa was murdered

(What were they all doing?)

And finally, what seemed to be the most important question of all:

How did the murderer leave the locked study?

I looked at my handiwork. Yes, that was a good list to be getting on with.

I looked out of the window, trying to think if I'd missed

anything. Everything outside was smooth and white, just as it had been when I went to bed the first time. Pristine. Not, I thought grimly, like the study floor which had been quite bloody.

The back of my brain started to itch again, telling me I WAS missing something from my list. But what?

I went back over all the events of the evening again, scanning the depths of my mind for anything that might be relevant, but nothing else floated to the surface where I could see it clearly.

I sat staring out at the white snow and the black woods for several long minutes, willing my brain to pull itself together and tell me what I *knew* I knew but just couldn't quite remember.

Eventually, I yawned so widely my jaw nearly fell off. Tiredness hit me like a sack full of bricks and I could hardly keep my eyes open. Whatever clue I'd seen wasn't going to be remembered that night, so I just drew a large question mark in my book to remind me. I'd ask Archie to help me in the morning.

I dropped off the window seat, drew the curtains, picked up Charles Darwin and clambered into bed, cosy still in my fur coat, and thankful to warm my feet under the eiderdown. And with question marks dancing behind my eyelids, I fell asleep.

EXHIBIT D: *A crumpled clipping from a newspaper printed 70 years ago.*

VE-NICE TO SEE YOU AGAIN!

GLITZ, GLAMOUR, AND GONDOLAS ON THE GRAND CANAL!

Special report by Hugo Slander   2nd APRIL

The social season started yesterday night with a bang — several of them actually, as the Facoltoso family kicked off their annual celebrations with a fabulous firework display over the Grand Canal in Venice.

The excitement at the exquisite waterside villa started several hours earlier with guests arriving in lantern-lit gondolas, the flotilla sweeping through the waters at sunset.

Crowds gathered in boats and on bridges, desperate to catch glimpses of the famous faces who have arrived in the romantic city for the annual party at the Facoltoso residence. Attendees were not just made up of representatives from the wealthiest Italian families, but from around the world, as well as several famous actors, singers, artists and some royal faces too!

Pictured below with their hosts, Signor and Signora Facoltoso are the opera star Mr Oscar Libretto (aged 50), who has been performing in Rome recently, Signor and Signora Ravioli — wearing her priceless 'Eye of the Storm' diamond necklace, and the Hon. Ignatius Gristle (aged 20) who is visiting the country from England as part of an extended worldwide holiday.

For all the gossip, gowns and details of the party see pages 3-18 for our exclusive and intrusive coverage!

PART FOUR:

AN ITCH AT THE BACK OF THE BRAIN

18th century egg cruets. Gold plated. Originally from the Palace of Versailles. France.

CHAPTER 23.
AN INVESTIGATION BEGINS

HECK IT! I'd overslept. I'd wanted to be up and at 'em to get stuck right into some detecting. I could tell Badger had agreed with me about the murderer being one of my family, and I wanted to make sure that I was on hand to help him find out who it was.

A quick sniff told me that despite the murder, Mrs Crumpet had turned out a good breakfast and I certainly wasn't going to miss that so I leapt out of bed, grabbed my murder book, pencil and Charles Darwin, and hoofed it downstairs.

I made a quick detour into the library (still smelling faintly and mysteriously of flowers) to grab the magnifying glass that lives on a table in there and shoved it in my pocket, then I headed to the hallway. I found Archie there, tinkering around with the telephone.

'Will you be able to fix it?' I asked. He frowned and waggled his hand about in a not-sure-yet sort of way.

'You'll do it, I just know you will!' I said encouragingly, then I dropped my voice to a whisper and sidled up to him closely. 'Listen, after breakfast we need to have a conference. I'm absolutely sure the murderer is someone in this house.'

Archie looked alarmed.

'Not you, of course!' I hissed. 'One of that lot in there,' and I cocked my head in the direction of the dining room from where a murmur of voices was coming. Archie looked worried and then slowly nodded his head.

'I've started making notes in here,' I said, patting my book, 'but we'll need to go through it together. I want your ideas too, OK?'

He nodded again, more confidently this time and I grinned. I knew I could count on Archie, even though he seemed a bit nervous.

'Look, I'll go and get some breakfast and then we'll slip off to our airing cupboard for a meeting,' I said. 'You keep your eyes and ears open out here and I'll spy in there.' We saluted each other and I dashed off to breakfast.

I skidded into the dining room and sure enough, my whole family were there around the table, even Muv, who usually has breakfast in bed. I have to say, they were not a pretty sight. They had faces like chewed slippers. It seemed that maybe I was the only one who had slept a wink last night. I was also the only one with an appetite. Some were toying with their food, but from the mounds still available on the sideboard, it appeared no one had eaten much at all. I was relieved because I was starving, so I tucked in.

'But how long ARE we going to be stuck here?' my sister Audrey was saying, in that whingy sort of voice that drives me up the wall.

'It'll be a few days yet, dear, I'm afraid,' said Aunt M.

She was dressed all in mourning black, which was quite a shock because usually she's resplendent in pastels.

'Nothing we can do until this snow stops or at least until what's fallen has thawed a bit,' said Lil, pouring herself a coffee. 'Completely impossible for any of our cars to make it down the drive or across the bridge into Much Maudlin. Would be dangerous to even try.' Outside, a very light flutter of snowflakes was falling gently across the glass.

Audrey growled and slammed her teacup down.

'Besides,' continued Lil, 'we'll all have to stay around to speak to the police when we can eventually notify them. They won't want us going anywhere.'

Muv growled now. Sometimes Audrey and her are very alike.

'Honestly!' Muv said, in a tight voice. 'This is really just too extraordinary for words! A murder in the middle of the night and now we are snowed in! It's like something from a dreadful book. And no telephone either! SUCH an inconvenience. Valentino won't have a clue what's happening. He'll be worried sick!'

'I think there are more important things to worry about at the moment than tennis lessons,' said Farv softly.

He looked dreadful. The bags under his eyes were the size of travelling trunks and his moustache was all limp at the edges. Muv snorted and sourly sipped her coffee.

Just then there was a sound in the hall – it was the front door opening and closing. Aunt M got up and clip-clopped out of the room. She returned a few minutes later with Badger, who I was pleased to see was back to his normal well-groomed self this morning. I'd hoped that he might be wearing a monocle and a very well pressed suit and gleaming shoes like my favourite detective in my murder book, but he wasn't. He was wearing a thick, beige cardigan and tartan slippers (he'd left his wellies in the hall). But at least he'd brushed his moustache.

'Sit yourself down and help yourself to anything,' said Aunt M, gesturing towards an empty seat. He sat and poured himself a coffee. Then Aunt M turned to address the room.

'Now, listen,' she said firmly, in the voice I recognised from hearing her talk to business people about The Jolly BonBon, 'we are all very upset about what happened to Daddy last night, so I've asked George if he'll help us.'

'Only until we can get the actual police involved,' said

Badger, slightly awkwardly. 'I'll just gather a bit of info together so that we can hopefully get all of this cleared up nice and quickly.'

'What's to clear up?' asked Muv, sharply. 'Someone broke in, murdered Ignatius and disappeared. No sign of them anywhere!'

Badger looked more awkward still. 'Well . . .' he said, and the way he said it made my ears twitch. So he DID think the same as me – the murderer was in the house!

Farv caught on to Badger's meaning.

'Surely you can't *actually* believe that one of us . . . ?' he said, nostrils flaring.

Badger held up a calming hand. 'I'll just gather some information – that's all,' he said. 'Find out what I can.'

This was my moment!

'And I'll help!' I said, thrusting a marmaladed slice of toast into the air, triumphantly.

'You will NOT, Edna, I forbid it,' said Muv sharply. 'This doesn't concern you. I don't want to see or hear another peep from you all day, do you hear me?'

'Oh MUV!' I protested and was surprised when support came from an unlikely source.

'Oh, let her have some fun, Ros!' said Uncle Roderick. The greenish look from the middle of the night had gone. In fact, I noticed he looked jollier now than he had all weekend. 'Most exciting thing to happen at Grimacres for years – a grisly, midnight murder!'

'Yes, well SOME of us are respectable people, Roderick,' said Muv primly. 'We don't all gallivant with gangsters and murderers and crooks like you . . .'

Uncle Roderick laughed. 'You should try it, Ros,' he said. 'Might melt that icy demeanour of yours a bit! And besides, whether you like it or not, it seems like you ARE now cavorting with criminals!'

'Nonsense! None of *us* killed Ignatius!' Muv cried.

'What other answer IS there?' he replied laughing uproariously, then suddenly he leapt up throwing his chair to the floor behind him and swung a pointed finger at all of us. 'WHICH ONE OF YOU SCOUNDRELS DONE IT?' he boomed. 'OR WAS IT ME? AM I THE DOER OF THE DEED MOST FOUL?'

Then he cackled like a sea witch.

I stifled a giggle behind my napkin.

'Roderick, do calm down,' said Aunt M, placidly. She turned to Badger and using her business voice again she said, 'Now I expect you'll want to talk to each of us and get statements or something?'

Muv snorted. 'What's to say? We were all asleep when it happened!'

Well, that's actually a bit of a fib, I thought. I knew for sure that quite a few people sitting around the table had been wide awake AND skulking about around the time Grandpa was done in with the narwhal tusk.

'Any information, however seemingly unimportant, will be very useful, Lady Gristle,' said Badger, standing up and dusting imaginary crumbs from his slacks. 'Now I think I'll make a start, Mildred,' he said.

'Of course,' said Aunt M. 'Who would you like to begin with? Me?'

Badger considered, then eyeballed me across the table.

'I think I'll start with Miss Edna, since she found Ignatius . . .'

I felt my cheeks flush with excitement. I shoved the last bit of toast into my mouth, dropped a hardboiled egg into the pocket of the fur coat for later and, grabbing my murder book and Charles Darwin, I followed Badger out of the room.

As I scampered past my family, I felt them glaring at me.

If their eyes had been deadly lasers, my head would have been sliced clean off.

CHAPTER 24.
THE APPOINTMENT OF AN ASSISTANT DETECTIVE
(SORT OF)

In the hallway, Archie goggled at me as I followed Badger into Grandpa's study.

I goggled right back. I couldn't believe I was being taken straight back to the room where it all happened. THE MURDER.

Of course *I* knew what Badger was playing at . . .

It could only mean one thing: Badger was appointing me as his Assistant Detective!

As I waited for him to unlock the door, I noticed that the broken panel I'd squeezed through had been hastily reattached. A great number of nails were firmly holding it all together. I nodded approvingly. *Good to keep the room secured*, I thought. Don't want anyone fiddling with evidence, do we?

I gave Charles Darwin a knowing look, which he returned.

Naturally we were in complete agreement.

I braced myself for seeing Grandpa dead again slumped in his chair, but when Badger opened the door I discovered he was no longer in the room.

'The body is being stored in the larder until the police can collect him,' Badger explained. 'Mrs Crumpet and Archie had a little clean up of the . . . er, mess.'

I gave a curt nod to show I understood, then pulled the magnifying glass out of my pocket and held it up to my good eye.

'Rightio!' I cried. 'Clues! Where shall we start?'

Badger looked at me, firmly but kindly and pulling on his gloves so as not to disturb any fingerprints, said, '*You* can start by standing over there and not touching anything, OK?'

Humph.

Disappointing.

But I did as he asked. It was important to be on my best behaviour in my new job. I slunk over to the big table that was piled with boxes of paperwork and waited as patiently as I could. I was bursting to run through everything I'd written down the night before, but I knew I had to wait for him to ask me. Badger had careful detective work to do, and since I was, at this stage, only his *junior* assistant, I didn't want to interrupt him.

I watched as he set about methodically looking around the room. I copied from where I stood. As I said, Grandpa had gone, and so had the narwhal tusk (probably still stuck in Grandpa). The narwhal itself remained hanging on the wall behind Grandpa's desk. I mentally made a note of how high up the fish was mounted. You'd need a good long pair of arms to hoik that down, I thought.

The sheet of paper that Grandpa had written '13' on had also vanished. I knew Badger would have collected that earlier before securing the room and I was glad it was safe. It felt important, even though I wasn't sure why. Everything else in the room looked to me exactly as it had the night before. The itch at the back of my brain telling me I'd forgotten something was still annoying me, but try as I might, I just couldn't think what it was that I'd missed.

I knew Badger had said for me not to touch anything, but sometimes I find it hard to look at things with just my eyes and not with my fingers. With his back turned, I took the opportunity to have a quick gander at the piles of papers and boxes beside me. Was there a clue in there? I wondered. But a quick peek told me there was not. It was just the Grimacres archive Grandpa had got out for Badger's book. Sheet after crumpled sheet of bills and receipts for things like banister spindles and cast-iron cooking pans. Pages of information about previous staff and employment dates and who paid what to the chimney sweeps stretching across centuries. There were a few pieces of paper referring to objects within the house, bought by my ancient ancestors – the enormous cannon, and the suit of armour, my old pal Clive, for example – but nothing that pointed to a murderer.

I shuffled a bit deeper into the mess and found a handful of very old, fading photographs. Most were of the house itself from long ago, but there were some with people in them. One was a picture of Old Mr Badger, Badger's dad, holding up an enormous turnip, another was of a young man (Grandpa, I realised) larking around with some tittering maids. I flipped the photograph over. There was writing on the back, names written in a tiny pencilled hand – Beverley Mopp, Georgina Buckett, Jessica Broom, Margaret Beeswax, Mrs Irongirdle.

I flipped the picture back around. I hadn't seen the old housekeeper in the picture, but after a good squint, sure enough there she was: her face stern, watching the group grimly from the shadows of one of the windows. I shuddered, glad that she was no longer working at Grimacres. Mrs Crumpet lets me run riot. I doubted Mrs Irongirdle would have stood for that at all.

I flipped to the next photo and had to quickly stifle a laugh. It was Great Aunt Priscilla in her younger days wearing an enormous old-fashioned feathery hat which, on closer inspection, had two live chickens and a parrot sitting on it. The parrot was cross-eyed.

I must've disturbed Badger with my laughing snort, because I noticed him glance my way, so I quickly slid the photos back on to the pile of papers and stood to attention.

'Hmmmm,' said Badger, appraising the space again. He tugged on his moustache and his brow crinkled. 'The problem, of course, is that so many people were in here last night. *Such* a disturbance to the crime scene . . .'

I nodded enthusiastically. 'Yes, really we should have had as few people in here as possible. If only I'd pulled myself together a bit quicker, I'd have got them all out for you.'

I stared at my feet. I felt I'd let my boss down, but Badger was quite kind about it.

'Not your fault,' he said. 'You'd had a shock.' That made me feel a bit better.

'Right, you'd better tell me everything you saw in here last night,' he said, still looking about, crouching down and exploring the room. 'Don't miss anything out. It's all very important.'

I stood to attention, giddy to finally launch in.

I started with Charles Darwin being mysteriously in the room and how I broke in. Then I told him about the inky message on the desk.

'Grandpa had written the number "13",' I said. 'But you've already collected that for evidence, right?' and I pointed to the blank fresh sheet on the desktop.

Badger's eyebrows shot up then his forehead crumpled into a frown.

'Oh – actually I haven't,' he said, almost to himself. I could tell he was wondering where it had gone because I was wondering the same thing. Then he said, 'Odd . . .'

I grinned. Clearly I was already being a big help! 'Well,' I said, 'if you're interested in odd, I've got a whole list of odd things that I've noticed since I've been here this weekend. For one thing, my sister is being stranger than usual, but I'm not sure why. Also, she was wearing a necklace I haven't seen before and I don't know how she got it because she doesn't have any money of her own so that's interesting, isn't it?'

Badger raised his eyebrows again, but didn't say anything. He gestured for me to continue.

I quickly flipped open my murder book to my List of Oddness and ran my finger down it.

'Also, Miss Bellissima has been snooping around. Mrs Crumpet said she found her in the library the other day having a good look at everything which might be suspicious, maybe?'

I looked up excited, expecting to have Badger's rapt attention, but he was just staring at the blank blotting pad stroking his chin, thoughtfully.

I continued.

'And of course, before you got here yesterday, Farv was hoping to see Grandpa for a <u>very</u> urgent chat. *I* think he wanted Grandpa to give him some money. I reckon we need it because all the people who help us at home have got new jobs and we only have one pot of horrible jam. Also, I think Gloria Blouse is a bit nervous. She's acting very str—'

Badger cut me off. He was looking directly at me now.

'What was that?' he said.

'About Gloria?' I said, 'She's very nervous and—'

'No, before that,' cut in Badger.

I thought back. 'About Farv asking for money? Yes, I think that was what he wanted to talk to Grandpa about. Farv told Muv they'd have to cancel Audrey's big birthday party and Muv's tennis lessons and she was very cross about it.'

'Hmmm . . . interesting,' said Badger.

I swallowed nervously. I hoped I hadn't just made my parents the lead suspects in a murder case? I carried on quickly with my list.

'And Uncle Roderick wanted money too . . .' I said hurriedly. 'And like I said, him and Gloria were acting very strange, and—'

'Thank you, Edna, you've given me a lot to think about.'

'Oh, but I've got more interesting things here,' I said pointing at my book. 'Shall I carry on? Something in here might be very important for our investigation, mightn't it?'

Badger shook his head. 'No thank you,' he said. He smiled and ushered Charles Darwin and I out of the door ahead of him. He locked it tight behind us.

'You've been *most* helpful, Edna,' he said. 'But I need to see the rest of your family now.'

'Shall I help with the interviews?' I asked. 'I can write notes!'

'No, thank you,' he said again. He tapped his trouser pockets and frowned. He was looking for a pen. I handed him my pencil, hoping he wouldn't mind the chewed end of it.

He took it gingerly and thanked me. Then he said:

'You . . . er . . . toddle off and play with a doll or something,' and he marched off to the dining room.

Play with a doll! I've never ONCE played with a doll and I certainly wouldn't play with one when there was a murderer on the loose!

HMPH! I wasn't happy at that at all. I felt quite frustrated. I had so much more to tell Badger. I hadn't even started on everyone gallivanting about the house around the time of the murder.

I sniffed. Play with a doll indeed! I knew exactly what I was going to do and it didn't involve any dolls. It involved jamming my ear up to the keyhole and earwigging like my life depended on it. I had a murder to solve after all and a little idea had just popped into my head that I thought was very interesting indeed.

Bakelite telephone receiver with slashed connecting wire.

CHAPTER 25.
PANEL TAPPING
AND KEYHOLE LISTENING

It had been the photo of Gappy in her feather hat that made me think of it. Something Gappy had said the night before about remembering the children crawling about the house looking for secret passages. Of course, I knew the rumours about Grimacres having a secret passage, but nobody took them seriously. None of the adults I'd asked about it before were any help. They just said it was a load of rubbish – like the stories of a ghost stalking the corridors – so I'd forgotten all about it and had concentrated on looking for the Grimacres buried treasure instead.

But what if there WAS a secret passage in the house?

It dawned on me that that must have been how the murderer got out of the room with the door still locked. One of the grown-ups in my family must have found it, kept it secret and then used it last night to commit murder! I'd have to find it now, but where to start?

Blast Badger for locking me out of the study! It would have been easier to look for a doorway in there because that must be where the passage ends. As it was, I now had the whole house to search for where the entrance to the passage might start.

Or did I?

On previous trips to Grimacres, Archie and I had made it our business to look everywhere for the buried treasure. We'd been inside wardrobes, trunks and window seats, pulled back rugs and eyeballed floorboards, looking for secret hidey-holes. Unfortunately, there hadn't been an X-Marks-The-Spot OR a secret door anywhere. BUT what Archie and I *hadn't* considered was that there were an awful lot of wooden panels on the hall walls and that any of them would make a cracking concealed door to the secret passage . . .

I scurried to find Archie and explain my plan to him. He was still in the hall, trying to fix the telephone. The way he waggled his eyebrows told me he thought my idea was a good'un. (I looked at Charles Darwin for his thoughts too, but he was too busy chewing my sleeve to offer an opinion, but that's tortoises for you.)

So Archie and I began searching immediately. Tapping and pressing. Pulling and heaving. We had to keep stopping though whenever one of the grown-ups came into the hall to go and speak to Badger in Aunt M's little office.

We'd jump away from the walls as they appeared, and Archie would pick up the broken phone and a screwdriver and I would pretend to help him. I'd put one hand on my hip and stroke my chin with the other and say, 'HMMMMM, YES THAT CERTAINLY *IS* A CONUNDRUM, ARCHIE!' very loudly so that the adults wouldn't get suspicious. They didn't catch on, of course – they were all too worried about speaking to a detective.

The moment they'd slip into Aunt M's office for their interview, I'd leap like a gazelle to the door and listen in. I wanted to hear how they'd all explain their bedroom lights being on and all the wandering about they'd been doing in the middle of the night around the time a murder was taking place. I borrowed a pencil from Archie and was all ready to make some fresh notes in my murder book as I earwigged.

I even wrote a nice title in caps and underlined it neatly. It said:

<u>NOTES MADE BY ME (EDNA GRISTLE)
WHILST LISTENING IN ON BADGER'S
INTERVIEWS WITH MY FAMILY ETC</u>

But I soon realised there was no point in making any notes at all because every single one of them said exactly the same thing –

'I was in bed fast asleep when the murder happened so it couldn't possibly have been me!'

Well, I knew for a fact that half of them were fibbing! Lying outrageously through their back teeth!

After the last one left the interview room, I peeked through the crack of the door and saw Mr Badger pulling on the ends of his moustache, meditatively. 'Hmmmmmm . . .' he said. Then he got up and left the room to join everyone in the drawing room where morning coffee was being served.

The minute the door closed behind him, I rushed over to the telephone table and tugged on Archie's sleeve for him to follow me upstairs to the airing cupboard.

It was time for us to have a conflab.

Ripped packet of Rhubarb and Custard Whirligig Suckables, made by The Jolly BonBon LTD's Development Kitchens, Mayfair, London.

CHAPTER 26.
THRASHING IT ALL OUT AMONGST THE LINENS

'They're all lying!' I said. 'Which I think you'll agree is very SUSPICIOUS!'

And I narrowed my good eye suspiciously.

Archie and I were in our secret cubbyhole, which is actually just the airing cupboard upstairs. It's just about big enough for the two of us (and Charles Darwin) if we squish together. We'd settled ourselves in amongst the folded towels and bed linens and got comfortable by the hot water pipe. After loitering in the freezing hall all morning, that little glow of warmth about the kidneys was a real treat. Charles Darwin was particularly thrilled by the change in locale. He backed his bum up against the heat and fell fast asleep.

In a tin tucked behind some very old, slightly mothy flannels, is where Archie and I keep our sweet collection.

Archie heaved it out, delighted to find some sweets still in there from my last visit. I popped a Rhubarb and Custard Whirligig Suckable in my mouth and Archie selected a Fizz Pop Lollipop (Pineapple Sherbet flavour) then we got down to business.

'Also,' I said, clonking the suckable against my teeth, 'someone's pinched a vital piece of evidence!'

Archie looked at me, agog.

'You didn't happen to notice a sheet of paper on Grandpa's blotting pad when you and Badger and Mrs Crumpet went back to the room later with the mop and bucket to, er . . . clean things up?' I asked. 'Grandpa had drawn the number "13" on it and it might be important.'

Archie wrinkled his brown for a moment – thinking, then shook his head firmly. He hadn't seen it which meant it definitely hadn't been there.

'So . . .' I said, rubbing the end of my nose thoughtfully, 'between when I found the body and when you went in to tidy up, somebody snuck in and took it.'

We nodded in unison.

'When Grandpa was being manhandled to the larder . . . But why take it?' The answer I felt was that there was a person in this house that considered it a very important clue. 'And what did "13" mean?'

Archie sucked thoughtfully on his lollipop, then, with a sigh, he shrugged.

'We'll come back to that!' I said.

I got my murder book out then and showed Archie all the notes I'd made the night before.

Archie read them slowly, running his finger under each word which helps stop them bouncing around on the page for him.

Then I showed him my list of suspects – the ones whose names weren't crossed out.

'The thing is,' I said, 'they've all LIED! They're telling porkers left, right and centre!'

Archie nodded and together we looked again at my notes. I had my pencil ready to add anything new as we thought everything out.

'Gloria *wasn't* in her bedroom, asleep,' I said, picking a name at random. 'She was in Uncle Roderick's room – I heard them talking, and from what I heard it sounded <u>very</u> suspicious to me! They were on about leaving in the night or first thing in the morning . . .'

I looked at Archie and Archie looked at me. We flared our nostrils at each other. Archie pointed at my pencil and I got scribbling.

Scribble! Scribble!

'And I actually SAW SOMEONE at the top of the stairs!' I said. 'It was either Farv OR Aunt M, I don't know which. You know how similar they look – especially when Aunt M's in her hair net. We definitely know ONE of them had been downstairs. But which one? There were lights on in both of their bedrooms . . .'

Scribble! Scribble!

Archie pointed to where I'd put 'MUV' on my list and looked at me questioningly.

'Well,' I said, 'I didn't see or hear her, BUT I know that she is a very light sleeper. There is no way she could have stayed asleep if a light was on in the room. Their bedroom at home is as dark as a grave.'

Scribble! Scribble!

Next: Lil.

Archie mimed using a stethoscope and then drew a question mark in the air and shot his eyebrows up to the ceiling.

'I know . . .' I agreed. 'I can't believe that a doctor would murder someone either, but . . . but she *had* been angry with Grandpa about how he bullied Aunt M! And before dinner in Aunt M's room, she slammed her fist down on the windowsill and looked LIVID!'

Archie's eyebrows crashed down into a frown as he considered this with a nod.

'And again, she lied too,' I continued. 'She said she was asleep in her bed when it happened, but I saw her slipping out of the bathroom that night, and she was drying her hands on her pyjamas.'

Archie thought for a moment, then his eyes went wide and he did a wonderfully vivid mime of murdering someone with a narwhal tusk and blood spurting everywhere, then daintily washing his hands.

I nodded. Archie was right. The murderer would definitely have needed a good hand swill. Was that what Lil had been doing? Or had she simply washed her hands after going for a midnight wee?

I didn't want to consider Lil as a murderer but reluctantly, I scribble-scribbled.

We continued.

Miss Bellissima – Giovanna.

'She also said she'd been asleep when Grandpa was murdered,' I said, 'and she certainly came running in last after everyone else, but was she fibbing? I know for sure she was snooping around earlier in the evening.'

Suddenly a thought struck me.

'Flowers!' I cried, making Archie jump. 'Last night on my Charles Darwin hunt, I smelt flowers in the library, which I thought was odd because Grandpa never has flowers in there. But I know what that pong was: it was Giovanna's face cream!'

Archie's eyebrows were on the roof again.

'I smelt it when I'd chatted to her on the landing after dinner,' I explained, 'AND I smelt it again when she'd wafted into the study later to faint on the carpet. Rose and Geranium!'

Archie's face lit up. He did another mime of washing his hands, then looked aghast at an imaginary watch on his wrist, then did a very convincing run and a swooning faint on to the pile of towels beside him.

'That's a very good point, Archie!' I said. 'She could very well have been late to the study because she had been washing blood off her hands.'

He grinned as I wrote it all down in my book. So Giovanna had definitely been awake and wandering about around the time Grandpa had been murdered . . .

'She did say to me that she wanted to look for something to read,' I said, 'so maybe that's what she was doing?'

But Archie looked at me with a dubious twist to his mouth.

'No, I'm not convinced either. Maybe she murdered him so she DIDN'T have to marry him?'

Archie slowly nodded.

'An interesting thought . . .' I said, waggling my eyebrows.

'Hmmm . . .' I said, reviewing our notes. 'A great number of potential suspects!'

Our list of suspects now looked like this:

MUV – LIED – light was on so not asleep

FARV – possibly lied – up in the night?
 Or was it Aunt M?

AUNT M – possibly lied – up in the night?
 Or was it Farv?

LIL – LIED – washing hands – blood from murder?

UNCLE R – LIED – talking to G. planning a getaway!

GLORIA BLOUSE – LIED – talking to Uncle R

AUDREY – snoring

GIOVANNA BELLISSIMA – LIED – snooping in the library, face cream smell

We looked at our list and both of us shivered with a thrilling mix of excitement and tremendous trepidation.

Archie tapped Audrey's name, which I'd crossed out, and he looked at me inquisitively.

I couldn't help but laugh.

'I just don't think she could have done it!' I said. 'When her head hits the pillow that's it. There's no waking her at all. A bomb could go off on her bedside table and she'd just roll over!'

Archie laughed. We were just going to move on when a thought struck me. 'But,' I mused, 'she *is* acting odd . . .'

I sighed. My head was a jumble. I rubbed my eyes and as I did, behind my scrunched-up eyelids, names and faces danced about. The number '13' floated around in circles and a vision of the narwhal mounted on the study wall swam in and out of focus.

Suddenly, something else occurred to me. My eyes snapped open.

'So,' I said slowly, thinking it all out, 'we've got that narwhal up high on that wall . . .'

Archie nodded.

'The murderer sneaks in, emerging from wherever the secret passage comes out, and has to reach up for the tusk. Grandpa would be asleep at his desk and then – STAB!'

Archie's eyes grew very large like saucers as he understood my meaning. He stretched his arms up like he was measuring something.

I nodded. 'Exactly, you'd need a good long set of arms on you, wouldn't you?'

Archie leant over and pointed to some names in my book.

FARV

AUNT M

UNCLE RODERICK

GIOVANNA

'Yes – all of them could reach the weapon!' I said.

He pointed to Lil and waggled his hand. 'She is a bit smaller,' I agreed, 'but not *too* small.'

We both agreed that Muv and Gloria Blouse were probably on balance just too titchy.

Muv just seems tall because of her enormous hair. To get

the tusk down though, they both would've needed either a running jump or to spring up like a gymnast, or had a ladder, which, of course, would have made enough noise to wake Grandpa and alert anyone else who was skulking around the dark corners of Grimacres that something fishy was going on.

'Not tall enough,' I said.

Archie tapped Audrey's name.

'Well, that's a funny one, isn't it?' I said, cogitating. 'She's not terribly tall but what she *is, of course,* is a ballerina!'

Archie mimed some beautifully fluid dance moves, including a few leaping pirouettes.

I agreed with him. 'She's used to leaping about with no noise at all. I've seen her do it. Might she have *danced* her way towards the weapon?'

We turned that idea over.

'Unlikely,' I said. 'But strange things do happen.'

I sighed. Everything about this whole situation was strange.

'And she *does* have something she doesn't want us to know about,' I said, and I explained to Archie about the necklace and the letter from home locked in the drawer along with something else I couldn't quite see.

Archie frowned.

'You're right,' I sighed, 'it's . . . SUSPICIOUS . . .'

I picked up the pencil and wrote:

FIND OUT AUDREY'S SECRET.

After that, Archie and I sat back, pleased. This confab had really pushed our investigation on from where I'd been with it first thing that morning.

However, something was still niggling at me. Something I'd seen last night that was Very Important that was still refusing to come into focus.

Was it something to do with the floor? The floor of the study? I squeezed my eyes shut again very tightly hoping that might help, but it didn't. I'd have to keep thinking . . .

'Well,' I said, eventually. 'We aren't ready to make an arrest *just* yet so we'll need to keep our eyes and ears open this afternoon!'

Then my stomach rumbled. It was nearly lunchtime. Mrs Crumpet would be looking for us to help lay the table soon. We leapt up, I tucked Charles Darwin into my fur coat and we let ourselves out of the cupboard to go downstairs.

'I wonder what grub Mrs C has made?' I said. I fancied a big pile of sandwiches and she makes good ones. No crusts.

Charles Darwin looked like he needed a radish.

We turned the corner on to the landing to see Badger plodding along towards us.

'Oh, hullo you two,' he said. 'Not causing trouble, are you?'

I hid my murder book behind my back and said, 'No, of course not' very sweetly. 'Just um . . . quietly practising our times tables.'

Archie gave me a boggle-eyed look.

'Good, good,' he said, 'just popping up to see Lady Priscilla. Occurred to me she might not know about the, er – about what's happened to Ignatius.'

Beside me Archie shyly mimed someone mixing something in a bowl and then pointed upstairs. Startled, Badger looked at me for a translation.

'He says that Mrs Crumpet's told Great Aunt P,' I said.

'Oh!' said Badger. 'Saved me a job.' He looked relieved. He turned and together we started towards the stairs.

And it was then that something happened that made our blood run cold.

Someone downstairs started to scream.

CHAPTER 27.
THINGS YOU FIND UNDERNEATH CHICKENS

It was Mrs Crumpet.

She was in the dining room, pinny on, standing in front of a lacquered cabinet, statue-still. We crashed through the door followed by the rest of the household, and it took a second for me to realise what had happened. I'd expected to see another dead body but instead Mrs C was staring at an empty cabinet.

'The silver!' she cried, hand to bosom. 'It's gone!'

And indeed it had. The doors of the cabinet were wide open and the shelves inside were bare.

'WHAT?' cried Badger. He looked flabbergasted and spun on his heel to face us all.

'I thought this whole house had been checked last night!' he said sharply. 'Who searched this room?'

Farv and Uncle Roderick stepped forward sheepishly.

'We did,' said Uncle Roderick quietly.

'And the pair of you didn't think to check this cupboard?'

'Well, I was going to . . .' said Uncle Roderick.

'To be honest with you, George, we were pretty cut up about Father, you know . . . BEING MURDERED,' cut in Farv angrily.

'Yes, it was quite a shock . . .' agreed Uncle Roderick. He looked like a lost lamb.

Badger eyeballed the pair of them hard for a good minute, then sighed and rolled his eyes.

'A murder AND a robbery!' he said grimly. 'Dear . . . dear . . . dear . . . back to square one!'

Muv was looking smug. 'See!' she said, cheerfully. 'I said last night it wasn't any of us! Someone came in, pinched the silver, murdered Ignatius and then left.' She folded her arms across her chest and looked incredibly pleased with herself.

I shook my head. 'No, that's not possible,' I said. 'We looked last night – no one had been in or out of the front or back doors at all, nor any of the windows. It had to be someone in the house.'

Muv snorted. 'So I suppose you're accusing one of us of stealing the silver too?' she cried. 'Hardly. Horrible old stuff anyway! Good riddance to it I say!'

'It *is* worth a lot of money though,' said Aunt M, fussing with her pearls. 'A LOT of money . . .'

'Well, sure I can't be standing around here,' said Mrs C, firmly. 'I've a lunch half made downstairs, so I'll let *you*' – she poked Badger on the arm here – 'solve this latest mystery. I've to get on. You'll all be eating with the old cutlery now. Archie, fetch a clean tablecloth from the airing cupboard would you, and *you*' – she turned to me here – 'had better come with me. I need a hand.'

I knew Mrs Crumpet just wanted to have a good old moan, so Charles Darwin and I followed her down to the kitchen.

'What in the name of my mother's (God-rest-her) anchovy blancmange is going on here?' said Mrs Crumpet as soon as we were in the kitchen. 'I thought that after all that business in February t'would be the end of it, but now look – the silver gone, I've a dead man in one larder and flock of hens in another, the weather's after wanting to encase us in this house like a snow globe, and me here up to my oxters in having to make food for you all.'

She sniffed before continuing, 'And I'll tell you this now – I hope you all like wedding cake, because I'm not throwing it out, wedding or no wedding, murder or no murder. You'll be eating it for weeks and I don't want to hear a single complaint, d'y'hear?'

I let Mrs C rattle on and made myself as useful as possible. I washed my hands and buttered some bread for sandwiches. All the time, Mrs Crumpet kept up a non-stop flow of talking.

'And aren't I just all at sixes and sevens today? Lunchtime

and not a bed in this house made!' she said. 'And Mildred's got Archie up there trying to fix that phone line so I'm completely on my own! My hair's a stranger to the brush this morning and I haven't even collected the eggs from under the chickens!'

'I can get the eggs,' I said.

Mrs Crumpet nodded and asked me to fetch a fresh jar of piccalilli whilst I was at it. It was in the larder with the hens; not, thankfully, the one containing Grandpa.

I dashed along, thankful to have a few quiet minutes with the chickens, who seemed to be enjoying the change of scene from their henhouse. They were nestled down in their old newspaper nests and cooing gently. I picked them up one by one and retrieved the warm eggs from under them. I was just collecting the egg from the last one, when something beneath it caught my eye. It was a sheet of the crumpled newspaper on which was printed a word I was very familiar with:

GRIMACRE

I retrieved the sheet of paper and smoothed it out so I could read the full headline.

VERDICT REACHED IN GRIMACRE WOOD MYSTERIOUS DEATH CASE.

I checked the date. February this year.

I knew then exactly what it referred to.

There was no doubt about it.

The Incident.

A jar of Forknum and Jason's 'Piccalilli from Piccadilly' piccalilli.

CHAPTER 28.
A WAYWARD ARROW

'What is it?' said Mrs Crumpet when I walked back into the kitchen. 'You look like you've seen – oh.'

She'd spotted the sheet of newspaper in my hand, and the headline. She sighed. 'Well, I knew you'd find out eventually!' she said.

'It was under a chicken's bum,' I said.

'It's amazing what you can find there . . .' said Mrs Crumpet. She took the paper from me, put her specs on and briefly read over the article, then sighed again. She folded the paper into the pocket of her pinny.

'*They* didn't want you to know,' she said, rolling her eyes in the direction of upstairs. 'Your mother said you'd only start nosing about and causing a nuisance. They wanted the whole thing cleared up as quickly and as quietly as possible.'

I waited for Mrs Crumpet to go on. She chewed her lip for a moment. 'Well, I oughtn't to say really, but I suppose there's no sense in hiding it now.'

She sighed and adjusted her bosom which I knew was a sure sign she was about to spill the beans, so I looked sharp and got comfy on a stool.

'It was dreadful!' she said. 'A complete accident of course, but still dreadful. 'Twas back in February, and your grandfather had been in an absolutely foul mood for days – even worse than usual! Almost bit the head off me every time I took the tea into him. Was like a crabbed old troll in that study, pacing around, or mooning over some letter he'd received or something. I thought to myself at the time, "That letter'll be from Roderick – what's the rascal done now?" because you know he can't help himself where trouble's concerned.'

I nodded. Roderick is a rogue.

'Anyway, on the day It happened, I was here on my own. Archie was over at Witt's End Farm fixing their fences after that storm, and Mildred was in town on business. Anyway, I'm halfway through a pile of laundry and in marches your grandfather. Coat on. "I'm out hunting!" says he. Well, what a thing for a man of his age to be doing! Out in the freezing cold, shooting at things he can barely see – I mean really! He was squinting at me, so heaven knows how he'd have seen a pigeon. But he was in a bad mood and was after taking it out on the world. There he was in front of me, ready to go. Before I could say a word, or tell anyone, he was out the door, bow and arrow slung across his back and off he went.'

She shook her head, lips pursed.

'Now, I remember thinking then that no good would come of it. For one thing I didn't think he had his right specs on, and secondly 'twas late in the afternoon and already the evening was drawing in. I carried on with my jobs and then back he comes an hour or so later, raw with cold and without an arrow to be seen.

'"Get anything?" says I, making conversation, you know. He grunts and says, "Nothing doing." And marched off back upstairs. He'd absolutely no idea what he'd done, of course. We didn't find her until a bit later . . . well, Archie did. The poor boy. Really shook him up it did . . .'

I was all eyes AND ears now. 'Found who?' I said, nearly falling off my seat with anticipation. 'Who did Archie find? What happened?'

'A woman – an elderly one,' said Mrs Crumpet with a sigh. 'Found dead in a clearing with an arrow in her back. Archie found her on his way back from the farm. I was scrubbing the table when he arrived back here as white as that snow out there, couldn't get the words out to tell me what he'd found. Took me a while to understand what he was trying to say. When we let Ignatius know what had happened, he said "People shouldn't be in my woods!" all snappy, but I think he was a bit shaken.'

My mouth was hanging open as I listened.

'But like I said,' Mrs C went on, 'he *shouldn't* have been out there hunting alone. Badger arrived then, thank goodness, and was marvellous. He'd been in Much Maudlin for some garden things – stuff for the slugs and wasps, and some flower seeds but he went back out to the woods to see what had happened. Then all his detective training came into play. Got the police out there immediately and organised everything.'

'But who was she?' I asked again. 'Surely there was *some* clue as to who she was?'

Mrs Crumpet shrugged her shoulders. 'Nobody knows. She wasn't anyone we knew from Much Maudlin. Badger checked her all over for anything that might tell us who she was, but nothing. The poor woman – she probably didn't know the area and was out there having a nice walk when she was twanged by a rogue arrow and that was that – dead. Nicely dressed apparently, white hair, dainty nose, blue eyes – startlingly blue, so they said – but deader than a doornail.'

She sighed again and looked sad. It *was* sad: someone minding their own business and WHACK! an arrow flies into her.

'Like I said – an awful accident,' said Mrs Crumpet, 'caused by your grandfather pinging off arrows willy-nilly. Stupid behaviour really – could have been Archie who got hit! And of course it was all in the papers. "Mystery Woman Found Dead in Grimacre Woods!" – even made the international news and we had photographers with their long lenses out in the trees. Your father was livid. All that fuss and scandal!'

I thought back to February. There *had* been a lot of fuss and whisperings and secret conversations that even my big ears had struggled to hear. And now that I thought of it, Farv *had* stopped reading the newspaper in the mornings at breakfast and had taken it up to his bedroom instead.

'Dr McDougal was a great help too,' continued Mrs Crumpet, slightly more cheerful now. 'She helped Badger and me keep everything as quiet as possible, and I know Mildred was very grateful. The very last thing your aunt needed was a lot of awful publicity. It was hard on her – managing The Jolly BonBon *and* keeping your grandfather under control. Oh! He was raging about all the fuss and the photographers, but between you and me – I think he enjoyed the attention. Livened up the days for him, y'know?'

I nodded. Grandpa *would* enjoy that.

'It had to go to court, of course, but thankfully it was ruled an accidental death. The woman was buried in an unmarked grave in Much Maudlin because no one ever came forward to identify her. After that, your father and Mildred decided that Ignatius needed to leave the country for a bit. Surprisingly, he agreed. Said he wanted to go to Italy for a while.

''Twas a blessed relief for all of us. After everything, a nice calm came over the house – Mildred kept the business going, Badger got on with his book, and Archie and I just carried on down here. Had to keep an eye on Archie though. He's not been himself at all since it happened.'

I nodded. 'Poor Archie,' I said. 'He's so gentle. Finding the poor woman in the woods must have frightened the life out of him, and the place crawling with police too!'

It was no wonder he'd looked peaky since Grandpa died. Two dead people in one year!

'Is that when he stopped talking?' I asked.

She nodded. 'Not a word since. An occasional whisper to the hens, but nothing to anyone else. Dr McDougal says not to worry, he'll come out of it in time, but still, it IS a worry.'

I patted Mrs Crumpet gently on the hand.

Mrs Crumpet pulled herself together. 'That's enough chit-chat!' she said, sharply. 'I've a lunch to get served!'

As she busied herself, I looked at Charles Darwin. He gave me a look that said, 'Very mysterious . . .'

Isn't it just . . . I thought.

But I already had a mystery to solve, and I didn't have time for another one right now. I promised myself though that my next case would be the unidentified woman in the woods. She deserved to have a name on her gravestone at least, and I would find it for her.

But first, I needed to get Grandpa's murder all cleared up,

and to do that I had to talk to Badger and let him know the truth: that everyone he'd interviewed was LYING.

Ornate 18th century carriage clock.
French. Made by Master Watchmaker
Mme. Madeline Quelquefois.

CHAPTER 29.
A LUNCHTIME TORNADO

Lunch was eaten in tense silence, then everyone retired to the drawing room.

A strange mood had settled on the house. The grown-ups were like caged animals: cooped up, suspicious, watchful and worried.

Lil got a good fire going, but even the roaring flames did little to ease the strange chill in the room. Muv and Audrey flicked through old, crispy-paged magazines while Farv and Uncle Roderick paced around not looking at each other. Gloria Blouse sat huddled like a mouse on the sofa next to Aunt M, who every so often would try unsuccessfully to coax a conversation out of her.

Badger sat quietly in an armchair puffing his pipe. I was desperate to speak to him, but with the stifling quiet in the room it was impossible to say anything without everyone's ears swivelling in your direction. So I hunkered down in my fur coat on the tiger skin rug with Charles Darwin in my lap, and waited until everyone dispersed to get ready for dinner.

A clock ticked.

Time went by.

One hour.

Two.

Suddenly, Farv let out an angry bear growl.

'This infernal snow!' he cried, looking out at the vast, pristine whiteness. 'Looks like we'll be stuck here for days and we can't get anything done. We *need* to get that phone fixed!' He cracked his knuckles loudly.

'Archie's trying his best,' I said, but everyone ignored me.

'Yes, it is awful, Bernard,' said Aunt M. 'But we'll just have to wait it all out.'

'There are arrangements to make, Mil!' said Farv.

Uncle Roderick laughed loudly, his face split into a Cheshire cat grin.

'Wanting to phone Grabbit and Co, the solicitors, Bernard?' he teased. 'Very important to get that will read pronto, isn't it?'

'Roderick!' said Muv, outraged.

'I *meant* funeral arrangements . . .' said Farv through

clenched teeth. 'It's . . . it's undignified for Father to be stuck in a larder!'

Uncle Roderick scoffed.

'Come off it, brother dear,' he cried, 'you're as eager as the rest of us to know where things stand, money wise. The wedding didn't go ahead, so this place is as good as yours! You'll be wanting to find out how much the old man left us and run off with your cut!'

They started to bicker.

Muv joined in.

'Don't pretend you haven't got your purse out ready for a nice big cheque to go in it!' snarled Uncle Roderick, making Muv shriek with outrage.

'That's ENOUGH,' cried Aunt M with surprising loudness. She turned to Gloria, her face a bit flushed above her twinset. 'Really, Miss Blouse, you must think we are awful,' she said, trying to sound light-hearted. 'I'm sure your family doesn't behave like this.'

Gloria Blouse looked flustered, her big, blue eyes blinking rapidly.

'Actually, I don't have a family,' she said quietly. 'My parents died when I was a baby. I had a great aunt who adopted me, but she died recently too.'

My ears pricked up. There were dead people popping up everywhere!

'Oh! I am sorry to hear that,' said Aunt M, relieved to

have something to talk about with Gloria. 'So you're adopted. How interesting. So is—'

But annoyingly I didn't get to learn who else was adopted (someone at Grimacres? I wondered) because at that moment Mrs Crumpet arrived with the tea tray which provided JUST the distraction I needed. This was my chance! So while everyone was fussing over tea and scones I sidled up to Badger. I was tempted to pull one of my plaits across my face above my lip like a moustache so he'd see me as an equal, but I resisted the urge. Instead, I hissed, 'PSST! Mr Badger, I need to have a word with you.'

Mr Badger tore his eyes reluctantly from the tea tray.

I cocked my head in the direction of the hall. 'Outside.'

With a sigh and a last mournful look at the scones, he followed me out.

Once the door was closed, I took a deep breath. 'Listen,' I said, looking him directly in the eyes with my good one. 'I know I should have said this before, and I did try, but well . . . I have something important to tell you.'

He looked at me hard for a few seconds and then said, 'Go on . . .'

I took a deep breath. It did feel a little bit like I was being a snitch, but if I was going to be a proper detective and get Badger to take me seriously, I *had* to tell the truth. The truth is very important when it comes to solving murders, so I swallowed hard and just said what I had to say.

'They're all fibbing.'

Badger's brow crinkled. 'Who is?'

'That lot,' I said, cocking my head at the drawing room door.

'What about?'

'Everything! They all said they were in bed asleep last night until they heard my scream, but they weren't!'

Badger stood quietly, stroking the ends of his moustache. Then, after a moment, he said, 'Right, I think you'd better tell me what you know,' and he motioned towards the stairs. Hitching his slacks up at the knees, he sat on the bottom step and I plumped down beside him and spilled the beans about everything – all the lights on and the walking about and the talking and the bathroom visits that I'd seen and heard that night after I left my bedroom.

Badger listened carefully and when I'd finished, he said, 'This is *very* interesting indeed. So you actually saw someone coming UP the stairs – possibly Bernard, you say?'

'Yes, but it could easily have been Aunt M, they look very similar in the dark.'

'Yes, yes,' Badger said vaguely.

'And several other people were up and about too . . . Lil, Miss Bellissima, Uncle Roderick and Gloria . . .' I said, and he nodded, a distracted look on his face.

The cogs were whirring in his head, I could almost see them. For a minute or two there was a companionable silence between us. Just a couple of colleagues having a think in the middle of a very perplexing investigation.

Then he sprang up energetically – or at least with as much energy as I'd ever seen Badger demonstrate. He's quite a mole-like person, truth be told – rather small, blinky blue eyes and bit of a twitchy nose above the moustache. But even moles can get the steam under them when they are after something, a big, juicy worm, for instance.

'Right, well, I'll have to talk to them all again,' he said, decisively and pulled out his notebook and the pencil I gave him earlier. 'Since they're all in the drawing room, I'll take the library this time, I think . . . And don't worry, I won't tell them it was you who gave me this information.'

I stood up too and was about to offer my services as note-taker-in-chief, but stopped myself just in time. I knew there was no way Badger would let me sit in on his important detective work, and besides, even if he did, it wouldn't do me any favours with my family. They'd soon connect the dots and realise I was the informant.

'Very good, Mr Badger,' I said, in my most police-constabley voice. 'Glad to have been of some assistance. Now if you'll excuse me, I'll let you get on. I'll go upstairs and play with my dolls.'

Badger nodded and returned to the drawing room just as Archie was returning to look at the phone again. He must have overheard what I'd said, because he was looking at me like the real Edna had been snatched away by a goblin king and in front of him was a changeling.

Quickly, because I knew I didn't have much time, I told Archie the latest developments.

'So you see he's going to re-interview all of them!' I said, a giddy quiver in my voice. 'Get them to stop fibbing and give us the FACTS!'

Archie frowned, then pointed at me and mimed rocking a baby.

'No, of course I'm not going to play with a doll!' I scoffed.

He held his hands up in a 'Well-what-the-heck-was-that-all-about?' sort of action.

I grinned. 'I just didn't want Badger to suspect even for a second what I'm going to do next,' I said.

Archie blinked, confused.

'Which is earwig like I've never earwigged before!' I whispered.

At last the penny dropped and a smile spread across Archie's face. He gave me a salute as I handed him Charles Darwin.

A rattling from the drawing room door told me that Badger was returning with his first interviewee.

'Right, I'd better scarper. I'll fill you in on everything later,' and with that, I dashed off.

I screeched down the hall and crashed into the library, then looked about for somewhere to hide.

A HA! The curtains!

I shuffled behind them. Thankfully there was plenty of room for me to park my bum behind the thick pleated fabric. I was just in time. No sooner had I plonked myself down than Aunt M and Badger entered the room.

I got my murder book out of my pocket, licked the tip of my pencil, pressed my good eye up against a very convenient moth hole, and got ready to note down everything that was about to be said. I knew I'd have to listen very carefully indeed because at any moment someone might drop a **_VERY_** important clue.

CONVERSATIONS OVERHEARD IN THE LIBRARY

INTERVIEWS BY: MR BADGER (DETECTIVE)
OVERHEARD BY: EDNA GRISTLE (CO-DETECTIVE)
(WHO SECRETLY NOTED THEM ALL DOWN IN TINY WRITING
IN THE BACK OF A BOOK ABOUT SOLVING MURDERS.)

NOTE: Cor! Grown-ups can't half go on. I'm only including the good bits here otherwise we'd be here all day.

AUNT M.

AUNT M: (FUSSING WITH HER CARDIGAN)

BADGER:

> Look, I'll be straight with you, Mildred, some new information has come to light and you'll understand how awkward this is for me, but I just need to know where you were around the time your father was killed. About 12.50 a.m. by Lillian's estimation?

AUNT M:

> But . . . but we've said already! We were all asleep

until we heard Edna screaming blue murde— I mean, screaming. I know I was certainly asleep.

BADGER:

(SCRATCHY SOUND OF HIM PLAYING WITH MOUSTACHE) Well, you see, the new information I've had says your bedroom light was on. It was seen spilling out from under your door. And well, someone in a tartan robe - and it's thought that it might have been you - was seen at the top of the stairs having just come up them?

(AWKWARD SILENCE)

AUNT M:

(HEAVY SIGH) OK . . . well, foolish of me to have lied - especially to you, George, you know us too well. The truth is I WAS awake. Just couldn't sleep. Tossing and turning. It was that awful argument! And Daddy going to marry Miss Bellissima and being so horrid to us all. Well, I tried to smooth everything over when I took him his medicine, but he just told me to get out - well, he didn't use those words if you see what I mean. Awful language. 'It's MY money!' he said and then told me to leave. Oh, the whole evening was horrendous. You heard it all!

BADGER:

    (NODS)

AUNT M:

    But I assure you I wasn't wandering the house. (SIGH)
    Lillian came into my room after a while. I'd heard
    her pacing next door the whole time I was in bed
    and I called her in. (You know this house as well as
    I do - you wouldn't get out from under the covers
    once you'd got warm, not for a million pounds.)
    Anyway, Lillian came in through the connecting door
    and sat on the bed with me and we just talked
    everything over. Making plans, you know. If
    Grimacres was going to be handed over to Miss
    Bellissima with that new will then I was rather
    worried about where I might live if she threw me out.
    So, we just sat and chatted.

BADGER:

    But why didn't you tell me this earlier, Mildred?

AUNT M:

    (SLIGHT PAUSE FOR HER TO BITE HER LIP BRIEFLY)
    Well, I suppose I lost my head rather. The shock of
    seeing Daddy like that . . . Lillian said to me before
    breakfast that he hadn't been dead long when little

211

Edna found him and well, my mind raced forward a few steps. You see, Lillian and I decided to call it a night and I remembered this morning that we parted ways just as the clock by my bed chimed quarter to one. In my panic I thought that if anyone had seen or heard her they might have thought SHE could have killed Daddy. Stupid really, because how she'd have got downstairs, gone into the study, murdered Daddy and found a secret way out within five minutes I just don't know. She simply couldn't have done it! (SIGHS)

I'm afraid that's really all I can tell you. I WAS cross with Daddy but not cross enough to want to murder him. I'm sorry I didn't tell you all this earlier. I was just so . . . so worried about everything.

(A SIGH.)

Shall I send one of the others in?

(BADGER NODS.)

DR LIL

(LIL MARCHES IN BRISKLY. SHE TELLS BADGER PRETTY MUCH THE SAME THING AS AUNT M)

NOTE: It seems a large part of being a detective is listening to the same thing lots of times . . .

BADGER:

Is there ANYTHING else you can tell me about the crime scene. You were there before me and when the real police come, they'll need all the details they can get.

(A THOUGHTFUL SILENCE)

LIL:

I've told you as much as I know - he'd been dead about ten minutes when we got there, stabbed with that narwhal tusk. It's hellishly sharp!

BADGER:

Anything else?

LIL:

(PAUSE TO CONSIDER)
Well . . . I'm not a detective, but from the angle of entry of the tusk, I'd say that whoever did it must have crept up behind Ignatius and got him from the righthand side.

(SHE POINTS TO HER CHEST TO INDICATE WHERE
THE TUSK WENT IN)
That's all I can say at the moment. The police
medical people would be able to tell you more I'm
sure, if only we could get them up here.

(SLIGHT PAUSE.)

How the killer left the room though, I really don't
know!

BADGER:

Yes, that's the question . . . And Miss Bellissima -
Giovanna? She'd fainted when I arrived. Genuine?
Not acting?

LIL:

(LAUGHS)
Oh, it was genuine alright! Absolutely conked! She'd
have to be a brilliant actress to pull a stunt like that
off and fool me!

AUDREY

(Audrey had absolutely nothing useful to say. She just

whinged on about wanting to get back to London)

<u>GIOVANNA</u>

GIOVANNA:

    I told you already – I was sleeping, heard Miss Edna scream and then . . . (HORRIFIED GASP) I saw Ignatius in the study. Dead. Then I fainted. PFFT – lights out!

BADGER:

    Yes, that's what you said this morning, but it's just, well, I've had some new information and I just need to check if your original statement is, well, actually true?

GIOVANNA:

    (HOTLY) Of course it's true! You think I'm a liar? Why would I lie? I was sleeping then I heard the scream and so I came down with everyone else.

BADGER:

    But by all accounts you were later to arrive than the others? Everyone was in the room before you.

GIOVANNA:

Yes, well . . . well, yes, I was a little later, but not much.

BADGER:

May I ask what caused your delay?

GIOVANNA:

(SIGHS) Mr Badger, I am new to this house and this country. I don't know if this is just a game they are playing or if . . . if they are trying to frighten me. They were very angry with me at dinner so I was in bed thinking, 'Is this them trying to scare me away?' So I waited and then when I heard them running and noises from downstairs I went to see too. You must believe me, Mr Badger, that was the reason.

BADGER:

Hmmm . . .
And when was the last time you saw Ignatius?

GIOVANNA:

After dinner. When I left the dining room, I looked into the study on my way up to bed.

BADGER:

And? Did you say anything to him?

GIOVANNA:

(SLIGHT THINKING PAUSE)
Only a little. He was ranting about his family. When he'd calmed down, he wanted to talk about the wedding but suddenly I felt a very bad headache coming on so I said goodnight and went to bed and straight to sleep.

BADGER:

Straight to sleep? You didn't see anyone else that evening or go anywhere else?

GIOVANNA:

No, not at all. I went straight to my room and got ready for bed. Oh! Wait a minute. Yes, I saw Miss Edna for a moment on her way down from taking dinner to Lady Priscilla. We chatted for a minute and THEN I went to bed.

BADGER:

What did you chat about?

GIOVANNA:

Nothing important. She asked me if I was excited for the wedding.

BADGER:

And were you?

GIOVANNA:

(FLATLY) Er . . . yes. I was. Very excited.

BADGER:

And you didn't leave your room again until the scream?

GIOVANNA:

No, not at all.

BADGER:

Not to come here – to the library?

GIOVANNA:

(CLEARS THROAT)
No, of course not. I was in bed, definitely, absolutely. And asleep too, for sure.

BADGER:

Hmmm . . . (pause) Interesting . . .

MUV

(LIBRARY DOOR IS FLUNG OPEN. MUV COMES IN, HEELS CLIP-CLOPPING ON THE PARQUET.)

MUV:

What's all this about? New information? From where? From whom? You're just meant to be gathering a bit of info for the police when they EVENTUALLY get here, but it seems like you're doing a full investigation by yourself? Do you REALLY suspect one of us killed Ignatius? Preposterous! It was BURGLARS! Surely the missing silver just proves it?

BADGER:

Won't you sit down, Lady Gristle. This will only take a moment . . .

(MUV SITS HUFFILY)

Thank you. Now please can you tell me again where you were at the time of Ignatius's death.

MUV:

I told you this morning - until Edna screamed. I was fast asleep. What that child was doing up wandering about like Pepper's Ghost I don't know! After the tortoise apparently. Must have got itself locked into the study by accident. Honestly, that tortoise has been trouble from the minute Roderick gave it to her. Typical Roderick - always a nuisance. Why couldn't he have got her something NORMAL for her birthday? A doll's house or something? Anyway, the minute we leave this dreadful house I'm hiring a governess! The child is wild.

BADGER:

Yes, well, I'm sure that will do her some good, but back to last night. I know you SAID you were asleep, Lady Gristle, but, er . . . a light was seen on under your bedroom door shortly before the murder was believed to be committed and –

MUV:

Surely, you don't think I was going around killing people in the middle of the night? I loathe being in these rooms during the day - nothing in the world would induce me to promenade around them in the dark.

BADGER:

Not even money?

MUV:

(GASPS) I BEG your pardon? What ARE you inferring,
Mr Badger?

BADGER:

I don't mean any offence, Lady Gristle, but last night
there was QUITE a bit of discussion about Ignatius's
new will, and well, now that he's dead it would seem
that you and Bernard are going to be rather wealthy
indeed.

MUV:

Well, yes, but we are very comfortable as it is, thank
you.

BADGER:

Really? Forgive me for prying, but I couldn't help
noticing that you don't appear to have travelled here
with any staff this visit? No chauffeur or maids, for
instance? You might as well tell me, Lady Gristle, as
you'll only have to tell the police later on . . .

(SILENCE FOR A MOMENT)

MUV:

Look, yes, all right, things have been . . . tricky, with

Bernard's businesses recently. A few things haven't quite, er, gone our way. But if you think that's reason for either of us to murder Ignatius then I must say I'm rather offended. I'm telling you the truth - I went to bed and didn't get out again until Edna screamed.

BADGER:

But your light was on?

(ANOTHER PAUSE, THE ONLY SOUND BEING THE CLOCK TICKING AND THE DRUMMING OF MUV'S FINGERNAILS ON THE ARM OF HER CHAIR)

MUV:

All right. Yes, the light <u>was</u> on. If you must know, I had a terrible headache after all the unpleasantness that evening. Couldn't sleep for it. And, of course, the dreadful worry of missing tennis with Valentino. So I sat up with the light on. And . . .
I sent Bernard to get me something so I could . . . er . . . take a tablet.

BADGER:

A glass of water from the bathroom?

MUV:

(QUIETLY) Well, no actually. I simply can't take tablets with water - never have been able to - I needed a glass of milk.

BADGER:

From the kitchen?

(MUV NODS.)

BADGER:

And this is why you didn't say anything about it this this morning - you realised Bernard had been downstairs around the time the murder was committed?

(MUV NODS AGAIN.)

MUV:

But you can't think HE did it? (A SHARP LAUGH.) He went downstairs and came back up. Simple as that. I mean yes, he WAS cross with Ignatius - but murder him? Never! You'll have to believe me about that.

BADGER:

(SHIFTS UNCOMFORTABLY) I will, Lady Gristle, but I

warn you the police might not. How long was Bernard
away for?

MUV:

(WAVES HANDS VAGUELY) NO IDEA - however long it
takes to go down to the kitchen and get some milk.
Five minutes? No, a bit longer perhaps - ten? I don't
know. Mr Badger you <u>must</u> believe me. Bernard didn't
murder his father. After that incident in February
with that woman in the woods, and the scandal we as
a family only JUST avoided, why would he risk putting
us all through it again?

(MUV exits the library)

BADGER:
(Quietly to himself) For money . . . ?

<u>UNCLE RODERICK</u>

(UNCLE RODERICK LOLLOPS INTO THE LIBRARY
HOLDING HIS HANDS OUT IN FRONT OF HIM.)

RODERICK:
(AS JOLLY AS A CIRCUS CLOWN)

Go on then! Clamp the handcuffs on me, Detective!

NOTE: Uncle R did not appear to be taking the interview v. seriously until Badger tells him he's been overheard talking when he claimed to have been asleep.

RODERICK:

Ah . . . Yes . . . well. You've got me there. I <u>was</u> talking to Gloria. She crept into my room — terrified, to be honest with you. This house — this family — is a bit of a shock to visitors, as you can imagine after the hoo-ha at dinner, and, er, I was just trying to calm her down . . .

BADGER:

Really? You were heard saying, 'LOOK, DON'T WORRY ABOUT IT. WE'LL GO FIRST THING IN THE MORNING BEFORE ANYONE CAN FIND OUT!'
What did you mean by that?

RODERICK:

(ANGRILY) Who's been telling you things? I bet it's Bernard?

BADGER:

I can't say.

RODERICK:

I bet it was. Always trying to stitch me up! What was he doing up listening at my door?

BADGER:

If you could just explain yourself, Roderick.

RODERICK:

(A PAUSE. A SIGH. THEN, IN A VOICE NO LONGER LIKE A CIRCUS CLOWN.)

OK. I did say something like that. Gloria's going a bit potty here and I think the row over dinner didn't help. Look, we'd done a lot of travelling that day – a flight, a long car journey, all that SNOW! and then – well, that dinner and all the fighting, made her nerves jangle. I just meant that I'd sort it all out and we'd leave in the morning. Not hang around for the wedding or anything.

(A GLANCE AT THE SNOW.)
Wishful thinking in this weather . . .

BADGER:

Are you sure that's what you meant? You also said, er, 'Before anyone can find out'.

RODERICK:

PFFT! D'you think I meant, 'Before anyone can find
out I'd murdered my own father'? Not at all – who
DOES that! I meant just what I said – that we'd slip
away in the morning before anyone can find out we're
leaving so we wouldn't have to stay for that terrible
wedding.

BADGER:

But why lie this morning?

RODERICK:

Because I knew you'd think exactly what you are
thinking now – that I'm a murderer. Everyone always
thinks the worst of me – Bernard particularly. You
don't know what it's like to have a brother everyone
thinks is wonderful – so good and proper. He's
loathed me since I was born. And Mildred – she's an
angel, of course – so efficient and excellent. Runs the
company like clockwork. I'm just the black sheep.
Baaaa-d to the bone!
(SIGHS)
I'm many things, Badger, and not all of them good,
but a murderer I am not.

FARV

(FARV ENTERS ANGRILY)

FARV:

I admit it was foolish of us all to say we were asleep when Edna screamed, but I just assumed – and rightly so – that if you knew I'd been up and about, you'd try to pin me for the murder, and probably this robbery too, I expect. Is that it?

BADGER:

Not at all, Bernard. I'm just after some facts. Rosalind said that you went to get some milk for her and you came back shortly before Edna screamed.

FARV:

Oh. Yes.

BADGER:

Hmmm . . .

FARV:

Do you think I'm lying?

228

BADGER:

Of course not, it's just Rosalind said that you were gone about ten minutes . . .

FARV:

(TUGGING HIS MOUSTACHE) And?

BADGER:

That's rather a long time . . . If perhaps you were a STRANGER to the house I could understand it — you'd have to find the kitchens, might get lost or sidetracked on the way — but, well, you know this entire house like the back of your hand . . .

FARV:

(FACE GLOWING RED LIKE A BABOON'S BUM)
And? So do nearly all the other people here!

BADGER:

Yes, but they weren't wandering about, Bernard. Don't be cross — I'm just anticipating what the police might say. They won't know you like I do and I think they'll find it very suspicious that you were wandering about around the time your father was murdered.

FARV:

I . . . I got the milk and, I . . . er . . . I don't know, I just sort of stood there in the kitchen for a while. It had been such a tense evening what with all that rowing - I just needed a moment. Catch my breath . . . you know?

You honestly think the police'll believe I murdered him? Miraculously behind a locked door? Come on, Badger. It's preposterous!

BADGER:

(QUIETLY)

I'm not sure they'll see it that way. You're the oldest child. You're going to be inheriting a lot of money now, Bernard. That's a very good motive for murder. And I understand you've had some financial difficulties recently . . .

FARV:

(SHORTLY) Our financial situation is nobody else's business! And I can assure you that even if things WERE a bit tricky, I'm not going to go around jabbing people with narwhal tusks!

(SILENCE)

FARV:

Badger, you CAN'T think I'D do a thing like that.
Roderick's the one who's always hanging around with
Undesirables - you know that.

BADGER:

You think he did it?

FARV:

(SNORTS) I wouldn't put it past him! If he didn't do it
himself, he'll have put someone else up to it. Got
someone to break in and do the deed for a cut of his
inheritance — or — or — let them steal the silver as
payment. You know what he's like. Up to his earholes
with money trouble and probably got half of the
gangsters in Europe after him.

BADGER:

Well, be that as it may, Bernard, we can't escape the
fact that you have the greatest motive to want your
father killed. And unfortunately for you, you were also
wandering about the house without anyone to back up
what you were doing whilst you were out of bed.

(FARV STANDS UP ABRUPTLY, SMOOTHING THE
CREASES OF HIS SLACKS.)

231

FARV:

> I've had enough of this. It's very good of you to turn detective for us, but I think I'd rather wait until the ACTUAL police arrive and speak to them.

(FARV CROSSES THE LIBRARY ANGRILY AND OPENS THE DOOR.)

FARV:

> Actually it MIGHT interest you to know that I thought I heard something — near here, or in the hall somewhere — when I was going back upstairs. But I doubt you'll believe that for a moment.

(FARV EXITS AND SLAMS THE DOOR.)

GLORIA

(GLORIA BLOUSE KNOCKS QUIETLY THEN SLIPS IN LIKE A VERY PEAKY MOUSE.)

BADGER:

> Ah! Miss Blouse - do sit down. Get comfortable . . .

GLORIA:

Sorry - I wasn't sure if this was the right door.

BADGER:

First time at Grimacres, isn't it? The place does take some getting used to. Bit of maze . . . Now, you and Roderick flew into England yesterday morning, didn't you? From Italy, was it?

GLORIA:

No, Spain. We'd been in Italy shortly before, but we - um - decided to go to Spain quite off the cuff for no real reason at all.

(NERVOUS LAUGH)

BADGER:

Have you always lived in Europe, Miss Blouse?

GLORIA:

Yes. Well, no - I grew up in England.

BADGER:

Oh?

GLORIA:

(QUIETLY) In – um – Great Torpid.

BADGER:

(SURPRISED) Oh, very close to here! Not far at all.

GLORIA:

No, I . . . er . . . I suppose it isn't . . .

BADGER:

Now, I know earlier you said you were asleep until Edna screamed, but before all that you didn't see or talk to anyone at all? Not even Roderick?

GLORIA:

Roderick? N . . . no – not even him.

BADGER:

You're sure?

GLORIA:

Oh! Actually, yes. Briefly. I was feeling rather nervous about the house and the arguments so we talked for a few minutes and then I went back to bed.

BADGER:

Straight back to bed?

GLORIA:

Er . . . yes. Of course.

(GLORIA FIDDLES WITH THE ARM OF THE CHAIR.)

BADGER:

Ah. I see. (Sighs) All right. thank you. That's all.

(GLORIA RISES TO LEAVE.)

BADGER:

Oh. just one more thing . . . Out of interest. how did you meet Roderick?

GLORIA:

(BLINKS) Oh. I met him at work.

BADGER:

You work at one of those casinos he likes to visit?

GLORIA:

Oh no. Not at all. I suppose it's quite funny really. I met him at the circus. I'm a gymnast.

A collection of objects including a number of coins and a women's silver chain with decorated pendant.

CHAPTER 30.
CONSIDERING THINGS ACCOMPANIED BY AN EGG

'Very interesting indeed!' I said to myself, as I watched Gloria leave the room through the moth hole in the curtain. Badger sat very still in his armchair for a moment, frowning and tugging thoughtfully at the ends of his moustache.

I thought my bottom was going to fall off with the cold that was creeping in from the frozen glass behind me, and my poor hand was throbbing from furiously scribbling notes in my murder book.

At last, after several minutes of quiet contemplation, Badger got up and left the room.

I leapt out of my hiding place and wiggled about a bit, to get the blood flowing again. There was a lot to think about. I'd heard so many interesting things and I was sure that in amongst them was a clue – several probably – that would help me solve Grandpa's murder and hopefully the whereabouts of the missing family silver too. I'd have to look through my notes carefully to see what it all told me.

Frustratingly, the Itchy Brain Clue was still a mystery. Nothing anyone had said to Badger had shaken *that* bit of information loose, but perhaps my notes would help lead me to it?

My belly growled, and I realised that on top of having a cold bum, all my eavesdropping had made me ravenous. It wasn't long until dinner. But could I wait?

Maybe there's time to nip to the kitchens for a little snackette to help my thinking? I mused. I was just slipping my murder book and pencil in the pocket of the moth-eaten fur coat, ready to set off in search of sustenance, when – hello! *What's this?* I thought. *A little something in my pocket!* I grinned.

Excellent work, Ed! I said to myself as I remembered that I'd stashed that spare hard-boiled egg at breakfast to have as a snack for later. Well, now it was later so I grabbed it, peeled it and gobbled it up. Then I shoved my hand back in the pocket to see if I'd got anything else nibbly in there – a Rhubarb and Custard Whirligig Suckable perhaps? I reached deep into the pocket, and one of my fingers found something else. A little hole in the silky lining of the coat. And, if I wasn't much mistaken, THINGS had fallen through it.

I ferreted about with my finger as best I could and

discovered that there were actually several things hiding inside the lining of the coat. It was tricky to remove them, but I managed eventually. There was some loose change (new and shiny) and something long and thin and slinky.

I fished it out and held it in the palm of my hand.

It was a ladies' necklace. A dainty, oval pendant on a length of silver chain.

'Now, what is this doing in a stinky old fur coat?' I wondered.

Whenever I put a coat on – mine or anyone else's – I ALWAYS root through the pockets immediately, in case there's some cash in there I can look after in my piggy bank. I knew for a FACT that I'd done just that the previous afternoon when I'd first put the coat on, and I was quite sure that the pockets had been empty then. I was also fairly sure that there hadn't been a hole in the lining either. Perhaps my sharp pencil had made it this morning? I put the coins back in the pocket and flapped the coat around a bit. It jangled – and it hadn't jangled yesterday.

'So all of this must have been put in there *after* Grandpa made me take the coat off at dinner, and BEFORE I'd put it on again when I went looking for Charles Darwin,' I whispered to myself. 'Meaning . . . someone had put these there around the time of Grandpa's murder!'

I was bewildered. Then I remembered that in my murder book, my favourite detective always said 'Consider

EVERYTHING'. So that was what I did, but I still couldn't make head nor tail of it.

Had someone else been wearing the coat? Unlikely, but if so, who?

I turned the necklace this way and that, letting it catch the dim light from an old lamp behind me. I noticed that the necklace was decorated with a dainty pattern of etched lines, like microscopic vines. It was obviously not new – it was rather tarnished – and although it was quite old-fashioned, it looked jolly expensive.

I pulled out the magnifying glass I'd pinched from the library earlier and studied the locket closely with it.

'Ah-ha!' I said. I'd spotted something.

There, in the middle of the beautiful, engraved foliage were two letters carved by a jeweller into the silver.

G. B.

I stood up straight.

My eyes narrowed.

One thing was certain – it was time for another conflab with Archie.

After the verdict, Lord Ignatius Gristle left the court room snarling at reporters. It's believed that he now is heading for an extended holiday in Sicily, Italy.

PART FIVE:
A CACOPHONY
OF CULPRITS
(MAYBE)

CHAPTER 31.
CONFERENCE (WITH GARIBALDIS)

'We need to sift through the facts to find the clues,' I said to Archie when I'd finished telling him everything. 'Like finding a teaspoon in amongst *this* mess.' I rattled my hands around in the soapy sink that I was up to my elbows in.

It was after dinner and Charles Darwin and I had slipped away to come and have a conference with Archie over the washing up. (Charles Darwin wasn't doing any washing up of course. Tortoises simply will **not** get involved with soap suds or dish cloths).

The atmosphere in the dining room had been so awkward that I'd thought at several points that I was going to have to reach down into my belly and turn myself inside out to cope with it all. It should have felt more relaxed than it was – in the end nobody had bothered to change for dinner, and we were using the everyday crockery and cutlery. However, after the interviews, everyone was more on edge than ever. Eyes darted from face to face and conversations fizzled out into long, painful silences. Only I made any headway with the food. I needed it to help me think.

After pudding (slabs of wedding cake), everyone went to the drawing room, which was when I slipped downstairs. I had much to fill Archie in on, so as soon as Mrs Crumpet disappeared to the attic with Gappy's dinner tray, I launched straight in over the washing up bowl.

Archie listened carefully, his eyebrows flying up at some parts then crashing together above his nose at others. When I got to the bit about the locket, he made a beard for himself out of the suds and stroked it.

'Yes, it IS very interesting,' I agreed.

As soon as we'd finished the washing up, we dried our hands, grabbed ourselves a glass of milk and sat down at the kitchen table with my notes and a tin of biscuits (Garibaldis) between us. Charles Darwin was busy with a cabbage leaf by the fire.

'So shall we go through our list of suspects again,' I said, 'in light of this new information?'

Archie nodded and with a finger drew a horizontal line in the air.

'I agree, it would be useful to scribble some names off. So – let's start with Aunt M and Lil. Aunt M said she heard Lil pacing all night, called her in and they sat talking, then Lil went for a wee, and shortly after, I screamed and they came down. This matches what I saw. I did see lights on in both rooms AND I saw Lil coming back from the bathroom, just as Aunt M said.'

Archie nodded.

'And I agree with Aunt M – Lil couldn't have run downstairs, murdered Grandpa, sorted out the locked door business, washed up AND got back to her room all in the time it takes someone to go to the loo.'

Archie nodded again, then crinkled his brow. He pointed to Aunt M's name in my book and then mimed running. I got his meaning.

'Could Aunt M have done it while Lil was in the loo?' I said. I considered this for a moment. 'She *is* tall enough to reach the narwhal, she had motive, and she may even know the house well enough to know where the secret passage is, BUT I just don't think it's possible in the time it takes someone to have a wee and wash their hands. Also Farv has already admitted it was him I saw in the tartan robe coming up the stairs. I think we can scratch Aunt M and Lil off our list?'

Archie agreed.

SCRATCH.

And we moved on to consider the next names: Muv and Farv.

'Muv is *still* saying burglars did it,' I said, 'and certainly the missing silver *is* a conundrum . . . but I wonder if the silver stealing is meant to flummox us and make us THINK the culprit's a burglar? Which it is doing, of course . . .'

We both had another biscuit.

'Muv says she was in bed and didn't get up until I yelled and that she sent Farv down for a glass of milk. But . . .'

Archie was on my wavelength. He mimed Muv running and stabbing. It was a very good impression.

'Yes, she might have been fibbing about her headache to get rid of Farv. She *could* have gone downstairs while Farv was gone and done the deed, but I just can't see it. She's too small to reach the tusk for one thing, and secondly, it just seems so . . . unlike her.' I pointed at the murder book in front of me. 'In here it says that murderers usually pick ways of murdering that suit their characters. If Muv were a murderer she'd pick something like poison. It's tidy. Muv wouldn't want to get her hands dirty and whoever did Grandpa in would have had actual blood on their hands.'

We crossed ~~Muv~~ off the list.

'Now Farv . . .' I said. My eyes met Archie's and we both pulled grim, worried faces.

'Yes, it doesn't look good for Farv,' I agreed. 'It was him I saw on the stairs, we know that for certain now.'

Archie rubbed his thumb and forefingers together and I felt my stomach tighten into a nervous ball.

'Yup,' I sighed. 'He has an excellent motive: he's going to

inherit heaps of cash AND Grimacres. The wedding would have ruined that.'

I sipped my milk, and suddenly felt my stomach tighten even further. I groaned. Archie looked at me questioningly. I didn't want to tell him what had just occurred to me, but he's my best friend and I knew to be a real detective I had to be truthful, even if the truth was uncomfortable.

'I just remembered something . . .' I said. 'When I saw that figure come up the stairs . . .'

Archie nodded, encouragingly.

'Farv . . .' I continued, my stomach squirming. 'He . . . he wasn't holding a glass of milk. His hands were empty!'

Crumble Crunch Teatime Medley biscuit tin (now used to keep housekeeping money in.)

CHAPTER 32.
IDEA SEEDS

Archie's eyes widened. I chewed my lip. Could Farv really be a murderer? Yes, he could be a big, grumpy bear, but to do THAT? I couldn't believe it. Beneath Farv's sometimes grouchy exterior, he was actually quite a gentle person. However, he hadn't been himself lately . . .

Archie patted me on the arm kindly, then scratched the back of his head.

'No,' I sighed, 'that's not Itchy Brain Clue.' To be honest, I'd forgotten about *that* conundrum what with everything else I'd learnt that afternoon, but having been reminded of it, the scratchy sensation at the back of my head immediately started up again. What *was* I forgetting?

'Well, we can't cross Farv off the list, but let's move on for now.' I cleared my throat, keen to put all thoughts of

250

Farv maybe being a cold-blooded murderer out of my mind. 'We can keep Audrey crossed off,' I said, moving on in a businesslike fashion. 'She slept through the whole thing. She doesn't know anything! Though I *would* like to know what her secret is.'

I considered for a minute, then I put another line through her name.

'Farv seems to think Uncle Roderick did it,' I said. 'Says he's always been a wrong'un and that the theft and the murder are *just* the sort of things he'd do.'

Archie rubbed his thumb and forefingers together again.

'Yes, money. And from what I overheard, Uncle Roderick needs it badly. Remember, Farv told Badger that Roderick's always hanging around with crooks and gangsters!'

Archie mimed paying people.

'Exactly! Maybe he's in some sort of trouble? With GANGSTERS! He might need the money to pay back whoever it is that he owes?' I suggested, and Archie nodded.

It was a good idea and I noted it down in my book, but as I did, I frowned.

It felt strange to consider Uncle Roderick as a murderer. He'd always been a bit naughty. I remembered Mrs Crumpet telling me once that when he was a little boy, he was always stealing things from her kitchen – apples, slices of cake, even the housekeeping money from the battered old tin above the fireplace. He'd got into frightful trouble for that.

Aunt M had also told me that on her 21st birthday, she'd convinced Grandpa to let her have a party and Uncle Roderick (who'd have been very young at the time – probably about six), had snuck into the cloakroom and stolen things from the pockets of people's coats. Caused quite the scandal apparently. I told Archie all about it.

'So, I could see him maybe stealing the silver, but murder?' I had to admit, I wasn't convinced. 'Besides, by all accounts, Uncle Roderick was in his room, not downstairs, when the murder was committed.'

Archie turned his hands into two beak-like mouths and flapped them open and closed.

'That's right, he was talking to Gloria, which brings us neatly to our newest suspect!'

Archie looked at me questioningly and I got out the locket.

'G.B. – or . . . Gloria Blouse? Gloria was VERY nervous talking to Badger,' I mused. 'She was a quivering jelly. AND . . .'

I paused to flick back through my notes. When I'd found what I was looking for I thrust a finger accusatorially at it.

'AHA!' I cried. 'THERE! She said in her interview that she's a trained gymnast, so she COULD have reached the tusk with an expert leap, and if this is her necklace, then it seems she *was* wandering about the house at the exact time that Grandpa was murdered! But the question is WHY?'

Suddenly Archie sat up straight and blinked. Then he leant

over and pointed at Miss Bellissima's name in the book.

'Yes, yes,' I said impatiently, 'we'll get to her in a minute. We're on Gloria at the moment . . .'

But Archie was insistent. He took my pencil and wrote G.B. and underlined it with three lines, then pointed to Miss Bellissima's name again.

I gasped. 'Giovanna Bellissima! G.B.! You're right, Archie, it could be her too!'

I thought back over her interview. 'She said again that she had stayed in bed until she heard my scream but I definitely smelt her face cream in the library, so she must have been in there AFTER she went to bed, meaning she just told *another* fib to Badger.'

Archie nodded sagely. Then he mimed someone looking around. Then he shrugged.

'I was just wondering the same thing,' I said. 'What *has* she been looking for? All this sneaking about she's been doing – has she been looking for the secret passage? Maybe she found it and used it to murder Grandpa so she didn't have to marry him! She'd lose out on the family fortune and Grimacres, but maybe it was worth it to not have to be married to Grandpa?'

Archie nodded, thoughtfully.

'Gloria Blouse of course would have no idea where the secret passage was since this is her first time visiting Grimacres. How would she know where to look?'

As I said it, my mind twitched as it tried to connect some ideas. I briefly wondered if in fact this WAS Gloria's first visit to Grimacres, but of course it was. The only other people besides family who came to the house regularly were Lil and the milkman, and Gloria was neither of those people.

She was also much, much too young to have been a maid here. My great-grandpa got rid of them before Farv was born. And anybody who'd been a maid back then would be an elderly woman now, not a young woman in her twenties with big, blue eyes in a thin summer frock.

Thinking about maids made me think of the photographs I'd looked at in Grandpa's office when I'd been in there earlier with Badger. Young women smiling with the terrifying Mrs Irongirdle grimacing in the background. The other photo had been of Great Aunt Priscilla in her funny bird hat.

I started. '*Great Aunt* . . .' I whispered to myself. I shook my head trying to work the memory loose. 'Someone said something about a great aunt earlier but I can't think who or when?'

Archie tapped Great Aunt Priscilla's name in my book and looked at me questioningly.

'No, it wasn't about her,' I said. 'I'm sure I'll remember in a minute . . .'

But no . . . The memory was fleeting and had disappeared like a frog in a pond.

'Of course, none of the interviews shed any light on why

Grandpa had written "13" on his blotting pad before he croaked it.' I sighed. I was beginning to wonder if it was even a clue.

'Still!' I said, trying to be positive, 'I think we are closing in on our main suspects – Uncle Roderick, the two G.B.s, Gloria Blouse and Giovanna Bellissima and . . .'

I said the next name quietly. 'Farv.'

Archie nodded.

We sat silently for a moment, each to our thoughts, then Archie picked up the necklace. He considered it closely, his eyebrows a V on his forehead. He ran his fingers along the edge of the pendant. He then tapped two tiny bumps on one side that I hadn't noticed before and raised his eyebrows at me. Then, giving me the necklace back, he mimed something opening, like a book, or a door.

'Hinges?' I asked, and he nodded. 'So this had a back to it? It's not a pendant at all but half of a broken locket!'

Quickly, I patted down the lining of the coat. There was still something stuck in a seam but it was long and thin like a stick of rock or a pencil. I couldn't get it out and other than that there was nothing else in there at all.

Just then down the corridor came the distant sound of Mrs Crumpet clumping down the stairs, so Archie and I hopped up and looked busy. The necklace and the murder book went in my pocket and Archie put the biscuit tin back where it should be and quickly swilled out our milk glasses.

By the time Mrs Crumpet entered the kitchen, we were smiling innocently like two little cherubs in an immaculate kitchen.

'Well, isn't it looking lovely in here!' she said, beaming. 'Won't you both have a biscuit now as a little treat for all your hard work?'

She reached for the tin that both Archie and I knew was now empty. I jumped up from the table and grabbed Archie's arm.

'Would love to, Mrs C,' I said, revving myself to skedaddle, 'but Archie and I were just going to . . . er . . . say goodnight to Great Aunt Priscilla.'

Mrs Crumpet said something about that being a nice thing to do, but I hardly heard her over the sound of mine and Archie's feet galumphing out of the kitchen and up the stairs.

'Come on! We've got half a locket to find,' I whispered to Archie, 'and some TOP SECRET snooping to do!'

Antique lacquered wood and mother of pearl jewellery box, originally from China.

CHAPTER 33.
A GOOD BIT OF SNEAKING

'We're looking for the back of that locket and . . .' I hissed, in answer to a very expressive piece of mime work from Archie asking me what we were doing, 'it *could* be very important. Especially if it has a photo stuck to it. It might even be a picture of the murderer! Although maybe that would be too much to hope for . . . Anyway – we should try to find it IN CASE it could be a clue.'

I tapped the book in my waistband.

'CONSIDER EVERYTHING!' I whispered.

Archie nodded.

'And . . .' I continued, 'we're also looking for anything else that might be a clue too, OK? Eyeholes wide open!'

Archie saluted.

We tiptoed along the upstairs corridor where all the

bedrooms were. I'd wanted to have a good old nose around Grandpa's study first to see if there was anything there that Badger and I had missed, however the door was still locked so instead Archie and I had dashed straight upstairs.

A murmur of voices was still coming from the drawing room below us, so I knew we had a bit of time before everyone started retiring to bed. My plan was to have a good look around everyone's rooms to see if there was anything in them that might help mine and Archie's investigation. The locket and the letters 'G.B.' were intriguing me and I had a bee in my bonnet about finding the back of it. Of course, if we also found something blood-splattered and suggestive of murder then that would be a terrific bonus!

Archie's face was pale as we crept along the landing. He's gentle and never likes to get into trouble. That's what was so horrible about the way Grandpa used to treat him. I suddenly thought about *The Incident* and how upsetting it must have been for him.

'Mrs Crumpet told me about what happened in February,' I said, quietly. 'It must have been awful, finding that poor woman in the woods. And I bet Grandpa was beastly afterwards.'

Archie grew paler still, opened his mouth and closed it, then nodded his head. I gave him a gentle punch on the arm. 'Don't you worry, though,' I said. 'I'm here now and I'll make sure you're OK and that we don't get into any trouble.

If we get caught snooping, I'll take the blame. OK?'

Archie smiled at that, and we crept on down the corridor.

'Right,' I said, as we reached the door to Muv and Farv's room. 'You wait outside and if you hear anyone coming upstairs, knock gently on the door to let me know. I'll dash out and we'll pretend we've just been to see Gappy, like we told Mrs C . . .'

I opened the door to Muv and Farv's room and was surprised to find a bright little fire flickering in the hearth. With Grandpa no longer around to object, Aunt M must have asked Mrs Crumpet to light them in the bedrooms. Good old Aunt M! I felt even more sure that she wasn't a murderer.

'If we *do* get caught, we can say we were lighting the fires!' I said.

Archie nodded and gave me a thumbs up. I could see he was still a bit nervous, but he squared his shoulders bravely and stood to attention by the door, on guard. I handed him Charles Darwin and slipped inside the room.

The fire, although lovely, was doing little to actually warm the place, but it did provide me with enough light to see what I was doing. My torch was in my bedroom and I hadn't wanted to dash there and back.

I snooped in drawers, in the wardrobes and cupboards, under the old trunk by the window and found . . . nothing.

I searched the vanity table in front of the window too, but

everything there was just as I expected – Muv's make-up and lotions, her reading glasses she refuses to wear in public, Farv's cufflink (the one with 'G' for 'Gristle' on it), a comb, a toothbrush, toenail clippers. Nothing at all to suggest a murderer.

With three more suspects' rooms still to snoop through, I crept on down the landing and continued my search.

There was nothing of much interest in Uncle Roderick's room or in Gloria Blouse's either. Her belongings were arranged more tidily than Uncle Roderick's (his room had worn socks strewn around the place), but there was nothing in either that got my detective nose twitching.

There was a small wooden box on Gloria's vanity table that briefly intrigued me. A good place to hide part of a broken necklace, I thought. I pulled my pyjama sleeve down over my hand so as to not leave any fingerprints and had a good look through, but the locket wasn't there, just a pair of earrings and some shiny costume jewellery that Muv would have called cheap.

I began to feel disheartened. I'd been convinced that I'd find something useful in the bedrooms, but so far: nothing!

I moved on to Giovanna's bedroom. It smelt of her perfume and her face cream. I shoved my nose into the bottle of Rose and Geranium lotion and took a big sniff.

Yes, that was definitely what I'd smelt in the library! No mistaking it. So what HAD she been doing in the library?

There was no time to consider this in detail right now so I got cracking with my search.

Again I'd found nothing of much interest, certainly no blood-stained gloves or a detailed plan of the murder, when I noticed that *she too* had a little jewellery box on her vanity table. Hers was much fancier than Gloria Blouse's – lacquered wood and mother of pearl. I carefully picked it up and shook it. Things rattled about inside, but the lid was locked tight.

The box in Gloria's room had the key in it, but Giovanna's didn't. That wasn't a problem for me though. I pulled my hair grip out and in a jiffy – *ping* – the lid sprang open. Sid, our old chauffeur, had taught me that little trick.

There were lots of jewels inside the satin-lined box. REAL jewels this time, gleaming brightly in the firelight. I had a good root around looking for the missing back to the locket, but I couldn't see it anywhere. I hadn't expected to really. The necklace I'd found in my pocket didn't fit in with all the other pieces in the box. They all looked very expensive and brand new – probably gifts from Grandpa – whereas the locket was tarnished and old.

I was about to shut up the box again and wipe it with my sleeve to get rid of my prints, when something made me suddenly stop.

My fingers had found something.

There, at the bottom, where the satin lining met the walls of the box, was a small loop of fabric. Quickly, I dumped the jewels out on to the table and had a good squint inside. The fabric loop formed a sort of little handle. I gave it a pull.

CLICK.

To my delight, the entire base lifted up, revealing a compartment underneath.

A very <u>secret</u> compartment.

'Well, well, well . . .' I whispered. 'What *have* we got here?'

A miniature leatherbound notebook with an equally tiny pen. Made in Italy.

CHAPTER 34.
SECRETS UNDER SATIN

Heart racing, I pulled the false bottom of the box up and peered underneath it.

The back of the locket wasn't there, but at that moment that didn't matter. Because what WAS hidden in the secret compartment was rather interesting indeed. There was a tiny notebook, a pen no bigger than my little finger, and some folded pieces of paper. These looked to have been snipped from books and newspapers.

I lifted them out and smoothed them on to the table in front of me, like exhibits in a museum or a court case.

EXHIBIT A: *A clipping from a book called:*

GREAT ANCIENT HOUSES OF ENGLAND: THE GOOD AND THE DREADFUL

by Felicity Wattle-Daub

(A quick glance told me that it was a brief description of Grimacres and the woods surrounding it.)

EXHIBIT B: *An extract from:*
A GUIDE TO THE BRITISH ARISTOCRACY
by Sir Henry Fox-Hunt

(My eyes widened as I read a short account of Grandpa's life. It also mentioned my grandmother and Grandpa's second wife – Uncle Roderick's mother. Farv's name was there too, as was Aunt Mildred's. For reasons I couldn't quite explain, my stomach started to tie itself into a knot.)

EXHIBIT C: *A collection of photos of Ignatius Gristle*

(It's not unusual for people to have photographs of people they like about their person. Farv's got a little collection of pictures of me and my siblings in his wallet and Muv's got an album of pictures of Valentino in her purse. I'm hoping to get a snapshot of Charles Darwin, but these pictures of Grandpa weren't proper photos. They'd been snipped from newspapers. Some were from a few years ago and the more recent ones were from earlier this year around the time of *The Incident*.)

EXHIBIT D: *A crumpled clipping from a newspaper printed 70 years ago. A special report by Hugo Slander about a party in Venice, Italy.*

(What this had to do with anything I wasn't sure. It was from so long ago – even before Farv was born. Then I spotted Grandpa's name under the photograph. There was a large man and a rather haughty-looking couple standing outside a grand palace on the edge of a canal. The woman was wearing an enormous diamond necklace and beside her stood a very young Grandpa. I looked at his face and marvelled. I'd only ever known him as a mean-spirited, wrinkly walnut of a person, but here he was at about twenty perhaps, looking rather handsome. Although, I noted, even then there was that malicious look in his sly wolf eyes.)

EXHIBIT E: *A little clipping from a newspaper, dated from last March.*

(This didn't tell me much. It just said that Grandpa was going to Sicily in Italy for an extended holiday.)

I ran my hand along the various papers, wrinkle-browed. What did these random snippets in Miss Bellissima's secret compartment mean?

I flicked through the tiny notebook. It was full of teeny tiny handwriting, page after page of it. It was written mostly in Italian but I could take a guess at what some words meant. There was a list of rooms but each of them had been crossed out.

La Casa Grimacres   (Grimacres House)

~~*La cucina*~~   (the kitchen)
~~*L'ufficio*~~ – *Lord Ingatius* ✕   (Lord Ignatius's office)
~~*L'ufficio*~~ – *Lady Mildred* ✕   (Aunt M's office)
~~*La biblioteca*~~ ✕   (library)

And on it went, listing, presumably, every room in the house.

After this there were lines and lines of neat, minute writing in Italian. Lists. What they meant I didn't know. The only things I could read and understand (because it was in English) were the words 'lost sight of it' and '*The Eye of the Storm*', Both phrases were accompanied by a question mark.

What this meant was also a mystery. The whole notepad was.

Had Grandpa *asked* her to make these lists for some reason? She *was* his secretary . . .

Mrs Crumpet had seen Giovanna wandering about the place with this very pad, looking at objects in the house and making notes. But why keep the lists here in this box? Surely they'd be more useful in Grandpa's study, on her little desk by the window? Did these lists have anything to do with Grandpa's new will? Perhaps Miss Bellissima had made notes so she knew what she was getting when the house became hers? I shivered. But then, if that was the case, she definitely wouldn't have murdered him.

I flipped to the back of the notebook and out fluttered another piece of loose paper. I picked it up from the floor and unfolded it. It was a small official-looking document about half the size of a postcard. It was in Italian again, and seemed to be a form of some kind. At the top was printed the name Francesca Ravioli and there was a very grainy, black and white photo next to it. It was a picture of the head and shoulders of a woman, dark hair scraped back into a severe bun, thick eyebrows, a pair of spectacles on her nose. She was rather a mousey looking woman with big eyes. Who she was I didn't know and yet the funny thing was she seemed vaguely familiar.

BONG!

The mantelpiece clock loudly chimed nine and I nearly leapt out of my skin. Then there came a quiet knock on the bedroom door. Breathing fast, I bundled everything back into the secret compartment, threw the jewellery on top of it and slammed the lid shut, then I raced to the door.

A panicked-looking Archie pointed down the stairs, and sure enough I could hear footsteps in the hall below, and they seemed to be heading in our direction. We ran back down the other end of the corridor towards my room, which was when I noticed the door to Audrey's room was ajar.

Together, Archie and I slipped inside.

'Phew!' I puffed. 'Just need to get my breath back!' As I did I had a little look-see around the room. Audrey was obviously desperate to get home because she hadn't unpacked at all and instead seemed ready for a quick getaway.

Exhausted after the excitement of nearly getting caught, I sat for a moment on her bed. It was unmade, of course. Out of habit, I slipped a hand under the pillows. That's where Audrey always keeps her secret diary at home. I didn't really expect her to have brought it with her but to my surprise, my hand brushed against something hard. I pulled it out, but it wasn't her diary. It was, I was sure, the flash of pale blue I'd seen her stash away in the drawer before dinner the night before. My eyes hadn't been deceiving me.

It was a book.

A slim, pale blue, hardback book.

My mind boggled. The only things Audrey ever read were the programmes we got each Christmas when Farv took us to see the ballet, and yet here she was with a book hidden under her pillow.

The back of my neck prickled with excitement. Had the pages inside been hollowed out to make a hiding place between the covers?

I opened it and as I read the title page my eyes widened to the size of dinner plates.

I called Archie over from the door with a loud hiss.

I pointed to the page I was holding the book open at. There was no hollowed out hiding place unfortunately, just the title of the book . . .

Tales from the Ballet
Edited by Coppelia Jeté

. . . and underneath it, in tiny handwriting was an inscription, and it was this that made mine and Archie's eyebrows practically dust the ceiling with surprise.

And just then, from behind us, someone snapped:

'What the hell are you two doing in here?'

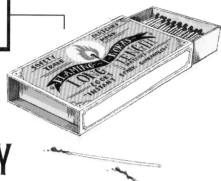

A box of matches labelled "Flaming Nora's Long Length, Cook's Matches. Instant Spark Guaranteed!" Made in England.

CHAPTER 35.
DANGEROUSLY FLARED NOSTRILS

Audrey.

HECK IT!

She was silhouetted against the dim light of the hall, nostrils flared like a charging bull.

As quick as a flash, we spun to face her and with the swish of my too-big fur coat I managed to cover me sliding the book back under her pillow.

I thought fast, remembering our earlier plan. 'Archie has VERY KINDLY been lighting fires in all the bedrooms this evening,' I said in a voice like treacle as I pointed across the room to the little flickering blaze. 'And *I* helped.'

'Oh,' said Audrey, obviously rather stumped.

Her temper was momentarily calmed but then suddenly flared up again. 'But the fire's over there. So what are you two doing skulking by my bed? Going through my things *again*? I know what you're like, Edna: trouble! Come on, out with it. What are you up to, you nosy little snooper?'

My brain whirred ninety to the dozen and thankfully crashed into an idea.

'Well, dearest sister,' I said, in a sugary sweet voice this time accompanied by a caramelly smile to match, 'I was *actually* just checking that you had a nice glass of water ready for bedtime.'

I cleared my throat for effect and said, 'A fire in the bedroom can be quite drying for the throat I find, and I wouldn't want you to wake up thirsty.'

Her eyes narrowed as she watched me make a great pantomime of checking her glass.

'You're up to something, Edna,' she said, dangerously.

I feigned outrage.

'Can't one sister look after another?' I gasped. 'Especially when there has been . . .' – I paused here and dabbed at my eye with the edge of my sleeve – 'a death in the family?'

Then I tucked my arm into Archie's and, with my head held high, we marched back out into the corridor.

Audrey frowned as we passed, clearly feeling a bit sheepish.

'Well,' she said, flummoxed by my brilliant performance, 'thank you for lighting the fire for me, Archie.' Archie nodded and looked at his feet.

'And thank you, *dearest sister*, for my glass of water,' she said, with a not completely convincing smile, and she went to slam the door behind us. But before she could, I wedged a foot against the skirting board to stop it closing.

'Oh, before we go, Audrey,' I said, like we were chatting at a bus stop, 'you haven't lost a necklace, have you?'

I pulled it out of my pocket and held it to the light.

Slowly, and very casually I said, 'It's got the letters "G.B." engraved on it?'

Immediately, Audrey's eyes sharpened and gleamed like an eagle's.

'G.B?' She gasped with a flicker of panic on her face. She reached out a hand to the necklace then drew back and instinctively touched a small bulge under her sweater between her collar bones. She relaxed.

'Never seen it,' she replied, clipped and haughty. 'Now get lost! And Edna – I don't know what you're up to but keep away from my room *and* my things, OK?' I just managed to move my foot in time before her slamming door crushed it to dust.

Well, that answers that. The necklace I'd found in my coat wasn't Audrey's. She was wearing her new one. But the mystery around the locket I'd found only deepened – especially after I'd seen the inscription in her book, which read:

With love from G. B.
x

The head of a full body polar bear specimen. Antique Victorian taxidermy. One glass eye missing. Some moth damage to his right ear.

CHAPTER 36.
CONSIDERATIONS
FEATURING A WILD BOAR AND A POLAR BEAR

For the next half an hour, Archie and I hunkered down in my room. We turned over the new developments this way and that way and also even a little bit upside down. The flickering light from the fire danced around the stuffed menagerie in my room and it felt almost cosy. I'd pulled the eiderdown off my bed on to the floor and we sat on that. Archie leant against the bottom of a wild boar with Charles Darwin on his lap, and I had my back against the legs of the eyepatch-wearing polar bear.

'There's something rather goose-pimply about Giovanna having those articles about us in that secret compartment,' I said. 'Has she collected them since being here?'

Archie shrugged, then pointed downstairs and mimed working on a typewriter.

'Hmm,' I said, catching his drift. 'You think Giovanna might have found the clippings amongst the paperwork when she's been in the study working?'

Archie nodded and shrugged again.

'But why would she keep those particular bits of information?' I said.

My mind whirred on. 'Unless . . .' I said slowly, thinking it all out, 'she had found those articles and things BEFORE she got here? Sort of like . . . research?'

An imaginary ice cube went down my back.

'If so, then that rather changes things, doesn't it?'

Archie nodded slowly, his eyes wide. He mimed reading a book then stabbing something.

'You think maybe she investigated Grandpa first, then came here to murder him?' I said, my eyebrows dancing up under my fringe. 'But why now? If she was going to murder him anyway, why not wait until AFTER the wedding, then she would have been rich? It just doesn't make sense.'

Archie threw his arms up and I sighed.

'And that notebook . . .' I mused, 'with the grainy photo in the back. Who was she? She looked familiar, but . . . ugh!' I huffed, exasperated. 'If only the picture had just been a smidge clearer . . .'

We scratched our heads.

'And what about "*The Eye of the Storm*"?' I said. 'Giovanna had it written in her tiny notebook, but I'm sure

I also saw it somewhere else . . . In one of the other clippings maybe?'

Another huff.

'HECK IT! I should have stolen those papers,' I cried.

Things were starting to feel a bit dispiriting. What I needed was a little pick-me-up. I'd had my hand shoved in the pocket of the fur coat trying to get out the long pointy thing that was wedged in there which I hoped, perhaps foolishly, was a stick of rock, but it was well and truly stuck so I gave up. Instead I lifted the loose floorboard by my cabinet, reached into my secret hidey-hole and pulled out the cache of sweets I had squirrelled away there, and Archie and I set to work on them.

'Of course the big problem we have now,' I said, sucking on an Ice Mint Sugar Spangle Chew, 'is Audrey . . .'

Archie and I exchanged worried glances. We'd both read the inscription in her book.

'G.B.,' I said. 'Again! We are being haunted by those letters, Archie! They're everywhere!'

Archie's eyebrows scrunched into a deep frown.

'Did Giovanna or Gloria give Audrey that book this weekend?' I said. I hadn't seen her talk to either of them. I shook my head. 'No, of course they didn't. I saw her put the book in the drawer before dinner. She hadn't had it at tea in the drawing room, so it must have been in her luggage, so she must have had it before we met either of them. So why are their initials in her book?'

There was silence for a moment, then Archie tapped his imaginary watch again and then made a backwards rolling motion with his fingers.

'Unless,' I translated, 'Audrey had met one of them *before*?'

He nodded. We sat thoughtfully sucking our sweets surrounded by the stuffed menagerie.

If Audrey had met either Gloria or Giovanna before this weekend, what on earth did that mean? Could this somehow explain Audrey's odd behaviour recently? If she knew Gloria or Miss Bellissima already, then why hadn't she said anything? Or why hadn't they?

Low rumbling snores were now coming from my sister's room and I wondered what secrets she was keeping in her sleepy head.

Just then a clock somewhere chimed the half hour and Archie leapt up. It was time for Archie to return downstairs. This was also a good opportunity for me to join him and see if there was anything midnight-snackish in the kitchen for me and also for Charles Darwin, who was moithering my eiderdown.

'We've got a big day of investigating tomorrow, Archie,' I said. 'Do you think you'll manage to get the telephone fixed?'

But Archie didn't turn round. He was staring wide-eyed at the snow.

He grabbed my arm and pointed to the window.

'Yes,' I said, 'it keeps falling, doesn't it?'

But he shook his head and pointed once more at the window and the world outside.

'What is it?' I said. As I stood up too, I noticed he'd gone ever so pale. I couldn't see what he wanted me to look at. There was just heaps of snow covering everything – the courtyard, Badger's cottage, the old stables, the coal house. All of it under a thick white blanket. Frantically, Archie made two of his fingers into miniature legs and walked them up the length of his forearm before pointing outside again.

I pressed my nose against the glass and peered intently out. I gasped, seeing what he meant at last.

There, leading from the dark mass of the Grimacre Woods, was a staggered line of tracks in the snow.

'Footsteps!' I cried.

They meandered about a bit, but eventually ended at . . .

Archie did a very expressive mime of a chicken.

'The hen house!' I whispered. 'There's someone in the hen house!'

Hurricane oil lamp lantern.
Edwardian. Bit battered.
Needs a polish.

CHAPTER 37.
AN EXPEDITION

We burst into the drawing room and I shouted to everyone what we'd seen. It took several minutes for them all to pull themselves together and understand what I was yelling at them.

'Someone? In the henhouse?' said Aunt M, incredulous, reading specs and tissues tumbling from her as she leapt up from her chair.

'What the . . . ?' said Badger, his moustache a bristling hedgehog under his nose.

'But who?' said Farv.

'The burglar!' said Muv.

'Whoever it is,' said Lil, practical of course, 'they'll not be in a good way out there in this weather. Could have hypothermia. Quick, we'd better go and find them!'

Everyone rushed to the hall to fetch boots and old waxed jackets from under the stairs, but Badger held up his hands to stop them.

'Wait!' he said, authoritatively. 'Now, listen – we can't all go crashing out there!'

'Oh, yes – they might be armed and dangerous!' said Muv. Gloria, her blue eyes enormous, squeaked in terror.

'And also they might be dead,' I said helpfully.

'Well, yes,' said Badger. 'Look, I'll go out and see, all right. The rest of you stay here. No point us all freezing to death.'

'I'd better come with you,' said Lil, and he agreed. 'Archie, run down to Mrs Crumpet and get her to put the kettle on, there's a good lad. We might need some hot water bottles filling, OK?'

Archie nodded.

Now, I know Badger hadn't specifically said I *could* go with him to look in the henhouse, but he also hadn't said I *couldn't*. And I was NOT going to miss out on this excitement. So whilst Badger handed Lil an old coat from the understairs cupboard, I ran down to the kitchens with Archie and shoved my feet into the old pair of wellies that sat mouldering at the back door. Then Badger, Lil, Archie (holding a storm lantern) and I made our way outside.

The snow was still banked thickly up against the back door and it took some minutes to get a path cut through it with the spade Lil had found leaning against the house. Once that was done, we trudged out into the night.

It was slow going. The snow was deep and frozen, and the cold night air stung my face and felt knife-sharp with each inhale.

The henhouse was a small brick building that, in the days when Grimacres had carriages and a stable full of horses, had been the office of the person in charge of all that business. Now it was where the chickens lived when they weren't pecking around the yard. We got to the door and found there were footprints leading right up to it, and that at some point recently, the snow at the foot of the door had been roughly pulled away.

My heart was pounding. Could there be a person inside? And were they, after all my investigations into my own family, really the person who had murdered Grandpa and stolen the family silver?

My brow wrinkled. If that was the case, where had they been hiding all this time? Surely not here? And, most perplexingly, why in that case did the footsteps lead FROM the woods towards the house and not away from it? If I'd stabbed someone with part of a stuffed fish and swiped some valuable heirlooms, I'd be hoofing it away as quickly as possible.

My thoughts were interrupted by Badger and Lil kicking at the newly formed ice in front of the door and pulling hard at the stiff, frozen handle. With a splintering crack the door swung open. The dusty smell of straw filled my icy nostrils.

Badger took the lantern from Archie and cast the light from it into the tiny room. And sure enough, there, on the floor, was the body of a man.

It was impossible to tell what he looked like, partly because of the shadows dancing about from the lantern, but mainly because he was huddled up under a coat thrown over him like a blanket.

Lil crouched down beside the figure, pressing two fingers to his neck, looking for a pulse.

'Is he dead?' I said. I felt a bit dizzy with excitement and intrigue – a stranger in the henhouse!

'Almost,' said Lil, 'but not quite. We got here just in time, but we need to get him back into the warm sharpish.'

The rest of us stood in stunned silence for a moment. I glanced at Badger and saw that he, like me, was thinking what on earth this meant for our investigation.

'NOW!' commanded Lil, and Badger hopped to it.

He grabbed the stranger's feet, and Lil took his shoulders. Carefully, they picked him up and carried him out of the henhouse. As they got themselves sorted outside, I motioned to Archie and we took the opportunity to do a sweep of the room with the lantern. It was soon clear that the family silver wasn't here. The only thing I could see other than the chickens' nesting boxes and half a sack of feed was a startled mouse diving into the shadows for cover.

'Come on!' shouted Lil from outside. 'I don't want to have to deal with you two icicles as well!'

We pulled the door shut behind us, and with Archie lighting the way, we marched back towards the house, carrying the stranger with us.

CHAPTER 38.
AN ANXIOUS FROG

The stranger was placed on one of the sofas in front of the fire in the drawing room. There was then a great palaver as the adults turned into a flock of unruly hens fussing about him. Snatches of conversations whirled around the room like a gymnast's ribbons.

'Who is he?'

'Darned stupid to be out there on a night like this, if you ask me!'

'In the henhouse? Extraordinary!'

'Hyperthermia!'

' . . . just in time, another hour and he'd have been dead.'

'No sign of the silver . . .'

'Must be the culprit. You ought to arrest him, Mr Badger!' (This was Muv, of course.)

' . . . to camp out in a henhouse in a blizzard? Bonkers!'

' . . . footsteps leading from the woods . . .'

'You don't think he's any connection to, you know, what happened in February do you?'

Whilst all this went on, Archie and I stood in a shadowy corner, watching. Lil checked the stranger over and took off his shoes and sodden coat. The man, whoever he was, needed warm blankets, thick socks and clean, dry pyjamas. Hot water bottles needed to be filled. Scalding tea wanted making and something to eat would be essential, said Lil – something sugary and easy to get down – for if and when the stranger came to. Lil also needed her doctor's bag. Soon the adults had dispersed to carry out these orders, leaving Archie and I alone with the mysterious new house guest.

'Quick!' I said, dashing over to the stranger. 'We haven't much time!'

Before anyone came back, I wanted to have a really good look at him.

He was a tall, young man.

'He's about Audrey's age, I reckon. About eighteen or nineteen?'

Archie peered down at him, then nodded.

He was slim and strongly built with broad, muscly shoulders. His breathing was very shallow, his chest barely moving, and I noticed that the thick ice was just starting to melt from his eyelashes. Even without touching him I could tell he was iceberg cold. The chill radiated from him, making the skin under my PJs go all cold and goosepimpled.

Next, I examined the fabric of his clothing.

'Hmmm . . .' I said. 'Well made and in good condition – despite being very soggy. Hang on, what's this? Blood?'

There was a splodge of something dark on the hem of one leg. Archie leaned forward and sniffed it. He shook his head and mimed pouring something from a little can.

I sniffed too. 'Oil!' I said, and Archie nodded.

I recognised the smell from hanging about in the garage with Sid the chauffeur. Quickly, I checked the material around his shirt cuffs, but they were clean.

'If he was Grandpa's murderer,' I explained to Archie, 'he'd have to have a bit of blood around his wrists. But nothing!'

Just then Lil arrived back with her bag and behind her came the rest of my family, arms piled high with suitably warm things gathered from elsewhere in the house. Archie and I jumped away from the mystery man. Archie fussed with some cushions and I put my hands behind my back and peered (seemingly fascinated) at a painting of a rhinoceros.

Lil got straight to work, and with Aunt M and Uncle Roderick's help, within a jiffy, the mystery man was out of his cold wet things and into a hodge-podge set of makeshift pyjamas.

The room filled with chattering again when Mrs Crumpet brought in a tray of hot sweet tea for us all. Everyone was so busy fussing around that we didn't notice someone else enter until they spoke from the doorway.

'What's going on?' It was Audrey, standing sleepily in her nightie with a makeshift, screwed-up toilet paper earplug still in one of her ears. 'I heard shouting and footsteps and—'

She stopped abruptly.

Her eyes had fallen on to the man laid out on the sofa. She stared at him, eyes widening. Her mouth fell open and her hand fluttered to her chest.

Then, in the croaky, startled voice of an anxious frog, she said: 'Gregory?'

CHAPTER 39.
A WET FACE
ON A COLD SHOULDER

So the mystery man wasn't a mystery after all.

Not to Audrey at least.

'He's . . . he's my boyfriend!' she cried.

A SECRET BOYFRIEND! Archie and I eyeballed each other so wildly our eyes nearly popped out.

Audrey told us all about him between sobs after she threw herself across the room and buried her wet face into the collar of his nice, warm pyjamas. She was caterwauling so loudly that it took a while for us all to understand what she was saying, and then another few minutes for Lil to explain to her that he wasn't dead.

The man – Gregory – for his part, just lay there. His eyes flickered a bit at the sound of her voice and his fingers tried to gently squeeze her hand as she schlumped on the floor beside him.

I looked at Muv. A vein was dancing on her forehead. I knew she wouldn't like this bit of news. She wanted Audrey to marry a duke or a prince, not someone who collapsed from the cold in henhouses.

'Boyfriend?' she said in a clipped voice. 'Since when? Who is he? Who are his parents? What's his title?'

Audrey's mouth flapped open like a landed trout. An angry red blotch started to bloom on her tear-streaked cheeks. A fearsome row was brewing, I just knew it.

Thankfully, Farv stepped in. He can be a teddy bear sometimes. Gently, he said in his kindest voice, 'You've had a terrible shock, Audrey, but well, he's here now, and safe, so why don't you tell us about him?'

The red glare dispersed. Audrey wiped her eyes on the sleeve of her nightie and in a quiet little voice told us all about the mystery man.

His name was Gregory Barre (A-HA! G.B.! Again, Archie and I exchanged knowing glances) and he was another dancer at Audrey's ballet school.

He had recently been accepted into a very prestigious ballet company – one that performed in the grandest of theatres all around the world. He and Audrey had been – as Aunt M coyly put it later – 'stepping out' for about six months. By that she meant 'kissing'.

'He gave me this,' she said, and after fishing under the

neck of her nightie, she pulled out the necklace I'd spotted at dinner on Friday. It was a slim silver chain and dangling from it was a tiny, silver ballerina. 'And a little book of ballet stories.'

I groaned internally. It seemed likely at this point that Gregory had absolutely nothing to do with the other G.B. locket, or the murder case whatsoever.

In that case then, who did? I thought. It seemed we were back to square one.

'This is all very romantic, Audrey,' drawled Uncle Roderick, 'but what the devil he was doing in the henhouse in the middle of a blizzard?'

That flummoxed her. 'I don't know,' she said. Then her eyebrows shot up. 'Actually, I do. Oh! The idiot!'

'Well?' snapped Muv.

Audrey's body language became all crinkled and nervous. In an even quieter voice, she explained.

'Well, on Friday morning, when Daddy got the letter telling us to come here, I also got a letter. An important one,' she said. 'Gregory thinks I'm a very good ballerina, and the company he's joined are looking for new dancers. Just in the chorus – playing swans and snowflakes and that sort of thing. He encouraged me to apply, and the letter I got that morning was calling me for an audition!'

'Oh, Audrey!' cried Aunt M, delighted. 'How thrilling!'

'It would be . . .' said Audrey bitterly, 'except the audition was today and I had to come here instead, so I've missed it. I didn't dare say anything, Mummy, because I knew how cross you'd be with me. I was going to just audition and see. They wouldn't have picked me anyway, but well, I couldn't go. So, before I left London I sent Gregory a telegram letting him know I wouldn't make it as I had to come here instead and I . . . I suppose he must have driven up to get me?'

'Ah, the foolish things we do for love . . .' sighed Uncle Roderick teasingly.

Muv tutted. She was NOT impressed by any of this.

'And he's been out there all day . . .' said Aunt M, looking at him anxiously.

'Actually, I think he's been out there since Friday evening,' I said. Everyone snapped their heads around to look at me, like bemused owls.

'Last night, before dinner, I saw a little light in the woods but then it disappeared so I thought my eye had tricked me. It hadn't though, obviously.' I pointed at Gregory.

'That would certainly explain these,' said Lil. She'd gone through his pocket and found a little broken torch, a packet of damp matches and a set of car keys.

'I wonder if it was his car we saw abandoned as we arrived?' said Uncle Roderick. 'Poor chap.'

'It's amazing that he's still alive if he's been out there that long!' said Farv.

The room filled with chatter again, Muv scolding Audrey

for having a secret boyfriend, trying to find out if Gregory at least came from what she called a 'Good Family', Farv telling Muv to stop interrogating her, everyone else mostly taking Farv's side apart from Uncle Roderick, who just laughed and provoked Muv further.

I didn't join in any of the talking. My mind was working overtime.

I'd had an idea. I sidled up to Archie.

'Even if Gregory *didn't* have anything to do with Grandpa's murder OR the theft of the silver . . .' I said. 'He has been near the house!'

Archie looked at me with a questioning brow.

'Well . . .' I said, working it out as I spoke, 'if Gregory had been walking in the woods towards the house on Friday night, then presumably he'd been watching the house, and if he'd been watching the house . . .'

It was then that I realised, a bit too late, that the conversation in the room had dipped. Suddenly, it had all gone very quiet so it was only me speaking when I said, '. . . then maybe he saw who murdered Grandpa?'

Everyone turned to look at me. They'd all heard what I'd said, and it was clear from what happened the next morning, that someone in that room found my idea very worrying.

Worrying enough to try something deadly.

PART SIX:
THE
PORRIDGE
THICKENS

Porcelain breakfast bowl decorated with the Gristle family crest filled with porridge. Spilt.

CHAPTER 40.
AN UNWELCOME ADDITION TO SOME PORRIDGE

How it happened didn't really become clear until much later, but let me tell you this: an attempted murder in your house at breakfast time is certainly one way to get you going in the morning.

I'd found it hard to sleep after all the excitement. Badger said that he was going to stay up with Gregory to make sure he was all right during the night. Lil said she'd join him and then so did Aunt M.

'We'll make a little party of it,' she said, attempting to be cheery. She nipped to her office and got a box of Jolly BonBon Jolly Bonbons (Raspberry Ripple flavour) to share, and a pile of company accounts, because fun for Aunt M is a great wodge of complicated sums to do.

Audrey had also wanted to stay up, but Muv wouldn't

hear of it, and neither would Lil. After the shock she'd had, Lil said she needed a good night's rest and so she sent her to bed with a mug of warm milk (with sugar) and a roasting hot water bottle.

And of course, *I'd* wanted to stay up too. Perhaps Badger and I might have sat up all night, just a couple of detectives thrashing the case out between us before arresting someone at dawn, but Muv (spoilsport) got wind of my plan and put her foot down.

My head was a merry-go-round as I got into bed. I'd already had a lot of things to consider before this evening's events, and Gregory Barre's arrival just added to my list. I lay awake for a while watching Charles Darwin march all over my eiderdown until he settled down and started to snore.

Eventually my eyelids drooped too, and I slipped into glorious dreams of solving the case before the police arrived and Scotland Yard awarding me and Archie big gold medals the size of dinner plates. What spoiled this was waking up to find I'd overslept again and hadn't solved anything at all!

I slapped on my eye patch, threw on the fur coat and ran downstairs, and although my stomach was gnawing at me with hunger, like a diligent detective I went to check on our latest house guest before going for breakfast. If he was awake, he might be able to talk, and if he could talk, he might have a very important clue for us!

I thundered downstairs with Charles Darwin and burst

into the drawing room to see how Gregory was doing, but to my surprise I was greeted by three very grave faces.

Aunt M, Lil and Badger were stood by the fire and I'd obviously interrupted them during an important discussion. They had the hollowed out faces of people who'd had no sleep. But there was more to it than that. My stomach squirmed with sudden nerves.

I glanced at the figure of Gregory still laid out on the sofa by the fire.

'Is Gregory . . . better?' I asked. Something told me he wasn't.

Aunt M swallowed. 'Yes, everything's OK, Edna, dear,' she said. 'Why don't you run along for some breakfast?'

She was keeping something from me, I knew it.

'What's happened?' I asked, growing more uneasy by the second.

'Nothing for you to worry about,' said Lil. 'Go on, you must be hungry.'

I walked slowly towards the door. With a furtive glance over my shoulder, I saw that the grown-ups had turned away from me to continue their discussion, so instead of shutting the door behind me, I squeezed behind the open door, ready to earwig.

'Why would anyone do this?' Aunt M was saying, her voice quiet and hurt. 'You're definitely sure it's poison?'

POISON? My heart leapt.

'Oh, no question about it, Mildred,' said Lil. 'Poison – disguised as sugar in the porridge. If I hadn't spilt some on my hand and licked it, I'd never have known. Discovered it just in time – I was about to feed him a spoonful!'

There was the sound of footsteps crossing the floor and a rattle. Carefully, I peered around the door to see Lil holding up a bottle from her medicine bag.

'These are the culprits,' she said. 'Not actual poison but a load of these, crushed up and mixed into the food would have the same effect.'

'But how did someone do it? We've been with him the whole time,' said Aunt Mildred. 'I can't understand it!'

'I think I can,' said Badger, looking very stern indeed. 'We were together here all night, but this morning we all left the room – you went to refill the hot water bottle, Mildred; and Lillian, you took out our dirty teacups. I should have stayed here of course but, *stupidly*, I went to get a cup of coffee from the other room. Whoever tried to murder this young man snuck in here then, took the pills from your bag, then took them down to the dining room.'

'But how did they get them into the food?' said Aunt M.

'I asked for someone to get a bowl of porridge for Gregory,' said Lil, clearly thinking it through. 'He needed something inside him and at least that would be warm and slip down easily.'

'Then I dished a bowl up,' said Badger, his eyes half closed

298

as he played through the scene in his head, 'but left it on the sideboard to cool a bit whilst I stood with my coffee at the window. I remarked to Bernard, who'd just come in, that the weather seemed to be clearing a touch. Rosalind wasn't there . . .'

'Breakfasting in bed today,' interrupted Aunt M, 'and *thankfully* Audrey is still asleep.'

Badger grunted an agreement and continued his rememberings.

'Roderick was at the table wolfing down a plate of eggs. Miss Blouse came in then and dithered by the food. I saw her reflection in the window, but she had her back to me. She spoke briefly to Miss Bellissima, who came in shortly after her. They considered the food for a bit thinking what to have, decided against anything, and then just poured themselves coffee. Not sure Miss Bellissima is keen on an English breakfast, really. Then Bernard came up and went straight for the sausages. He was there a few minutes. Asked me over his shoulder if he might be able to get some documents from the study today so he could start making arrangements for Lord Ignatius's funeral, and I agreed. Then you came in, Lillian, and we took the porridge in here, but blast it, I'd had my back to them all the whole time so I didn't see anything. Too busy wondering when this ruddy snow will thaw . . .'

'And so at any point during that time in the dining room

the crushed up pills could have been slipped into the porridge!' said Lil. She shook her head in disbelief.

Aunt M suddenly looked very tired and sad.

'What is happening to this family?' she said with a sigh. 'Why would someone want to poison this nice young man?'

Behind the door, my heart was beating fast. *I* had a pretty good idea why someone would want to do it.

Carefully, I slipped out from my hiding place and down the hall.

Archie was stood fiddling with something by the telephone table. I tugged on his arm and, after quickly checking the coast was clear, I told him to follow me.

Antique Victorian cuckoo clock, originally from the Black Forest, Germany.

CHAPTER 41.
DUSTY LUNGS

'You know what this means, don't you, Archie?' I said.

We were crouched in the cupboard under the stairs. It was as cramped and dingy as ever. Within the first few seconds of being in there, I'd felt something small and spidery crawl nimbly over my ankle, and we'd breathed in enough dust to turn our lungs into the inside of a Hoover bag.

'The murderer is panicking,' I said. 'Someone heard me say last night that Gregory might have seen something the night of the murder and decided to shut him up forever!'

Archie gasped.

'And if I've learnt anything from reading my murder book,' I continued, 'it's when a culprit thinks they could get caught they become Very Dangerous!'

For a moment, we both sat in the gloom, the whites of

our eyes glowing, taking this in.

I tried to remember what I'd overheard in the drawing room.

'If we can assume that the person who tried to poison Gregory is the same person who murdered Grandpa . . . ?'

Archie thought about this and nodded.

' . . .Then the good news is, we're down to three suspects, because by all accounts only three people had the opportunity to put poison in the porridge,' I said slowly, piecing it together. 'Muv and Audrey were upstairs, and Aunt M and Lil were busy downstairs with Mrs Crumpet at the time when someone slipped poison into the porridge. Uncle Roderick was also eating eggs at the table. So it can't be any of them. Then Gloria and Giovanna came in and were both by the sideboard where the porridge was. Then, of course . . .' I paused. I didn't want to say the next bit out loud. It was too awful to consider, but as a detective I had to deal with facts.

'There's Farv.'

I sighed. Badger had said that Farv had asked about getting some papers from the study. Did my father really want them or did he only ask as a distraction whilst he poured crushed up pills into Gregory's porridge? My stomach knotted itself and I felt a bit queasy. Farv couldn't possibly be the poisoner, could he? Could he really have tried to murder his daughter's boyfriend, as well as his own father? It was too horrible to contemplate! And yet here were the facts: he was without a doubt one of the three possible poisoners.

'Look here, Arch,' I said, trying to shake the terrible thought from my head like a dog drying itself after a bath, 'you were in the hall at breakfast time – you didn't see anyone sneak into the drawing room to take those pills, did you?'

Archie shook his head and pretended to fix an imaginary object.

'I know, I know, you were busy with the telephone,' I sighed.

He nodded sadly.

'Don't worry,' I said, 'you weren't to know someone was about to poison an innocent ballet dancer.'

We sat in silence, turning everything over. Every bit of me felt uncomfortably spiky, like a cat whose fur has been brushed the wrong way.

'There's someone very dangerous at work in this house,' I said. 'And if the case isn't solved soon, goodness knows what deathly mayhem will occur! We almost had a second dead body on our hands this morning. The murderer could try something again! We need to do something!'

For a moment, Archie, Charles Darwin and I sat chewing our lips and thinking.

'Right,' I said eventually, having made some decisions. 'Here's our plan: your job is to get that telephone back up and running as soon as you can. Things are getting out of hand, and whether we like it or not, the fact is we need reinforcements, so the sooner the police can get here, the better. How long do you think you'll need?'

Archie screwed up his face and waggled his hands around to say that he didn't know for sure but that he thought perhaps he wasn't far off from getting it sorted.

'Good!' I said. 'Sterling work! You keep on with that – that's *very* important. In the meantime, what I really need is to get back into Grandpa's study. If I could just be in the room again, I could try to visualise what happened on the night of the murder and see what it is that I've missed. I'm sure if I was there, the Itchy Brain Clue would come back to me. Obviously the murderer thinks that there IS something that Gregory might have seen, so I need to get in there and work out what that is. And with the study door locked tight, there's only one thing for it . . . I HAVE to find out where the secret passage is!'

And as I said it, I knew just who it was I needed to talk to.

A pair of dainty Edwardian embroidery scissors in the shape of a stork. Property of Dame Priscilla Gristle.

CHAPTER 42.
SNIP SNIP

I knocked and waited for Gappy to say, 'Come in . . .'

'Oh hello, Mildred, dear!' she said, cheerfully when I popped my head round the door. She was sitting up in bed with a tray across her lap busily doing a jigsaw. Well, sort of. What she was actually doing was holding up the pieces and trying them against each other. If they didn't fit, she trimmed them to size with a pair of dainty embroidery scissors. The breakfast tray was a mess of jigsaw pieces and curling cardboard cuttings.

'It's me,' I said, 'Edna.'

She looked at me a moment, confused, then said, 'Well, it's very nice to meet you, Edna. Won't you sit down.' She gestured to the end of her bed and I sat. Obviously Gappy was in one of her foggy moments, but that didn't necessarily matter for what I needed from her.

'Now, can I offer you something to drink?' said Gappy, with the air of someone who suddenly found themselves hosting a cocktail party. 'I'm sure Mrs Irongirdle could bring us some sherry?'

'Don't worry about that, Great Aunt Priscilla,' I said, 'I won't be here long. I just wanted to ask you something?'

'Oh yes?' said Gappy, resuming her task again. 'If it's about what flowers to do for the table on Christmas day, I always think cabbages can be very decorative.'

I stifled a laugh. 'No, it's not that,' I said, then I took a deep breath. 'When I came to see you the other evening with your dinner—'

'Oh yes!' beamed Gappy, grinning at me. 'I thought I recognised you! You're the new maid, aren't you. Replacement for Whatshername . . .' Her sentence petered off. I decided it was best not to correct her.

'Yes, that's it,' I said, 'and we had a chat and you said something about a secret passage? About the children looking for it?'

Gappy's face lit up with an indulgent smile. 'Yes, those three are always on the hunt for it. Of course, I looked for it myself as a child . . .'

'And?' I said, eagerly.

'Never found it!' she said as she snipped the bumpy bit off a jigsaw piece. SNIP.

HECK!

'But the children? You said that the . . . er . . . the other day you found them hunting somewhere in the house for it?' I urged. I knew in reality that this memory of Gappy's must have been from years ago, but I had to play along. 'Can you remember where?'

Her brow crinkled. 'The hallway, I think,' she said. 'Or near there. I was on my way out and was looking for my umbrella. Someone – and it CAN'T have been me – had put it in that cannon and NOT in the elephant foot umbrella stand where it should have been.'

She grinned again.

'The children – Mildred and the other ones, er . . . Whatshisname and Dooodah? They were always looking for the secret passage! Convinced each had found it and was keeping it, well – a secret!'

My stomach squirmed. Farv. Could he really have found the secret passage as a child and kept it a secret all these years? I felt suddenly like my heart was made from lead.

'So it was in the hallway?' I said, struggling to keep my voice light.

'Hmmm? Yes, yes!' said Gappy, distracted by her snipping. 'It was in the cannon, not the umbrella stand where it should have been.'

I could tell the fog was descending again. But I'd got what

I needed. It had to be one of those panels in the hallway. Perhaps I was trying to open them the wrong way?

I got up, still feeling leaden with worry about Farv. 'You've been very helpful,' I said. 'Thank you.' I was about to leave when I had an idea.

I reached into my coat pocket and pulled out the broken locket engraved with the initials G.B. I held it out to my great aunt. She took it with her little bird hands and turned it this way and that. I could have been mistake but for the briefest of moments I thought I saw something like recognition in her eyes.

'It's not yours, is it?' I said, but she shook her head. She handed it back to me and for a moment her mouth flapped like she was going to say something, Then she folded her lips in on themselves and picked up her scissors again.

SNIP SNIP.

Whatever she was going to say, she had decided not to.

I put the locket back in my pocket and got up to leave, thanking Gappy again as I did. But when I got to the door, Gappy suddenly said:

'My brother, Ignatius – he's dead, you know?'

I turned. She was still happily snipping.

'Yes, I know,' I said, gently. 'I'm very sorry.'

She looked up then glanced about conspiratorially. Her voice dropped to a whisper.

'Murdered someone!' she hissed. 'That's what I heard.'

Well, she got that back to front, of course, but how could I tell her that? Not an easy thing to tell someone whose brain gets foggy that their brother was stabbed with a narwhal.

'I'm not allowed to talk about it,' she continued, and she clamped her lips shut and with her spare hand mimed a cross over it.

She started clipping again. 'That poor woman,' she said.

I gasped. Did Gappy know about *The Incident*?

'Who told you about that?' I asked. I was sure Mrs Crumpet wouldn't tell her such a terrible thing, nor Aunt Mildred.

Gappy closed her mouth firmly and started snipping again. SNIP SNIP.

I remembered my earlier idea that perhaps someone – possibly Miss Bellissima? – had been up here to get information. 'Has someone been up to see you?'

'Oh yes,' she said, cheerfully.

My stomach somersaulted. I had to ask.

'Did . . . did my father tell you?' I said, wincing in preparation for the answer.

'My father?' said Gappy. 'Oh no, HE couldn't tell me. He's dead. Like my brother. And that woman.'

I sighed and decided to change track.

'Was it an Italian woman who came to see you?' I said, casually. 'Very glamorous?'

Gappy considered, her scissors held aloft.

'I've never been to Italy,' she said, eventually. 'It sounds lovely – I'd like to try spaghetti.'

I pondered this. Had Giovanna been up here talking to Gappy about her home? There was another option, of course.

'Was it a small woman, big blue eyes, blonde hair?' I asked. 'Called Gloria Blouse?'

'Blouse?' said Gappy. She looked down at herself. 'I'm wearing a nightie.'

'No, Gloria Blouse is a person,' I explained.

'Oh,' said Gappy. 'I don't know a Blouse. Used to know someone called Buckett, but you can't wear a bucket can you?'

I shook my head. It was clear I wasn't going to find out what I wanted. The fog had rolled in and Gappy was lost in it again. I was accidentally knotting her up in a confusion and I didn't want to get her all upset or worried by muddling her unnecessarily. Instead I thanked her, gave her a little kiss on the cheek and went to go. She looked me up and down as I stood in the doorway in my pyjamas and the old fur coat.

'I'm not sure about these new maid uniforms, dear,' she said. 'Most unusual if you ask me.'

And she carried on cutting up her puzzle.

CHAPTER 43.
CONSIDERATIONS ON A HOT WATER PIPE

I fetched Charles Darwin from where I'd left him in my bedroom and together we went to the airing cupboard. He had a wander and I perched on the hot water pipe.

I felt sick. It was clear from talking to Gappy that the entrance to the secret passage was somewhere in the hall. My next job would be to find it. But what was concerning me was what she'd said about the younger two children pestering Farv as if he knew where it was. Could Farv really have kept quiet about it for all these years and then used it for murder? A horrible thought.

'But then of course, there's the locket . . .' I said aloud. 'SOMEONE who was sneaking around at the time of Grandpa's murder dropped it in the pocket of this coat. But who?'

I looked at Charles Darwin but he was no help.

'I'm sure Gappy recognised it a little. Has she seen it before? Or has someone asked her about it? Someone who'd lost it perhaps?'

It was certainly clear that someone other than me, Mrs Crumpet and Archie had been up there to see Gappy recently, someone who had told her about Grandpa's death, and *The Incident*, although why they'd done that I didn't know. And had they also asked her about the secret passage?

Could that person have been Giovanna? Or Gloria?

I clung to this idea, desperate to believe that someone other than Farv was the murderer.

I looked down at the notes I'd made in the back of my murder book. They were a jumble. The writing went this way and that, upside down, and all in cramped little letters. And yet in amongst them somewhere **must** be the answer.

Perhaps I was a bit scared to look at them too closely. My brain was coming to conclusions that made me feel very uneasy indeed. What if the answer I found was a dreadful one?

I thought of Farv wielding the narwhal tusk, then shook the vision out of my head and directed my thoughts back to the other two suspects: Gloria Blouse and Giovanna Bellissima.

Mentally, I crossed out Gloria. What did she have to gain from murdering Grandpa?

But Giovanna? I already KNEW she'd been snooping around the place. Had her snooping taken her up to Gappy, and had she got her talking about the secret passage?

I was suddenly narrow-eyed with suspicion.

I looked vaguely over my jumble of notes.

Giovanna had lied to Badger, twice.

She'd been in the library just before the time of the murder.

She had a secret dossier on Grandpa in a secret compartment in her room.

Her initials were G.B.

It HAD to be her, didn't it? SURELY Giovanna Bellissima was the murderer and not Farv?

If only I could find the secret passage, maybe there'd be a clue there that would prove my suspicions, or at the very least I could use it to get into Grandpa's study and look at the crime scene again. And once there, I was sure the Itchy Brain Clue would come back to me – I was convinced it held the key to everything.

I let my breath out, noticing that I'd been holding it anxiously. I realised it must almost be lunchtime. Some food would help set me up for an afternoon of hunting around the hall again for the secret passage. I stood up and untangled Charles Darwin from the towels he'd got himself muddled in.

I left him safely in my room then walked down the landing towards the stairs. On my way, I noticed Giovanna's door was ajar. She was seated at her vanity table, fussing with her hair in the glass.

Further down the hall, Gloria too was in her bedroom, standing at the window wrapped in a blanket looking out at the snow.

I crept by the pair of them not wanting to be spotted, then hurried on downstairs towards the kitchen. But I never made it there, because something stopped me in my tracks.

It was the door to Grandpa's study.

And it was open.

Heavy, solid glass paperweight containing a scarab beetle. Originally from Egypt.

CHAPTER 44.
SOMETHING LOST BEHIND AN UNLOCKED DOOR

It was only open a teeny, tiny amount. So tiny that anyone who wasn't an eagle-eyed detective like me might have thought it was still locked.

I glanced quickly around the hallway and found it deserted. But I needed to be sure I was alone.

I crept cat-like across to the drawing room door and pressed my good eye against the crack. Gregory was propped up on the sofa, still very weak with his eyes half closed. Audrey was sat next to him, holding his hands, and on the other side of him were Badger and Lil, keeping guard. Muv was in an armchair, filing her nails, Uncle Roderick was at the window and Farv as usual was pacing anxiously.

I heard Lil ask Gregory, 'So you're sure you didn't see anyone near the house? Or anything suspicious at all?'

Gregory shook his head. 'Nothing,' he said weakly.

So that was it: it was all down to me now to crack this case. With everyone occupied, I had the opportunity to snoop and I didn't waste a moment. I dashed across the hall and slipped silently into Grandpa's study.

I stood with my hands on my hips, surveying the room.

It was exactly as I remembered it – Grandpa's desk, the other little one by the window, the table piled high with the Grimacres archives.

I walked over to the window. It definitely looked out towards the woods – no wonder the murderer was nervous. If they'd had a torch or a light on in here and someone had been looking, they could well have been seen.

As I crossed the room again, I accidentally bashed into the table with all the archives on it and one of the wobbling piles of paperwork fell, causing an avalanche that spilt across the floor. HECK IT!

I bent to pick it all up. It was mostly boring documents: a letter confirming the sale of a pig called Gertrude, a list of who worked here when the house was full of maids, a ticket from when Grandpa set off for his round-the-world trip all those years ago, the paper so old it felt brittle in my hands. There were some old photos too, black and white snapshots of moments in time long gone: Mrs Irongirdle livid in an Easter bonnet, a little boy with his parents at the door of the gardener's cottage, and a very striking young woman with a nice smile and big pale eyes that even in black and white I could tell would have been blue. The uniform she was wearing told me she was one of the maids from decades ago. I flipped it over. Written in faded sloping writing was *G. Buckett*. I thought perhaps I'd seen her before . . .

From outside the room, I heard the sound of voices. Someone crossing the hall. A door closing. I shook myself. I didn't have time to stand around gawping at old photos. I shoved everything back on the table in an untidy mess and continued my search of the rest of the room.

What *had* I missed?

I closed my eyes and visualised the room as it was on the night I found Grandpa. He'd been at the desk and I'd been looking for Charles Darwin with my torch before I found him.

Opening my eyes again I retraced my route around the room, looking for anything that might be the source of my brain itch but . . . nothing.

I slipped behind the desk and slid into Grandpa's seat with only the slightest of shudders. To distract myself I tried opening the drawers on either side of me, but they were all locked. I contemplated opening them with my hairpin trick, but I knew I didn't have much time. Instead I inspected the top of his desk. It was almost exactly as it had been on the night of the murder. The spilt ink had been cleaned up leaving only a dark stain on the wood, but everything else – the pot of pens, the lamp, the glass paperweight, the scattering of old arrow heads he'd been polishing when he'd stormed in here after dinner were right where they had been.

The big difference was the fresh sheet of blotting paper in front of me when on the night of the murder, of course, Grandpa had drawn the number '13' cryptically on a now vanished piece of paper. I glanced in the empty fire grate in case it had been sizzled up in there. I hoped a scrap might have helpfully remained, but no luck. The fireplace was as clean as a whistle. Where *had* that gone? I blew my cheeks out with frustration. It was a mystery, like everything else, and the Itchy Brain clue still failed to return.

I twirled around in the swivelling seat, chewing a strand at the end of my plait whilst contemplating the narwhal on the wall. Without its tusk it just looked like a big fish, but I couldn't help feel there was a slightly malevolent look in its dead, glass eye. I shuddered and spun back round.

A bad mood now descended on me like a falling piano. I'd hoped coming in here would help me find that missing clue, the one that would crack the case and seal the fate of the murderer once and for all. Besides that, of course, I wanted to find something that would prove definitively that the person who everything seemed to be pointing to, the person with the biggest motive, who knew the house and all its secrets and had the most to gain, WASN'T in fact the culprit at all. SURELY there was something in here that would incriminate Giovanna Bellissima instead?

But there was nothing helpful in the room at all. Outside in the hall Archie banged the gong calling us to the dining room. I got up and headed to the door. I glanced over my shoulder, once more willing there to be something – ANYTHING – when to my surprise a glint of winter sunlight came through the window illuminating an object beneath Grandpa's desk. It was only a brief flash before the clouds scudded over the sun again, but it was enough.

I bounded towards it, my heart thumping. Naturally, I'd looked under the desk after I'd found Grandpa, but only with my torch, which was rather dim. Badger had looked under the desk too but it seemed that we'd both missed something. It was hiding behind one of the wheels of the heavy office chair.

I crawled under the desk to fish it out. My hands tightened around the object. Small and gold, I knew what it was even before I looked at it. I turned my palm over. My stomach turned into a cannon ball, heavy and leaden. I was sure I was about to be explosively sick.

'I thought I said that this room was out of bounds for *everyone*!' came a sharp voice.

The surprise made me straighten abruptly, walloping my head on the underside of the desk. CRACK. I crawled out, head throbbing.

HECK IT!

Badger!

He was standing in the doorway, his icy eyes glaring angrily at me from behind his little specs.

'Oh!' I said, desperately trying to think of a fib as to why I was in here. I couldn't use Charles Darwin again – he was upstairs in my room. 'I . . . er . . .'

'What's that in your hand?' said Badger suspiciously.

I squeezed the object tighter.

'Oh, nothing!' I said, attempting to sound bright and breezy. 'A . . . er . . . tissue . . . Coming down with a cold, I think . . .' I did a big, dramatic sniff as I stood and started towards the door, but Badger stopped me. He'd seen right through my pretending. He placed a hand on my shoulder.

'Now listen,' he said conspiratorially, 'if you've found something in here you need to show me. You've been a great help so far with this case, but we can only be detectives together if we work as a team.'

Despite the cannon ball in my stomach, I felt a flutter of pride. So Badger DID think I was a detective . . . And he was right, of course – we *had* to work together.

Slowly, I opened up my fist revealing the object within.

We both looked at it. I saw it all in my head then. Everything became clear. The pieces slotted into place.

Badger sighed. He closed his eyes for a moment and looked almost sad. He'd been thinking the same way I had and this new clue only confirmed it.

He opened his eyes and his shoulders drooped heavily.

'Could you call everyone into the drawing room please?' said Badger, gravely. 'We have a case to close.'

Ornate 19th century bone-toothed moustache comb. Made in Belgium by Poirot and Sons.

CHAPTER 45.
AN ABANDONED MEAL

Of course, I knew what he meant.

In my murder book, when the detective has solved the case, he calls all the suspects together and reveals the facts, unmasks the culprit and that's that: CASE CLOSED. The murderer is led away in handcuffs.

It's always the most exciting part of murder stories, but I didn't feel excited. I felt awful. And sick. This wasn't just a story I read by torchlight under the covers, this was real life with real people – and the real people were my family!

Reluctantly, I went into the dining room where everyone was seated at the table, everyone except Gregory and Audrey, who were still in the drawing room.

'Mr Badger says can you all come to the drawing room, please?' I said. 'Um . . . Now?'

Everyone looked at me. Questions were asked – 'What's this about?' 'Can't it wait? The food will be go cold.' – but I just repeated what I'd said and pointed towards the door. With much tutting and huffing they eventually got up from the table.

They bustled into the drawing room. Gregory was still dozing on the sofa with Audrey on the floor beside him, so we all took up positions elsewhere – in armchairs, on the edge of tables, against walls. Uncle Roderick lounged against a sideboard, Gloria perched on a pouffe, Farv paced as usual, pausing occasionally behind Muv's chair. Giovanna stuck to the shadows at the back of the room as did I.

After a few minutes Badger entered the room with Archie trailing behind him. Archie came to stand by me looking as worried as I did. I knew what was coming and there wasn't anything I could do to stop it.

'Come on then, Badger,' said Uncle Roderick in his loud, jokey voice. 'Gathering us all together to do your detective bit, are you? Going to reveal which one of us dunnit, eh?'

He laughed, but on seeing Badger's stoney, serious face, he stopped abruptly. The energy in the room shifted. What had been a perplexed sort of interest quickly turned to an awful violin twang of tension. All eyes were on Badger, who stood with his hands behind his back, twisting his mouth this way and that, as if trying to decide how best to start.

'Has something happened?' asked Aunt M nervously.

Badger cleared his throat and set his shoulders.

'I'm afraid so, Mildred,' he said. He took a deep breath.

'I'll start from the beginning. In the early hours of Saturday morning, Lord Ignatius was violently attacked – murdered,' he said. 'The following morning, you, Mildred, asked me to gather information to give to the police when they got here, which I agreed to do – reluctantly, I might add. We're old friends, Mildred, and I have known many of you all your lives, so to put you all under investigation, as it were, has been rather difficult and uncomfortable. However, I am a detective – retired, yes, but once a detective always a detective, and I had to do my duty. A detective must deal with facts, and so facts are what I've been gathering.'

He took another breath. Tweaked the edges of his moustache.

'So the facts are these: Lord Ignatius was found stabbed in his study by his granddaughter, Edna.' All eyes in the room shifted for a moment to me. I didn't know what to do, so for some reason I decided to wave.

'She'd had to break into the study due to it being locked from the inside. An inspection of the room told me that not only was the door locked, but the windows were all sealed shut and no attempt had been made to open them. There were also no other signs of anyone breaking into the house. No footsteps outside, no broken windows, and the back door in the kitchen had a thick, undisturbed snowdrift piled high against it. So the fact is that whoever murdered Lord Ignatius was – and is – in the house.' He paused here, casting an eye around at everyone. 'The murderer is someone in this room.'

An uncomfortable quiver of apprehension vibrated around the room.

'A murderer needs a motive,' Badger continued, 'and the dinner before Ignatius's death provided plenty. He was about to marry Miss Bellissima and he revealed that upon doing so a newly made will would come into effect. Upon his death, the entire Grimacres fortune and the house would be passed solely to his new wife.'

Beside me Miss Bellissima looked like she wanted to melt into the wall as everyone turned to look at her with ice-cold stares. She stepped back from the light and a dark shadow rippled across her face, momentarily changing it entirely. Then she lifted her chin and the Hollywood star returned.

'I'd wanted to leave when the row began, but, Mildred, you asked me to stay which meant I heard all the arguments of that night. You were all furious about the upcoming wedding and in your anger you revealed to me reasons why many of you might want Ignatius dead. Of course, I could discount several members of the house immediately. What reason would they have to murder Lord Ignatius – Mrs Crumpet and Archie for example. Yes, Ignatius was a difficult person, but neither of them had reason to kill their boss, besides, they were both asleep at the time. And Miss Blouse

– a new visitor to the house and a stranger to the family clearly had no motive. And as for Miss Bellissima – well, why dispatch your fiancé on the eve of you becoming sole heiress to one of the country's largest fortunes? But the rest of you . . .'

Badger turned to look at Farv, Aunt M and Uncle Roderick.

'Money was an excellent motive for all three of the Gristle children. Suddenly everything they thought one day would be theirs would, on the day of the wedding, be snatched from them. Further investigations led me to understand that the two sons, Bernard and Roderick, had both arrived at Grimacres with the hope of getting money from their father (which he wouldn't give them) as they were both in tricky financial situations.'

'Mr Badger! You've no right to talk about that in front of everyone!' snapped Muv, an angry red flush colouring her pale cheeks. 'That's private information.'

'That might be so,' said Badger, 'but it will all have to come out to the police whether you like it or not, so it won't be private for long.'

Muv snorted.

'And these financial difficulties meant you had a motive too, Lady Gristle. You were very angry the night before the murder at the idea that you and Bernard would be left without the inheritance.'

An angry growl came from Muv. Aunt M leant over to

place a calming hand on her arm. Badger turned to her.

'And you, Mildred, I'm afraid you too had a motive. The new will would remove you from the home you've lived in all your life. Not necessarily a problem, as you wished to live with Dr Lillian, but with the removal of Grimacres from the family, there was a possibility that the business too would be taken from you. The business you have toiled to keep successful, and the fortune your hard work has added to – surely on Ignatius's death some of that money at least should go to you, not someone your father has only known a few months?'

'Well, yes . . . I mean, no, but—' Aunt M stammered and her eyes filled with tears.

'Oh, come off it, Badger!' laughed Lil. 'Surely you can't think Mildred murdered Ignatius? She was upset with the news of the new will, understandably, but there's a big leap from being cross to sticking a narwhal tusk in her father!'

Badger nodded. 'Indeed, indeed,' he said, 'but I had to consider the possibility. And of course, I had to consider you too, Lillian. Another strong motive for murder is love. You love Mildred, but Lord Ignatius didn't want his daughter going off to live in a doctor's house in town. You were angry about that, and angry also that after all her sacrifices, Mildred was about to lose everything she had worked so hard for. Mildred might be a gentle soul, but you are a determined person, Lillian, and your temper was high that night.'

I saw Lillian attempt to keep another flicker of anger in check now as she sat on the arm of a sofa being accused of possibly committing murder.

Badger began pacing on the tiger skin rug.

'So there were motives, but what about opportunity? The murderer had to have had the time to sneak into Ignatius's study and kill him, so that was the next set of facts I needed to uncover. But apparently, you'd all been sleeping peacefully until you were disturbed by the scream. Lies, of course, as I found out soon enough.'

He paused here to glance in my direction. My face burned as I was walloped by another wave of angry glares from my family.

'And so it was a case of working out where each of you were . . .'

'And?' said Uncle Roderick.

'You,' said Badger, turning to look at him, 'were overheard speaking to Miss Blouse in your bedroom.'

He turned to Aunt M. 'You were with Lillian apart from the five minutes when she nipped to the loo. And you,' he continued, turning to Muv, 'were in bed with a headache, which leaves me with one person. One person who was by their own account roaming the house at the time of the murder. Isn't that right, Bernard?'

All eyes were now on my father, a bead of sweat on his brow.

'You can't be serious!' he said, attempting at a chuckle. 'You think *I* killed my father?'

Badger looked sternly at Farv, the two of them facing each other, two bears with their moustaches twitching.

'The thing is, Bernard,' said Badger quietly, 'you had the opportunity – you were seen at the top of the stairs after the murder AND you admitted to not being in bed around the time Ignatius was killed. And as for motive – <u>you</u> were the one set to lose the most. As the first child, you would inherit the house and the largest share of the fortune, so long as your father died before the wedding.'

Farv's hands turned to claws gripping the back of Muv's armchair.

'THIS IS PREPOSTEROUS!' he roared. 'COMPLETELY PREPOSTEROUS! I told you I was up getting Rosalind a glass of milk!'

'You took an awfully long time to do that, it would appear,' said Badger, meeting Farv's dark flashing eyes with his own steely blue ones. 'More than enough time to commit murder.'

'YOU HAVE ABSOLUTELY NO PROOF!' shouted Farv. 'NONE WHATSOEVER!'

Badger cleared his throat. I felt the blood slowly draining from my face because I knew what was about to happen.

'I'm afraid that's where you're wrong,' he said, softly. 'Your daughter found this in Ignatius's study, very near to where his body was found.'

He opened his hand which for the duration of his speech had been clamped behind his back.

In his palm was the small shiny object he had been holding, the one I'd found on the study floor.

Everyone leant in to see, but I didn't have to, because I knew.

It was one of Farv's cufflinks.

Solid gold engraved cufflink.
Made by Gleam & Glint
Gentleman's Jewellers, London.

CHAPTER 46.
A VERY DEADLY
MIME PERFORMANCE

Those hecking cufflinks!

It was one of the ones I'd seen Farv struggling to do up before dinner the night Grandpa had been murdered. Then one had flown across the table later that evening when Farv had angrily thumped his fist down during the row over the wedding. I'd seen him twiddle it back into place afterwards, but it must have flown off again later in the study when . . .

I gulped.

When I'd been snooping around the bedrooms upstairs, I'd seen only one cufflink in Muv and Farv's room. I hadn't thought anything of it at the time – I just assumed the other one was there somewhere, but it wasn't. All this time it had been lying on the floor of the study at the scene of the crime.

'You can confirm that this IS one of your cufflinks?' said Badger.

Farv stomped across the room and peered at it in Badger's hand.

'Yes . . . Yes of course it is,' said Farv, a bead of sweat on his forehead, 'but—'

'And it couldn't be anyone else's?' said Badger.

Farv shook his head. I knew it couldn't be either. The cufflinks each had a letter engraved on them.

B for Bernard. G for Gristle. The one we were all looking at had the B engraved on it.

'The facts speak for themselves, Bernard,' said Badger. 'Motive, Opportunity, and now Proof.'

He sighed sadly. 'I'm sorry, I really am,' he said, gently.

Farv ignored him.

'This is UTTER MADNESS!' he shouted. He huffed for a moment and then, quite a surprise to us all, he suddenly laughed.

'This has got to be some sort of a joke,' he said. 'Father was killed in the middle of the night. If I were the killer, why would I murder him in the shirt I was wearing at dinner? I was in my pyjamas at the time the murder occurred. I don't know what you wear in bed, Badger, but I assure you I don't wear cufflinks with my nightshirt!'

I had to admit Farv had a good point there.

Farv folded his arms across his chest and smiled rather

smugly around the room.

Nobody said anything. The clock ticked.

Badger twitched his nose for a moment, making his moustache dance.

'Look,' he said, 'this is what I think happened. Frantic at the idea your inheritance was about to be taken from you, you went to bed, but didn't get changed. You sat up brooding a while, then later you went downstairs, into the study where you found Lord Ignatius at his desk asleep. You took the tusk from the wall and then . . .' Here, he swung his right arm high into the air, pretending he was holding the murderous fish horn in his hand, then – WHOOSH! – he brought it down fast, miming thrusting it into an unsuspecting pensioner. As he did so, he dropped the cufflink from his hand to demonstrate how it must have fallen to the floor. It landed with a thud on the parquet.

I had to admit it was pretty convincing. But something – something I couldn't quite put my finger on – wasn't right.

'The cufflink had already flown off your wrist once that evening,' continued Badger. 'It hit my glass at dinner. Then, once you'd committed the crime, you locked the study door, and left by other means, stopping briefly in the kitchen to wash your hands before returning to your room upstairs.'

I closed my eyes, remembering Farv that night at the top of the stairs. He'd been mainly in shadow. I knew that he was wearing a dressing gown, but under it? I had no idea.

Had he been in his pyjamas? Or was he still wearing his tuxedo from earlier? He certainly hadn't had a glass of milk with him.

My stomach twisted. I took a deep breath. For the briefest moment a strange thought flitted across my mind. It was too quick for me to fully catch it, but something in my head had definitely shifted. I glanced at Archie and saw that he too was frowning. I tried to examine what the flitting thought could have been, but across the room Muv suddenly leapt up from her armchair. Her face was puce.

'Now you listen to me, Mr Badger,' she snapped. 'I was in that bedroom and I saw Bernard get changed for bed the minute we all retired for the night. I saw him! That's proof for you!'

She put her hands on her hips and smiled a tight, lipstick smile at the detective. Badger sighed.

'I'm afraid you saying that won't cut it with the police,' he said, gently. 'You are bound to back up whatever Bernard says – you're his wife and you are set to jointly inherit all the money.'

'So I'm a liar?' Muv snapped. 'Is that it? Well, I've never been so insulted. I'm telling the truth! He was downstairs getting me a glass of milk, and then he came right back to bed.'

Had I been mistaken or had there been the briefest flicker of a look between my parents. Mentally, I groaned. *Please tell me they aren't in on this together*, I thought.

Muv turned to the rest of the room. 'You all saw Bernard in his pyjamas when we came down later, when Edna screamed, didn't you?'

She looked around frantically for back-up.

Lil spoke up. 'We did, Rosalind, but . . .' she sighed, 'that *was* later.'

More than enough time to have changed out of a blood-spattered shirt, I thought.

Farv had now sunk into the chair vacated by Muv. 'And supposing I *did* do what you are accusing me of, please tell me how I was supposed to have left the locked room?' he said, dryly. 'A magic trick? Am I a ghost?' He patted himself down to check he was real which I thought was quite a good touch.

Badger cleared his throat. 'Through the secret passage,' he said.

'Secret passage indeed!' Farv laughed, but I saw the sweat damp on his forehead. 'What nonsense! MILDRED! You'll back me up – we spent all out childhoods looking for that, didn't we? And we never found it! It's pure myth! Tell him, Mildred!'

Aunt M was silent for a moment. She was chewing her lip, her forehead a rippling expanse of frown.

'Well,' she said, eventually, '*I* never found it . . .'

Her meaning was shockingly clear to all of us. *She'd* never found a secret passage in the house, but she was wondering now, faced with all the evidence, if perhaps Farv had, and had kept it from her for all these years.

Farv looked like he was about to explode. I braced myself for one of his big bear roars, but instead Farv's voice came out low and dangerous-sounding.

'Huh!' he snorted. 'So, my own sister thinks I did it!'

Aunt M tried to protest, but Farv waved her words away. He stood up and rounded sharply on the rest of the room. 'I'm being set up!' he cried, making Gloria squeak. 'One of you is trying to frame me!' All around the drawing room, glances were exchanged. The awkward silence was sickening.

'The facts speak for themselves, Bernard,' said Badger again.

'Facts be damned!' shouted Farv. He threw himself back into the armchair. 'We'll see what the *real* police think of your so-called facts when they get here. They'll have a <u>lot</u> to say about these ridiculous stories you've made up! You've lost your touch, old boy. Retirement's turned your brain to toffee, Badger! You'll see . . . when the police get here in a few days' time, they'll see you're wrong!'

Satisfied, Farv settled back into the chair.

'Actually,' said Badger, calmly, 'the police will be here in the morning.'

A gasp went around the room. Audrey grasped Gregory's arm so tightly he woke up with a snorting, startled snore before settling back into slumber. My goodness, the man could sleep!

'The phone line's fixed and I've just spoken to them. They are sending a rescue party to dig a way through to us.'

Everyone gasped again.

Farv's confidence faltered for a moment.

'Oh,' he said, his mouth a stunned little circle. 'Well, good! Sooner they get here the better. Get this nonsense sorted out properly!'

Badger stood awkwardly by the fire.

'The thing is,' he said, 'Chief Inspector Gladys Truncheon has given me the authority to, well, er . . . arrest you. She's asked me to lock you into a room until she gets here.'

'WHAT?' said Farv and Muv at the same time. Everyone else looked shocked too.

'She agrees that you are the prime suspect and are as such a, er, "danger to the household", in her words. You've already committed murder and attempted a second with this young man here by slipping crushed up pills into Mr Barre's porridge. Gladys says she can't risk you doing anything else.'

'You can't be serious!' hissed Muv. She looked positively green.

'He is,' said Uncle Roderick, looking at the detective's stern face. 'Old Badger, locking up Bernard, CRIKEY!'

'Where shall I put him, Mildred?' said Badger.

Aunt M stood up, dithered with the buttons on her cardi.

'I'm sure this isn't necessary,' she said. She looked sadly at Farv who had his head in his hands. 'But . . . but if that's what the Chief Inspector has said then . . . I suppose you'd better go to my office. There's a lock on the door, but there is also a comfortable chair for you, Bernard.'

Farv didn't move.

'Do as you're told, now, Bernard,' said Aunt M softly to Farv. 'Best to comply with the police. Don't worry we'll, um . . . sort all this out.'

Farv didn't say anything but allowed himself to be led from the room. As if in a trance we all shuffled into the hallway. The glass eyes of all the stuffed deer heads stared down on us like some kind of macabre jury. There were murmurs of disbelief from my family.

Muv began loudly protesting, but I didn't really hear any of it. My mind was elsewhere. The flash of a thought that had skittered across my mind a few minutes ago had returned and was slightly clearer now. I examined it from one way then another. My heart began thumping. The more I thought about it the sharper into focus it was becoming.

'Wait!' I cried, excitedly. Everyone turned to look at me. 'I've just thought of something!' I said. The idea was twisting and forming in my mind, squirming like a fish in a net. I wasn't completely convinced of it, but there was enough there for me to <u>have</u> to say something.

'Not now, Edna, dear,' said Aunt M, kindly but firmly.

'But—'

'Be QUIET, Edna!' Muv snapped. 'You've caused enough trouble this weekend! In fact, it would be better if you kept away from all of us for the rest of the night. Might stop you from being more of a nuisance than you already have been.'

Clearly she blamed me for Farv's predicament because I'd found the cufflink, but what I'd just thought of might actually *help* Farv, if only I was allowed to speak.

'But, I—'

'GO TO YOUR ROOM!' she said, pointing towards the stairs with a crimson nail.

I stood my ground for a moment, but Muv was furious.

'NOW!' she growled.

I swallowed hard, then thundered up the stairs. At the top I turned back just in time to see Farv walk, like a prisoner to the gallows, into Aunt M's office. At the door he turned too and looked up at me on the stairs, his face all crumpled and hurt. Then Badger closed the door, put the key in the lock and turned it.

Click.

I turned away, my eyes prickling, and ran straight to my room.

CHAPTER 47.
ANOTHER PERFORMANCE
THIS TIME INVOLVING A STUFFED TURKEY

As a rule, I am not much of a one to cry. It only leads to a damp eyepatch.

However, as I slammed my bedroom door shut and slid down behind it on to the floor, I could feel my eyes filling with hot, angry tears. I let them come. I allowed myself one full minute to sob. It was fury and frustration that had caused my eyes to leak so uncharacteristically, as well as the awful image of Farv, so dejected, being locked into that room. I'd made him feel so wretched. Me – his own daughter, had sealed his fate by finding that cufflink.

Yes, he could be a bit of an old grouch, but he was my Farv and to see him like that made me feel very sad and cross. Especially as I was now almost entirely convinced that despite all the evidence, Farv <u>hadn't</u>

murdered Grandpa at all.

ALMOST entirely convinced. I needed to think.

That flash of an idea I'd had downstairs had now turned into a full theory, but was it right? I had to prove it one way or another.

With my crying minute up, I rubbed my snotty nose on the sleeve of the fur coat, dried my eyes and set to work. I stood up and paced the room.

'You see, Charles Darwin, it was the mime that Badger performed that set me off,' I said to my tortoise, who was also promenading around the bedroom.

'It was during his demonstration of the crime that I realised something. Something important. Of course, Mr Badger was only performing what he *thought* was correct, but I've got a feeling he's been blown off course by someone in the house being a very devious little sneakster . . .'

I consulted my notes in the back of the murder book, running a finger across the tiny lines of scrawled text.

'AH! That's it!' I cried. 'In her interview yesterday, Lil said:

"*Hmm . . . well, I'm not a detective, but I'd say that whoever did it must have crept up behind Ignatius and got him from the righthand side . . .*"

Which is interesting, isn't it, Charles Darwin?'

I decided that I'd have to try my own performance of the crime. I looked around my bedroom at the stuffed animal menagerie and picked a subject to play the part of Grandpa. I chose a very dusty stuffed turkey because its annoyed expression and droopy neck made me think of Grandpa. I apologised to it as I positioned it in front of the (unlit) fireplace in an approximation of the scene I'd discovered downstairs that night, then I got ready.

'RIGHT!' I said to Charles Darwin. 'This turkey (Grandpa) is asleep at his desk and according to the evidence, the culprit crept in like so . . .' (I tiptoed up behind the turkey.)

' . . .Took the tusk from the wall . . .' (I mimed that.)

' . . .Then lifted the weapon high in the air . . .' (I swung the imaginary narwhal spike up high with my right hand.)

'And then . . . LUNGED!' (I mimed this. Poor turkey.)

'URGH!' I said afterwards looking at my hand. It wasn't the crime that disgusted me in that particular moment, but rather how awkward and strange it had felt to do the action with my right hand when normally I do everything with my left.

'Just like Farv . . .' I said.

I tried the reconstruction again with my left hand. Swinging the tusk felt much more comfortable now, *but* for it to have struck Grandpa at that same angle as the real tusk had, well, to do that with the left hand was completely impossible. I tried and I tried – it just wouldn't work.

Charles Darwin gave me a look that I chose to believe was full of pride and admiration.

'So I _am_ correct!' I said, excitedly. 'Farv _couldn't_ have killed Grandpa. IF Farv had done it he definitely would have used his left hand in which case the narwhal tusk would have been sticking out the other way!'

And then I thought of something else.

'And what's more,' I said to Charles Darwin, 'if he HAD done it with his right hand, as the killer did, then the cufflink that flew off would have been the one he wears on his right wrist – the one with the "G" on it – not the one that I found, which was the one with the "B" on it, which is the one he wears on his left wrist!'

I stood in the middle of the room, surrounded by my audience of dead animals, thinking hard. I narrowed my eyes.

'Which means . . .' I said, 'as I suspected – someone in this house has been playing a very clever game attempting to frame Farv for something he couldn't have done. But who . . . ?'

I rubbed my chin.

'That, Charles Darwin, is exactly what we have to work out . . .'

PART SEVEN:

LITTLE GREY CELLS

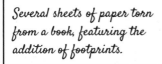

Several sheets of paper torn from a book, featuring the addition of footprints.

CHAPTER 48.
PUZZLING OUT THE PUZZLE PIECES

I was a whirl of action.

I tore the pages of my scribbled notes from the back of my murder book and spread them out in front of me. The answer surely was hidden there, I just had to get it all organised. As my favourite fictional detective was always harping on about: I had to use my 'little grey cells'.

Someone had presented Badger and I with a very compelling case that pointed squarely to Farv being the culprit, but they'd slipped up. Farv COULDN'T have done it, and so I was back to square one . . . or not quite. I already had all the pieces of the puzzle, I was sure of it. So all I now had to do was work through the pieces and see how they slotted together.

I picked up my pencil and turned to a fresh sheet of paper.

With Farv eliminated, I decided to turn back to my two

other suspects – the two G.B.s – Giovanna Bellissima and Gloria Blouse.

I looked around the room and decided to pick two of the taxidermy animals to stand in for my two suspects. A crow for Giovanna, all dark and sleek, and for Gloria Blouse? I picked a tiny bushbaby in a wooden case wedged behind a fox and the mounted badger. Its huge eyes reminded me of hers, except of course its eyes were brown and hers were pale blue.

I eyeballed the two animal substitutes. It was good to have something to focus my mind on.

I scribbled:

GIOVANNA BELLISSIMA.

- G.B. like on the locket I'd found
- Was up around the time of the murder
  (I smelt her face cream in the library)
- Was at the sideboard near the porridge too
- But what reason has she got to murder Grandpa BEFORE her wedding? She had no claim at all on the Grimacres fortune now

I chewed my lip, thinking it over.

There was, of course, that strange collection in her secret

compartment, all those old newspaper clippings, and that picture of Grandpa aged twenty at a party in Italy standing next to an opera singer and that woman with the extraordinary necklace.

I closed my eyes and took myself back to being in Giovanna's bedroom, snooping. I thought hard to remember each object in turn. One thing after another.

The clippings . . .

The newspaper articles . . .

The form with the mysterious woman's photo attached . . .

CLICK.

Suddenly some of the puzzle pieces slotted together in my mind.

'Well, well, well . . .' I whispered, opening my eyes again. 'Very interesting . . .'

I turned next to the bushbaby and focused my brain on to Gloria.

GLORIA BLOUSE.

- Another G.B. like on locket
- Was awake at time of murder
- Had opportunity to poison the porridge

What else?

She'd hardly said a word all weekend so it was hard to think of important things to scribble down. I scanned back through my notes.

Gloria had been talking to Uncle Roderick at the time of the murder, except . . .

Hmmm . . . I gave my jumbled notes another look over. Something I hadn't seen before leapt out at me.

Very interesting, I thought. I tried to remember when else I'd heard Gloria speak that weekend. I lay back on the floor with my eyes closed, thinking hard. She'd squeaked a few times at tea and at dinner, then again in the study later that night with everyone, but other than when Badger interviewed her (something about being from near here?) and a brief chat with Aunt M (something about having no family?) she hadn't said much else.

She'd just sat there blinking her enormous blue eyes and squeaking.

Blue eyes . . .

CLICK!

Again, some puzzle pieces in my mind clicked together.

I frowned. An idea had popped into my head, and although not quite formed yet, it seemed to want my attention. I explored it.

In my head, puzzle pieces started to gather. They turned, revolving around and around. Were they starting to slot into place very neatly?

I got up. The cold wasn't letting me think straight. Without a fire the room was arctic, so I shoved my hands in my pockets and wandered around the room trying to warm myself up. I went to the window and looked beyond the courtyard at the gloomy dark mass of Grimacre Woods.

From my pocket, I pulled out the coins and the locket and examined them again, hoping they would give up another clue. Why were they there? I wondered for the millionth time. What could a tarnished old necklace and some coins tell me? I thought and thought and thought until I started to feel frustrated. A Rhubarb and Custard Whirligig Suckable would really have helped in that moment but my sweet cache was empty.

Suddenly I brightened – the stick of rock! It was still wedged in the seam of the coat. I could feel it. Desperate times call for desperate measures. I took my pencil and using its point, I slashed a hole in the ratty silky lining then gouged about inside with my fingers to free the sweet.

However I soon realised it wasn't a stick of rock. I picked and pulled and tweezed and twisted and out came a . . .

Oh.

My shoulders slumped. A pen. An ordinary, boring pen. I scribbled with it on the back of my hand. Blue ink.

I groaned, but fished around in the coat lining again just in case there was something else. Nothing.

I twisted the pocket upside down and gave it a shake.

A load of dust fell out then – *clunk*. Something else fell out too.

Something silver and slightly tarnished.

The back of the G.B. locket! I connected the two pieces together and they were a perfect, if broken, fit.

I examined the newly found part. Engraved in the same swirling style as the front were the letters:

I. G.

'Grandpa's initials . . .' I whispered. 'So Grandpa *has* got something to do with this locket! But what?'

He'd never met Gloria Blouse before so the G.B. couldn't refer to her, and as for Giovanna Bellissima – well, he'd only met her a few months ago after *The Incident*. This locket was much older than that. The coins, by contrast, were fairly new.

I sat thinking for a long time.

The clock ticked.

I mentally turned over each clue as I toyed with the pen.

I turned to a fresh sheet and absentmindedly doodled all over it as I willed my brain to work harder: to slot the puzzle pieces together. I knew the answer was right in front of me, but I just couldn't see it.

Growing frustrated, I got up and paced around, then stood staring out of the window a while at the snow.

Gregory had been out in that snow. The murderer had been worried he might have seen something. But what? My brain itched, exhausted from all the thinking I was doing.

I flopped down on the floor again and glanced once more at my notes. As I did, I saw for the first time what I'd been doodling in the book. My hands must have been thinking about the inky clue Grandpa left on his desk because I'd drawn '13' over and over and over again. So many times, in fact, that it started to look like something else . . .

The fog in my mind started to clear.

And I saw something else. Charles Darwin had decided to get involved with my investigation. He'd obviously been having a lovely time exploring around the fireplace as there was now a dusty line of charcoal dark marks across my papers. I smiled at the black, tortoise-y footprints when suddenly

CLICK.

I sat up straight like I'd been electrocuted. As I stared down at the grubby marks my heart started to thump. The puzzle pieces in my head were tumbling quickly and instead of turning this way and that trying to find ways of fitting together, they were now clicking firmly and neatly into place.

CLICK. CLICK. CLICK. CLICK. CLICK.

I gasped.

The Itchy Brain Clue! The one that had eluded me since the night of Grandpa's murder: I now knew exactly what it was!

Sneaking kit – a torch and a screwdriver. Property of the Hon. Edna Gristle.

CHAPTER 49.
ANOTHER MIDNIGHT SEARCH

I sat for a long time on my freezing bedroom floor, my notes clasped in my hands as my little grey brain cells bounced around, slotting everything into place.

Despite my excitement, a horrible sicky feeling was forming in my stomach again. I could hardly believe what I was thinking, but the more I explored my new idea, the more it came together.

Click! Click! Click!

'The audacity of it all!' I fumed as everything sharpened in my mind. 'The absolute cunning!'

I shook my head.

'What we need now, Charles Darwin, is proof!' I said. 'Proof of several things actually, and I think we can get it. It'll involve another night-time excursion though, and this time you'll have to stay here, I'm afraid . . .'

I looked at the clock beside my bed. Hours had passed since I'd been sent to my room and it was now gone midnight. A quick peek out of my door told me that the entire house was shut up tight for the night.

I ran back into my room and scrabbled around in my hidey-hole. I grabbed my torch and shoved my screwdriver down the back of my socks. I had to get into Grandpa's study one way or another and if my PLAN A didn't work, PLAN B would involve prising that panel off the door again. I hoped I wouldn't have to though, not if my thinking was correct.

Once ready, I saluted Charles Darwin and set off.

Like on Friday evening, the corridor was pitch black, but this time no one was awake. No talking. No one else creeping about. No lights shining under doors.

I tiptoed along the landing trying to avoid creaking floorboards, then hurried downstairs as quietly as I could. I crossed the hall and headed to the door leading down to the kitchens.

For a moment, I thought perhaps I'd heard something in the darkness. I hadn't dared put my torch on yet and I didn't want to now, if I could help it. I paused and listened carefully. *Had* I heard something moving? Or was it just my heart thumping under my pyjamas? It was probably that, I decided, and continued on my mission.

Down in the kitchens, Mrs Crumpet's snores rattled

through the air. At Archie's door, I knocked gently, then snuck in. He was fast asleep. I called him quietly and even tapped him on the shoulder. He stirred slightly, but didn't wake up.

HECK, I thought, backing out of the room and closing the door behind me with a soft click. I'd wanted my friend to come with me, but I didn't have the heart to wake him when he was in such a deep sleep. I'd have to go on alone.

I scurried back up to the main hall, where Gappy had said the secret passage was.

I had a pretty good idea of where the entrance to it might be now, but was I right?

I checked again that I was alone and once satisfied, I opened the door to the cupboard under the stairs and slipped inside.

This had been the only place in the house I *hadn't* thought of looking; not this weekend, or on previous visits when I'd been searching for the Grimacres buried treasure. Why look in a boring cupboard filled with junk? I just hadn't considered it. I considered it now though, hoping I was correct.

Once inside, I crouched down and flicked on my torch. The battery was low making the glow very weak. I scanned the floor where Archie and I had sat earlier for our conflab. The place was full of junk – old tools, dried up cans of paint, broken furniture. My dim spotlight illuminated them all but stopped suddenly on an object. An object different from the others in its newness was bunched up on the floor. It was some white fabric, scrunched into a bundle. I smiled a just-as-I-thought sort of smile as my fingers felt the row of little buttons in the darkness. Yes, I was on to something!

I stood up. Hanging from hooks in front of me was the collection of ancient coats and stinking waxed jackets I had plucked my fur coat from on Friday. I rummaged amongst them until I reached the back panel of the cupboard. I put the torch in between my teeth, held my breath, and with both hands I gave the wall a firm shove. For a split second, nothing happened. Then there was a quiet *clunk*.

And the entire wall gave way into darkness.

Small metal oil can.
'Original Grease Monkey SQUEAK BEGONE!
Multi-use formula.' (Rusted.)

CHAPTER 50.
INTO THE DARK

My heart leapt. Here, hiding in a space so ordinary and dull that it had been overlooked, was the entrance to the secret passage. I gave myself a brief moment to marvel at my discovery then pushed on. I slipped through the wall of coats and into the passage beyond.

It was dark in there, even with the feeble glow from my torch. The floor beneath my feet was made from wonky old stone and the air was cool and musty. Carefully, I inched my way along, bracing myself to get smacked in the face by cobwebs, but there weren't any. It took me a few seconds to realise that whoever had been down here on the night of the murder had presumably had to face the spiders before me. And I didn't just mean Charles Darwin, although this did explain the dusty state I'd found him in.

Good! I thought. A mouthful of spiders was the least the murderer deserved.

I carried on, and soon came to a dead end. I thought initially that in front of me was either a stone or brick wall, but running my hands along it I realised it was made from splintery old wood. I felt for a latch and found it tucked neatly to the side. I gathered myself to give it a good shove to get it going but to my surprise it slid aside easily and without a single squeak. A flash of my torch revealed a small can of oil by my feet.

Well, well, well, the murderer had been very organised indeed . . .

The wall swung open and I slipped out, as expected, into Grandpa's study. Looking behind me, I realised that the door to the passage from this side was disguised as one of the bookcases in the alcove to the left of the fireplace. In front of me was the back of Grandpa's chair, above me to the right was the narwhal. How easy it would have been (if you were tall enough or able to leap up and get it) to reach for the tusk and then—

I shook my head. *Don't get distracted, Ed . . .* I had information to find, urgently. I needed my evidence gathered and ready for the police in the morning.

As I didn't know what opened the passage from this side (a book presumably?), I left the door open slightly behind me so I could find my way back easily. I then dashed quietly across to the table containing all the boxes full of the old Grimacres paperwork. Now that I stood in front of it, the task felt huge. The proof I needed to solve the case was, I knew, hidden amongst it all. I'd seen some important things already. I just had to find them again and then uncover the rest of what I wanted, but the mountain of papers in front of me was intimidatingly ginormous. There was only one thing to do and that was to just hecking get on with it.

In my hand, the light from my torch flickered. The battery was running very low now. I didn't dare put one of the lamps on as I didn't want to get caught in here. I'd have to work fast.

I put the torch on the floor and began searching. The avalanche I'd caused earlier hadn't helped matters. At the time, I'd just shoved everything back willy-nilly into rough piles not thinking that I'd have to go through it all again, but now here I was up to my elbows in the stuff. I rustled through it all and in a few minutes I'd found some of the things I needed. I held them up to my light to make sure. Looking at them now, I marvelled at how I could've missed what was so obvious. I shoved them in my pocket for safety. The final piece of my puzzle, however, was proving harder to find. Or rather re-find.

I dumped a pile of the papers on to the floor and kneeling down with the torch beside me, I got to work. It wasn't easy, as with every second the torchlight was fading. As the glow became dimmer and dimmer, my searching grew more and more frantic until suddenly – I saw it! The thing I needed!

I snapped my fingers with glee.

And just as I did that, the light from the torch died and the room was plunged into darkness.

And that's when I heard it.

A floorboard behind me creaked.

I held my breath, my heart pounding.

Someone else was in the room.

Green bankers' lamp. Brass and glass. With a weighted base for stability.

CHAPTER 51.
DANGER IN THE SHADOWS

Foolishly, I tried to do two things at once – grab the torch and leap to my feet. I managed the latter, but as I did the torch went spinning across the room into the thick, velvety darkness.

I listened. My heart was thumping and my breath fast and ragged. It was hard to hear over the noises coming from my own chest, but yes, a floorboard had definitely creaked and yes, someone was definitely in the room. I could hear them breathing.

My good eye slowly became accustomed to the darkness and I was glad of a very faint glow of moonlight coming in through the thickly frosted windowpanes. It wasn't enough to illuminate the room, but it helped highlight the edges made soft and confusing in the gloom. I could see the bookshelf door now – it was standing wide open.

'Who's there?' I hissed, even though I could guess the answer. 'I know you're here!'

Then, from much closer than I'd anticipated, a shape peeled away from the shadows, barely a couple of feet from me. I shoved the papers into the pocket of my coat and made a run for the passageway entrance. I knew going to the proper door would be useless. It was locked and the key wasn't in the room. The passage was my only way out.

I set off, hands out in front to help guide me, but my foot landed on the torch and I flew through the air bumping down with a thud and walloping the back of my head on the floor. I sat up, everything spinning and the vision in my good eye dazzled with pinpricks of coloured lights.

I staggered back to my feet, but a hand suddenly grabbed my arm, holding it painfully tight. I shook it off and dropped to the floor again hoping to crawl away but again I was grabbed – by my ankle this time. I kicked out and my foot connected hard against something – a shin? A chin? Who knew, but my foe cursed and let go momentarily allowing me to escape.

Up I got and off I ran. My head was throbbing where I'd hit it and I was slightly disorientated. I ran hard into something. A desk. Giovanna's by the window. I ran in the opposite direction towards Grandpa's desk, towards the bookshelf door, but my pursuer was behind me again. They grabbed at my arm but once more I wiggled free and dropped to the floor and scrambled away like a crab to hide under Grandpa's desk.

From my hiding place, I saw the dark shapes of two legs stalk by me.

'Come out!' hissed a voice, harsh and full of icy venom. 'Stop thinking you can outsmart me, you stupid child!'

Not on your nelly, I thought, and I busied myself as silently as I could tracing my hand up the length of cable that hung beneath the desk. It connected to the lamp sitting above me. If I could just find the switch, I could click it on. Light would flood the room and my pursuer – Grandpa's killer – would be exposed.

Inch by inch, my hand went up the cable. I held my breath trying to be as quiet as possible. The switch was nearly in my hand then – OUCH! – a foot crunched over my other hand that was on the floor. Pain shot up my arm and in my surprise, I pulled sharply on the wire making the lamp fall to the floor – SMASH! – followed by a tinkling sound as the light bulb exploded covering the floor in front of me with tiny shards of broken glass.

A second later, I was grabbed roughly and dragged from my hiding place and before I had a chance to yelp a hand was slapped firmly over my mouth. The glass on the floor scraped my hands as a knee on my shoulder pinned me to the floor.

'You just couldn't leave things alone, could you?' said the voice. 'Well, now I'll have to shut you up for good.'

An arm swung up into the air, something heavy grasped tightly in its hand. The arm began to move towards me at speed. I felt the air rush. I braced for its impact, but then suddenly the hand stopped as another voice from behind the desk, from the entrance to the passage, cried:

'EDNA!'

Early 20th century wall mounted electric light switch.

CHAPTER 52.
A SURPRISE ARRIVAL

The surprise slowed the descent of my would-be murderer's hand just enough for me to wiggle free.

'ARCHIE?' I shouted. Relief washed over me. He was here in the room – and his voice had filled the air! I got a brief glimpse of his striped pyjamas in the moonlight as he raced towards me. He took hold of my sleeve and pulled me up from the floor, steering me towards the passageway door, but we didn't get far before the murderer was on us.

A pair of hands gripped us tightly. For what felt like a lifetime, Archie and I struggled against our attacker, fists and legs pumping, punching like hares, kicking like mules. One second we were free, the next we'd been pulled to the ground again. Furniture skidded across the floor and objects fell from the walls as we wriggled desperately to get free. All was a blur and utter confusion. Glass from the broken light bulb crunched under our feet, our knees, our hands, but we didn't give up.

Where is everyone? I thought, frantically. *Why isn't anyone coming to help us?*

But we didn't have time to wait for assistance – we were stuck in a room with a dangerous murderer! We'd have to rescue ourselves, but getting out of that room seemed impossible. I ran once more at the attacker whose outstretched arms were grabbing dangerously close to Archie's throat and pulled at their hands with all my might.

WALLOP!

An elbow hit me right in the face and sent me reeling across the room. A mountain of paperwork from the table fell, burying me under it all.

'Edna! HELP!' croaked Archie. I couldn't see what was happening, but I knew it wasn't good. I scrabbled out from the sea of paper and looked about. In the corner, I saw the dark shadowy shape of Grandpa's murderer hunched over Archie.

Panic! My friend was in danger! I had to stop them. What could I use? Suddenly something on the floor nearby caught my eye. It had landed there after falling from the wall.

The stuffed, tuskless narwhal.

I grabbed it – shocked by how heavy it was – and threw it over my shoulder.

Then, with a furious war cry, I charged across the room, swinging the narwhal violently above my head.

I built up speed then –

WHACK!

I smacked it hard against the murderer's head.

A pause.

And then our attacker crumpled on to the floor.

Knocked out cold.

I leapt up and ran to the light switch on the wall by the main door and I turned it on.

CLICK!

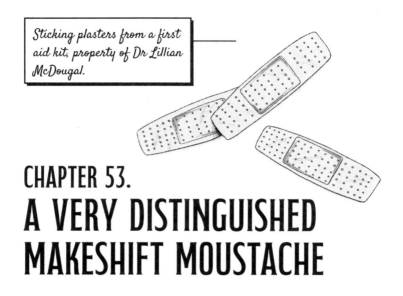

CHAPTER 53.
A VERY DISTINGUISHED MAKESHIFT MOUSTACHE

'Come on, Edna, get on with it!' said Muv.

A pale wash of grey was starting to scrub away the darkness outside, and once again the entire Grimacres household was gathered in the drawing room. A newly lit fire was burning in the hearth and I was standing in front of it in what I considered to be a particularly rakish way.

My hands (now bandaged) were clasped behind my back. I'd tried draping one of my plaits across my top lip as a makeshift moustache, but decided I didn't need it. I was, however, looking very dramatically into the middle distance.

A lot had happened in the last few hours. Firstly, the moment I turned the light on, the study door had been smashed down and suddenly there was everyone, standing in the doorway, looking in at the scene of chaos in the room.

Then there was a lot of confusion, yelling and blustering, shouts and rushing about. Lil had seen the state of Archie and I and had immediately pulled us out from it all and got to work on us. Thankfully, there was nothing seriously wrong. The cuts on our hands and legs from the smashed glass looked worse than they were and the bump on my head was nothing to worry about either.

'No permanent damage done!' said Lil, cheerfully. 'No brain leaking out or anything!'

Good old Lil! She always knows how to make me feel better.

Once some semblance of calm had descended on the house, everyone gathered in the drawing room where they were all sat now in their pyjamas looking like they'd been put through a mangle backwards. Every eye was fixed on me.

'Yes, come on, Ed!' said Uncle Roderick. 'You need to explain what the devil's going on!'

And so I began.

'You'll see now that the wrong person has been blamed for the murder of my grandfather,' I said, and nodded to the armchair where Farv sat. He nodded back. Was that a little twinkle of pride in his eye? I think so.

'It was,' I continued, 'an easy mistake to make. All the evidence, as detailed earlier this evening, certainly *did* point to Farv. But I realised that Farv couldn't possibly have done it for one very good reason,' – I paused dramatically –

'because he is left-handed.'

Here I was greeted, not with the applause I'd hoped for, but with blank, blinking faces.

I sighed.

'Gregory,' I said, 'please could you come up here and help me? I'd like to murder you.'

Gregory, who had been sitting beside Audrey looking bemused, stared at me with round, wide eyes.

'Not really, of course. It'll be pretend. Come on now. That's it.'

Worries soothed, up he got. My goodness, he was tall! I'd not seen him vertical before so his height came as rather a surprise.

I perched him on the edge of a low foot stool and demonstrated, as I'd done for myself last night, how given the position and angle of entry of the tusk, Grandpa had to have been attacked by someone holding the tusk with their right hand, and how awkward – impossible really! – it was for a left-handed person to do that. If I'd had a narwhal tusk in my fist rather than just thin air, it would have clattered to the floor.

'That's right, isn't it, Lil?' I said as I did the demonstration, and she nodded, admiringly.

I thanked Gregory and told him he was a real brick and let him glide back to Audrey.

'Impossible for Farv to have committed the murder then,'

I continued. 'Also, the cufflink I'd found was the wrong one. Farv's cufflinks have his initials engraved on them. One on each cufflink. The one I'd found was the "B" one, which is the one—'

'I wear on my left wrist,' interrupted Farv.

'Exactly,' I agreed. 'And if you'd used your right hand to commit the crime, it would have been the "G" that should have flown off.'

'Yes,' said Farv. 'But it's the "B" with the loose fitting, and that I can never do up again, being left-handed.'

I turned to the rest of the room. 'And so it became clear to me that Farv had been framed for a crime he didn't commit!'

I let that sink in for a moment then carried pacing across the tiger skin rug with my hands behind my back. How I longed to be in an immaculate tuxedo delivering all this and not my crumpled pyjamas . . .

'So, who could have done it?' I continued. 'As has been previously stated by my colleague, Mr Badger, there were lots of people who would have liked Grandfather dead, not least of all his three children. Uncle Roderick the rogue was the obvious choice.'

Uncle Roderick stared at me fiercely.

'But no, it wasn't you. And it wasn't you, Aunt Mildred – you're left-handed too. And not Farv either? So none of the children. Then who?'

I paced a bit more. I liked the sound of my feet on the

floor, the crackling fire, the fizzing tension in the air.

'A CONUNDRUM!' I cried, making everyone jump. 'But then Gregory arrived. You almost getting poisoned, Gregory, was a real boon for me! It cleared up a few things. As Mr Badger said earlier, only three people had the opportunity as the porridge sat on the sideboard to slip in the goods. There was no reason for it to be Farv if he hadn't killed Grandpa, so then there were two: Miss Bellissima and Miss Blouse.'

The two women said nothing.

'I *had* dismissed them as suspects – what was their motive? – but with that latest development? Well, well, well – I was forced to examine them more closely and the more I examined, the more I was convinced that at least one of them was connected to the case. The puzzle pieces were starting to fit. And, of course, there was this . . .'

From the pocket of my coat I pulled out the locket and held it in the air. Everyone leant closer to get a better look. At the back of the room, Mrs Crumpet quickly cleaned her specs on her pinny to make sure she didn't miss anything.

'A women's necklace, old, broken, but engraved with the letters G.B.,' I explained. 'I discovered it in the pocket of this coat the morning after the murder. It hadn't been there the previous evening and so someone must have hidden it there during the night, someone who had been sneaking around the house at the time of Grandpa's murder. But who? Could it belong to G.B.: Giovanna Bellissima?'

In her shadowy corner, Miss Bellissima's mouth opened to say something then closed suddenly.

'My new step-grandmother . . .' I continued. 'If she was the murderer, surely, she'd have waited until *after* the wedding to do it. But I had to look at the facts. And the facts were interesting.

'Mrs Crumpet told me that since her arrival here a week ago, Miss Bellissima has spent an awful lot of time snooping about the house, making notes. Had she been searching for the secret passage so she could use it to murder Grandpa? Also, on the night of the murder, I had assumed that she was asleep in bed because her door was locked, but when you are a detective, you mustn't assume anything. How stupid of me! She could, I realised, have locked the door from the landing side and spent some time wandering about the house, which, in fact, you did, didn't you, Miss Bellissima?'

All eyes flicked to Miss Bellissima, then back to me.

'I smelt your Rose and Geranium face cream in the library before I discovered Grandpa – proving that at some point around the time of the murder you had been prowling around the house. I dug a little further into exactly who you were. And I discovered some THINGS hidden in a secret compartment in your jewellery box.'

I turned to look directly at her.

'Would you like to explain why you had a file of information about us in your room, Miss Bellissima? Or should I use your real name?' I paused for a moment.

A good dramatic moment.

Then I said: 'Miss Francesca Ravioli . . .'

Priceless white gold and platinum necklace set with the Eye of the Storm diamond. Originally from Italy.

CHAPTER 54.
THE EYE OF THE STORM

Silence.

All eyes swivelled across the room to where Giovanna Bellissima was glaring at me, hard.

I waited.

I knew I was right. It was earlier, when Badger was accusing Farv of murder, that my brain had started to fit things together. Miss Bellissima had recoiled away from the light of a table lamp and for the briefest of moments, the shadows had altered her face. A dark line had crossed her forehead giving the illusion of thicker eyebrows, bringing to mind another face, one I couldn't quite put my finger on in that precise moment. But later, up in my room, it had come back to me – the grainy black and white photograph attached to a form in the secret compartment! I remembered the photo and now suddenly I recognised the face. Thinner eyebrows, no glasses and her hair released from the tight bun in the photograph had worked wonders for disguising Francesca Ravioli.

She sighed.

'All right,' she said, 'you've caught me.'

She drew herself upright in the chair, jutted her chin proudly.

'My name is Francesca Ravioli, and it's true that I have indeed got myself here under false pretences.'

Everyone leant in.

Miss Bellissima-slash-actually-Francesca-Ravioli took a deep breath, and then said:

'Long before I was born, my grandparents went to a party in Venice – a glittering affair with many people coming from all over the world to attend. My grandmother, my nonna, wore our family treasure that evening – a necklace containing the famous and priceless Eye of the Storm diamond – an enormous jewel which gets its name from the story of its mysterious discovery. It washed up on the beach after a ferocious storm and has been in our family for centuries.

'Anyway, years later my nonna wore the diamond to this party in Venice, during which it was stolen from her neck – gone! Vanished into thin air! Nobody could find it – the work of a master thief. I grew up being told the story of the missing diamond, and in me grew a passion for finding hidden treasure. As an adult I worked briefly as an actress, but then a new career opportunity presented itself to me. I now work for an organisation that tracks down lost treasures – objects believed stolen from private homes, museums, galleries – all sort of places.

'I've been investigating a large collection of items for months and believed many of them to be in a house in England called Grimacres. I did my research on the owner, gathering information from any books or newspapers I could find that mentioned the family. Amongst them I found a photograph of Lord Ignatius at that party in Venice so long ago. He was actually standing beside my grandmother and she's wearing her famous necklace. I wondered, could *he* be connected to the diamond theft? I tried to think how I could get myself into Grimacres to search for it, but it seemed impossible. And then, just a few weeks later, who should arrive in Italy, but Lord Ignatius himself. This was my chance! I got the job as his secretary, and six months later here I am in Grimacres itself and able to look for my grandmother's missing diamond. I'm *sure* it's here, because Lord Ignatius bragged about stealing it when I slipped the diamond into a conversation, but where it is he wouldn't say. Just said he'd lost sight of it which I don't think's true for a second. It's priceless!'

She paused as we all goggled at her. Her disguise had been very clever – her hair, make-up, clothes, those eyebrows. Of course I'd vaguely recognised something in the black and white picture of the young woman attached to the form in the secret compartment, but she looked very different to the person sitting in front of us now.

'You must believe me when I tell you that I didn't have anything to do with Lord Ignatius's death,' she said softly, and I nodded. I knew she didn't. 'I'm here for my nonna's necklace, that's it. I never dreamed he was going to ask me to marry him! I was so surprised I couldn't even answer. He just assumed I'd said "yes" when I hadn't. On the night he was murdered I *was* up, looking for the diamond. I had to find it quick so I could escape as soon as the snow thawed enough for me to leave. I wanted the diamond, but I certainly wouldn't have murdered for it.'

She sat back and looked at me with her nice dark eyes.

I nodded, business-like.

'I believe you,' I said. 'Lil said your fainting was genuine and I don't think even an excellent actress could knock themselves out like that on cue. So . . . where did this leave me? Well, there was ANOTHER person close enough to the porridge to poison it and whose initials also matched those on the mysterious locket . . .'

I swivelled on my heels.

'Gloria Blouse.'

Ladies' lace edged handkerchief,
embroidered with the initials G.B.

CHAPTER 55.
AND THEN THERE WAS ONE

'Gloria Blouse,' I repeated. 'The other G.B.'

Gloria said nothing. She just sat there, worrying at the edge of her frock and blinking her big, blue eyes at me.

'Of course, I'd dismissed you from being involved in Grandpa's death almost immediately. You'd been in Uncle Roderick's bedroom talking to him when I walked down the corridor . . . but wait!'

I paused, taking a moment to have my back to everyone so I could spin around dramatically to face them for the next bit. If I'm honest my spin *could* have been a bit smoother but I pushed on regardless.

'Facts. It all comes down to facts,' I said, addressing the room. 'What I'd *actually* heard was JUST Uncle Roderick's voice. NOT Gloria's, meaning she might not have been in the room at all! She could have been downstairs sticking a fish tusk into Grandpa!'

Uncle Roderick scoffed. 'And I was in the room talking to myself?'

'You might have been!' I said. 'Or you might have been talking in your sleep.'

I stood and looked distinguished and ponderous for a moment.

'But it did just seem so unlikely that Gloria was the murderer. What reason did she have? Money? She wasn't set to inherit any of the Grimacres fortune. Yes, you'd be a lot richer, Uncle Roderick, but would Gloria really find having access to that bit of the money worth murdering someone for? I could see HOW she would do it, of course. Gloria, you told Mr Badger in your interview (which I just happened to overhear because I was behind the curtain in the library at the time er . . . looking for, well – er, something . . .) that you used to be a gymnast. It's not hard to imagine you being able to leap or clamber up to the weapon without making a sound despite you not being very tall. So that was the HOW, but what about the why? ANOTHER conundrum! Then something you said to Aunt M after lunch yesterday made me wonder if there could be another motive for you to kill Grandpa . . .'

The heads of everyone in the room swivelled between Aunt M and Gloria Blouse like they were watching a tennis match.

Aunt M looked perplexed.

'Just a little comment,' I said, 'but important nonetheless. You, Aunt M, said that you bet Gloria's family didn't behave like we all have this weekend. Then Miss Blouse said that she didn't have a family. Only a great aunt who had adopted her as a baby, but had recently died. Well, that got my ears pricked! Because despite you all trying to keep it from me, I found out what happened in Grimacre Woods in February. Yes, I know all about . . . *The Incident.* It was on a sheet of newspaper I found under a chicken's bum: an article about a mysterious woman Grandpa accidentally shot with an arrow. It made me wonder: had I got the motive for Grandpa's murder entirely wrong? Might it not have been money after all, but REVENGE?'

I stood passing the G.B. locket from one hand to the other.

'Could the woman in the woods have been Gloria's great aunt?' I said, excitedly. 'You said when talking to Mr Badger in the library that although you've lived abroad for a long time you actually grew up close to Grimacres. Had your great aunt been a maid here a long time ago? If she had, she might have found the secret passage and told you about it!

'Could this locket have been hers? It certainly seems old enough to be, and perhaps you'd been named after her so had the same initials? It all seemed to fit – Gloria had also been around the porridge AND was upstairs when I found the door to Grandpa's study unlocked so had the chance then to plant the cufflink she'd presumably stolen earlier . . . and yet . . .'

My shoulders slumped.

'There was something missing. Something which didn't quite tie everything together as neatly as it needed to. When I returned to my room after finding Grandpa dead, I couldn't shake the feeling that I'd missed something important. I knew I'd seen it but just couldn't think what it was. It was a crucial clue and the effort to remember it made my brain itch. It kept flashing into my mind but before I could capture it – *pfft* – gone! I *needed* to remember it. I was sure that whatever it was would be the missing piece to complete this puzzle and tie Gloria to the murder absolutely.'

I paused.

I looked around the room.

Everyone was staring at me, agog.

'Then earlier this evening it came to me – what my brain had been itching to tell me.' I took a deep breath. 'I'd been looking out at the snow, thinking about Gregory and how the murderer was obviously panicking that he'd seen *something* – but he hadn't. What I realised then was that I was looking for my clue the wrong way around. I was looking for *something* when really the clue was actually something I SHOULD have seen the night of the murder, but DIDN'T!'

Blank faces blinked back at me again. I soldiered on.

'It was Charles Darwin who put me on to it when he

walked over my notes. That pointed me in the right direction. A direction I hadn't even considered – none of us had – and yet the minute I remembered it, all the puzzle pieces started to click together neatly revealing the full picture of exactly who had murdered Grandpa. And it wasn't you, Gloria.'

I stopped and looked directly into the darkest corner of the room, where two icy blue eyes were glaring at me coldly from the shadows. I glared back, fierce and unafraid.

And then I said:

'It was you, wasn't it, Mr Badger?'

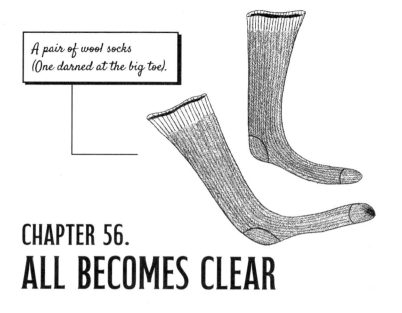

A pair of wool socks
(One darned at the big toe).

CHAPTER 56.
ALL BECOMES CLEAR

He didn't say anything.

He just sat there in the armchair sneering and with his eyes, furious, fixed on me. There was a large red lump on his head from where I'd walloped him with the narwhal.

His hands were bound tightly with his belt. Lil and Uncle Roderick had done that after they'd broken down the door and found Archie and I standing over him. At first, no one could understand what had happened. Then Mr Badger had come to and started to say that he thought we were intruders. The lying woodlouse! I, in my excitement and confusion, had then shouted something about him being dangerous and that I needed handcuffs but no one believed me at first except Lil. It was on her instruction that he'd been bound with makeshift restraints.

'I think you'd better tell us all about it, Edna,' said Aunt M. 'We'll have to have all this straight for when the police arrive.'

I took a deep breath.

'Footprints,' I said. 'That was the clue. I'd been so busy thinking that I'd seen SOMETHING and had then forgotten whatever it was, that it hadn't occurred to me that instead, I should have seen something, but hadn't. Something very important.'

I grinned, but quickly realised from my family's blank, blinking expressions that I hadn't explained myself very well, so I started again.

'When I went back to bed, after Grandpa had been murdered, I noted down everything I'd seen. I sat on the window seat in my room running through it all making sure I'd got everything right. From my window, I could see across the courtyard and the old stable block and Mr Badger's cottage and the henhouse and beyond it the woods. The blizzard had stopped for a while and everything was covered in a white blanket of thick snow which was quite calming to see after everything that had happened.

'That was when my brain started to itch, and I realised I'd missed something important. Stupidly, I thought it was something in Grandpa's study, but it wasn't. In fact, I was looking right at it: besides Archie's partially filled in tracks from earlier in the afternoon when he'd brought in the chickens, the entire courtyard was as smooth as an iced cake, which meant Mr Badger couldn't have gone home that night or come back over here after I screamed!'

Aunt M shook her head. 'But I saw him leave when I went to get Daddy's medicine,' she said slowly.

I nodded. 'So did I,' I said, 'but in reality he just slipped out of the front door, waited in the porch under the gargoyles and then slipped back in again when the coast was clear. You know that front door is never locked. Is that right, Mr Badger?'

He didn't say anything but one of his eyelids began twitching angrily, so I knew I was correct.

'I think what happened is this,' I continued. 'Mr Badger then hid in the cupboard under the stairs, put his gloves on and waited until all was quiet. Then, using the secret passage, he slipped into the study, murdered Grandpa, locked the study door from the inside and then left through the passage again. Charles Darwin must have wandered downstairs and found the cupboard door open and, unbeknownst to Mr Badger, followed him into the study and got trapped there. It would explain why Charles Darwin was covered in cobwebs when I found him . . .

'I imagine the plan had been for Mr Badger, once the crime had been committed, to then slip off home and wait there until the body was discovered in the morning, but unfortunately Farv, Miss Bellissima – I mean, Miss Ravioli – and I were all wandering about, so he was stuck. He must have heard us from the cupboard. Then of course I went and broke down Grandpa's office door to rescue Charles Darwin, meaning he had to think on his feet and come up with a plan!'

'But he was in his pyjamas when he arrived?' said Uncle Roderick.

I shook my head.

'He wasn't,' I said. 'He said he'd got dressed quickly and had run over from his cottage when he heard my scream, when in fact it was the opposite. When you all came running downstairs, he was in the cupboard stripping off his shirt so he was just in his vest. He messed up his hair, took off his socks, put his shoes back on, threw on his coat and then, when everyone was in the study distracted, he came in, panting as if he'd come running from his house. We were all so shocked by finding Grandpa and in such confusion with Miss Ravioli fainting that none of us questioned it. And why would we? He's good old reliable Mr Badger, the retired detective and celebrated private investigator.

'Of course he had to be here, you see, to make sure no one suspected anything and to manage it all. His plan had been thrown out of shape, so he needed to be in charge to pull it back into order. I know all of this is true, by the way, because tucked away in the cupboard you'll find a discarded white shirt that has a bit of blood on the cuff. I found it earlier. I expect his socks will be somewhere there too.'

Everyone sat looking at me with their mouths open.

'And as for poisoning Gregory – easy,' I continued. 'He took the tablets from your bag, Lil, when you and Aunt M left the room, and then in the dining room it was HIM who ladled the porridge into the bowl and, with his back to Uncle Roderick (who was the only other person there and was busy eating his eggs), he crushed the tablets up and popped them in. He then took himself across the room, leaving the bowl where Farv, Miss Ravioli or Gloria – anyone really – could be near it so that later he could point the finger at them, which he did. We just didn't think to investigate him because he was investigating us!'

'But why should Mr Badger want to murder Ignatius?' said Muv, wrinkling her brow in a way she would hate if she'd had a mirror in front of her.

'For the same reason I thought Miss Blouse did,' I said. 'I thought back to that conversation Aunt M had with you, Gloria. You revealed you'd been adopted, and Aunt M started to say something – she was going to tell you that someone else here was adopted too, but she was interrupted. I wondered who that might have been? Could she have been about to say Mr Badger?'

Aunt M put her hand to her mouth in surprise and looked across the room at the bruised detective.

'Oh!' she said quietly. I was right!

'Then I remembered something Great Aunt Priscilla had

said when I was up in the attic with her. I'd been asking her if she knew where the secret passage was. She said that the three children had been looking for it and I had assumed she meant Farv, Aunt M, and Uncle Roderick, but I was wrong! I hadn't thought about the facts!

'Uncle Roderick is heaps younger than you two so when he was a child you were both practically adults. But Badger grew up here. He lived in the gardener's cottage with Mr and Mrs Badger. He'd had plenty of time to search the house for the passageway as a child – more than you two really as he's a bit older than you both, so he could have found it and kept very quiet. It would have been so easy to just keep directing you – Aunt M, and Farv to the wrong places to search when you were children.'

'I'm still perplexed,' said Muv. 'So he's adopted, lots of people are, and he grew up here, fine – but why kill Ignatius?'

'It all comes down to this,' I said, holding up the locket again. 'G.B.'

I looked over at the detective.

'Shall I tell them, George, or do you want to do it?'

CHAPTER 57.
MYSTERIES KNOTTED
AND UNKNOTTED

The grey light of dawn outside was getting brighter. It cast long shadows into the room illuminating the shadowy corner in which Badger was sitting. After a few moments, he started to speak.

'I discovered the G.B. half of that locket amongst my parents' belongings after they died when I was eighteen,' said Badger. 'It was tucked away with a lot of my baby belongings. With a note from Beryl Badger – my mother. She told me I'd been adopted, which I'd guessed anyway, and said that the locket had belonged to my birth mother. No name though, so who she – this G.B. person – was I had no idea. Didn't care really. As far as I was concerned, Alfred and Beryl Badger were my parents, but a mystery involving myself – well that was like catnip to me then. I was planning on becoming a detective and so being given a clue was very intriguing!

'I joined the police, became a detective and, as you know, then went on to become a successful and rather wealthy private investigator. But through all of it, I kept the necklace in my pocket with me at all times, and whenever I had a quiet moment at work I would put my detecting skills to use trying to track down who had left it for me and therefore who my mother was. Unfortunately, I never got anywhere. There was no one at Grimacres I could ask – all the staff had left ages ago when I was a baby, so it was the greatest mystery I'd ever faced.

'Then, earlier this year, that elderly woman turned up in the woods. Doing my bit to help Ignatius out, I dealt with the situation. I checked her for any identification, but nothing – only hidden in her pocket was a small silver disc.'

I held up the missing half of the locket. Everyone looked. Then George Badger continued.

'It was the back of *my* locket. A perfect fit, but what on earth did it mean? Who was this mysterious woman? My mother? She must have been, but why was she here? And who actually was she?

'I decided to keep quiet and investigate privately. Luckily, Ignatius was soon out of the way in Italy and, under the guise of researching the Grimacres family history for my book, I had access to all the documents I needed. But it wasn't until I spoke to Priscilla in the attic that I got the information

I was after. I told her about *The Incident* – everything – but she was no help at all. Or so I thought. Just kept asking if I knew where her maid was – Georgina. Wanted to know if she'd come back yet or had been replaced . . .

'I then realised that this was exactly the clue I needed. A quick check through the Grimacres estate archives and a look at some old photographs told me who my mother was . . .'

'Georgina Buckett,' I said, picking up the story. From my coat pocket I took out the photograph I'd found of her in the study – a young woman in a maid's uniform with pale eyes, and around her neck, just visible, was the locket.

'Great Aunt Priscilla thought I was her replacement which started me off thinking about who this Georgina might have been and why she needed replacing. Where had she gone? Her name – Georgina – made me think of George – the only other G.B. in the house after Gloria and Giovanna had been crossed off my list. Georgina had named George after herself. I knew I was on the right track, but I just needed proof. That's what I was looking for in the study tonight. And I found it.'

I pulled out more old papers from my pocket. Yearly lists of who worked here when the house had had a full staff.

'Georgina worked here and then suddenly she didn't – she left at exactly the same time George was adopted and went to live with Mr and Mrs Badger in their cottage. After that it seems Grandpa's dad got rid of all the other maids and never hired any more, probably to avoid that all happening again.'

'But why kill Daddy, George?' said Aunt M, perplexed. 'Revenge for him shooting her with an arrow?' She shook her head trying to get it all straight. 'But . . . but . . . that was an accident!' she said.

'Revenge? Pff! What did I care about her? I didn't know the woman!' snarled George. 'And anyway, what makes you so sure that shooting was an accident?'

'Of course it was!' cried Aunt M. 'Daddy didn't go around shooting people on purpose! He was shooting at birds and by sheer bad luck she got in the way! He didn't even know she was in the woods.'

'We'll never know for definite,' I said, 'but I think Grandpa DID know she was there. Mrs Crumpet said that he'd received a letter a few days before and it had made him angry. I reckon Georgina had written to him a few days before *The Incident* and asked to meet him. It would have seemed very odd him suddenly inviting a so-called stranger into the house – he hated strangers! – so I think he suggested they meet in the woods to keep it a secret.'

'H-he did,' a little stammering voice piped up then. To my surprise, it was Archie.

'When I was on my to Witt's End Farm,' he continued, looking not at all of us but at Charles Darwin, who was sleeping on his lap, 'I saw Lord Ignatius talking to the woman.

I heard them arguing – not everything they said, just bits. She was shouting if he wanted her to keep quiet about everything he must give her the diamond. OR ELSE . . . He seemed very cross about that. Then later when I came back from the farm I found the woman dead. I was so frightened I'd be in trouble if I said anything, so I just . . . didn't say anything at all.'

We were all silent for a minute after that. I gave Archie an encouraging little grin. I was VERY proud of him for telling us what he had.

Then Farv said, 'What did she mean "keep quiet"?'

'Well,' I said, 'that all comes down to the final clue. Actually – the first clue. Grandpa gave it to us himself. He wrote the whole answer to this entire case on his blotting paper just before he died. Only it went missing . . .'

'But we've found it now,' said Archie. From his pocket he pulled out a notepad. It was Mr Badger's. It had fallen out in the fight and when the lights came on, Archie had swiped it.

From inside he took out a folded sheet of blotting paper and opened it out.

On it was written the number 13.

CHAPTER 58.
THE NUMBER 13

'13?' said Audrey, piping up from the sofa.

'That's what I thought to begin with, but why would Grandpa write that number down? Why was "13" so important to tell us in his last moments?' I said. 'But when I was doodling it over and over again in my book I realised it wasn't "13" at all but a capital "B".'

I used the pen I'd found stuck in my coat to show everyone what I meant by writing the letter in Badger's notebook.

'The murderer had to make sure no one else saw it. It told us exactly who the killer was . . . B for Badger. I think he didn't make my mistake but straight away saw it as a B so possibly, if I hadn't opened my big mouth about the 13 clue to Mr Badger, he may just have got rid of it. However, I think he then saw the potential of it to help further frame

Farv, so kept it. I'm sure that piece of paper would have suddenly turned up at just the right (and very useful) moment. But of course, as we've said already – it couldn't have been Farv who murdered Grandpa because of him being left-handed. So it had to be a B. B for Badger.'

'I still don't understand why you would do it, George!' said Aunt M.

'I do . . .' said Mrs Crumpet, narrowing her shrewd eyes and looking first at Badger and then at Farv. 'Didn't see it before, but now I do . . .'

Everyone then turned to look at Badger. Then their eyes flitted across to Farv. Realisation slowly dawned on them all. I couldn't blame them. I hadn't seen it either until I thought about it upstairs in my room. The similarities between them – both bear-like, the way they tugged at their moustaches. The big difference, though, was their eyes. Farv's were dark whereas George had inherited his pale blue eyes from Georgina.

'You're our brother?' cried Uncle Roderick.

Badger nodded.

'Yes. Ignatius Gristle was the I.G. engraved on the back of the locket. He'd given it to her. I expect he'd stolen it and had it engraved. Ignatius enjoyed thieving from an early age. Anyway, he and my mother were young when they had me. Priscilla told me when I questioned her later in one of her less confused moments. There had been a terrific row about it at the time. Of course, this was a long time ago and there would be an enormous scandal if people had found out they weren't married . . .

'Eventually, I got the full story out of Priscilla. Alfred and Beryl adopted me, which they were delighted to do. They'd always wanted a baby and they gave me all the love I could ever have wanted. Then Ignatius's father sent him and Georgina away. Separately, of course. Forbade them to be together. Well, I made some investigations after that and discovered that they'd disobeyed that order and instead they met up in Europe and travelled around together. It's interesting that everywhere they went, there seemed to be a spate of thefts at the same time. Soon, they found themselves in Italy at a party in Venice. Where a priceless diamond went missing and I think suspicions were raised. Ignatius and Georgina decided to part ways and scarper. Shortly afterwards Ignatius had to come home – he'd inherited Grimacres and the business and had to be a respectable businessman and get married.

'But he was a person with a secret past. One secret is reasonably easy to keep but more than that it becomes rather tricky. And Ignatius had several – a secret scandal, a secret baby, and a secret career as a sneaky thief. Georgina was paid a lot of money to keep quiet about it all which she very happily did. She had a fabulous life of parties and adventures, but I think she must have come back all these years later because she really wanted the diamond. But ultimately I think it came down to this: Ignatius did not like sharing his precious things and so . . .'

Badger made a horrible mime of someone shooting a bow and arrow.

'So murdering Daddy WAS revenge . . .' said Aunt M, grimly. 'For shooting your mother?'

To our surprise, however, Mr Badger guffawed.

'Revenge?' he cried. 'No . . . Like I said – what did I care? I didn't know who she was. Of course, when I found out, I was glad that my mystery was finally solved. It felt nicely organised in my brain. And naturally it was *rather* unfortunate that Ignatius had shot her with an arrow, but no no, revenge wasn't my motivation . . . I wasn't interested in that at all. I was very interested in something quite different . . .'

Everyone looked at him.

The penny dropped.

'Money!' said Farv.

'The will!' said Uncle Roderick.

'You're . . . *you're* the oldest child!' said Aunt M.

'You'll inherit – nearly everything!' cried Muv forlorn.

Suddenly, Badger changed. He stopped laughing. A darkness fell across his face. The eyes turned ice cold.

'Yes,' he snarled. 'I'd planned on telling you all who I was when Ignatius eventually croaked it. Make it seem like I had stumbled across the information as to who I was completely by chance whilst writing my book, but then on Friday night, when Ignatius suddenly announced his ridiculous plan to marry the next morning, I could see everything crumbling in front of me. This house and most of the fortune too – gone! Suddenly, this Miss Bellissima person would get it all. It's funny – after a life catching criminals, I never thought I would become one. However, I wasn't going to let some interloper get all my money! So, as you all rowed with Lord Ignatius, I sat in the drawing room quietly concocting my plan to take matters into my own hands and find a way to get MY money! It was just as *she* said.'

He pointed at me.

'I hid in that cupboard and waited. I'd found the passageway before you were even born, Bernard, and kept it to myself. I thought about telling you many times but there was something fun about having a little secret all of my own. I never imagined then how useful it would be. My plan had been of course to put the blame on burglars or Giovanna to ensure she never got a penny, but when I heard so many of you wandering about in the night, I decided to lock the office door from the inside. Give the police when they got here a nice little locked-door mystery to solve. Of course, it did mean that someone in the house would eventually be blamed for the murder, which . . .' he sighed, 'was unfortunate. I rather like you all, but it couldn't be helped. I had to do what needed to be done, if you see what I mean. And anyway, with Ignatius dead, the new will he'd made wouldn't count and so the house and the money would come to me!

'It was only later that I saw the opportunity of pinning the murder on Bernard, especially when I discovered that he had been prowling around the house around the time I'd committed the crime. Easier still to steal the cufflink from his room. A cufflink had hit my drink at dinner and I suppose that was what gave me the idea.'

'But why pin it all on Bernard?' asked Muv. 'You've always been quite friendly with each other.'

'Greed,' I said. 'Why stop at getting the house and the money when he could get Farv's share too? Farv wouldn't get anything if he'd killed Grandpa.'

I frowned for a moment, thinking.

'I think in the long run, Mr Badger would have found a way to get you and Uncle Roderick out of the picture too,' I said, looking at Aunt M, 'so he could get ALL of the money, and not just a share of it. Poison, I expect. He has some wasp killer in his garden shed that would do the job marvellously. By chance he'd bought it the day of *The Incident*.'

I looked at Badger, who nodded eagerly.

'Of course, Gregory's arrival threw me a bit,' he said. 'What if he said that he hadn't seen me run over from my house after Edna's scream, or that he hadn't noticed any tracks in the snow? I was unsure how long he'd been outside the house. So I needed to get rid of him too. And my plan would have worked except for Lillian spilling some porridge on her! I knew then that I had to act fast. Those two horrible children were nosing around. I didn't think they'd get anywhere, but it was still a concern. Fortunately I saw an opportunity. I realised what a stinking little nose-poker Edna is. I forbade her to go in the office but purposefully left the door unlocked. I planted the cufflink in the office and left the door open knowing that she' – another angry point at me – 'wouldn't be able to resist snooping. And I was right.'

He thumped his bound fists on the arm of the chair.

'If only I'd remembered that Bernard is left-handed, I'd have gotten away with all of it!' he roared. 'And if it hadn't been for you . . .' he spat, turning to glare at me. Then suddenly he was up on his feet. He started to run towards me but – *wallop!* He crumpled to the floor as Mrs Crumpet's outstretched foot tripped him up.

I turned to look at her and found she was not alone.

'I wouldn't try anything stupid, George,' she said. 'There are some people here that want to speak to you.'

From the floor he looked over his shoulder. There behind Mrs Crumpet was a collection of very snowy, very damp looking people, all bundled up in big coats and each holding a shovel. They'd heard everything from the hall. From amongst them, a small but fierce woman stepped forward, and pulling a thick scarf away from her face, she said, 'I'm Chief Inspector Gladys Truncheon, and I'm arresting you for murder.'

EPILOGUE.
SURPRISES

It's several weeks after all that now and an awful lot of things have happened since then. There have been quite a few surprises too which I'll get to in a minute.

After the police led Badger away from Grimacres that morning, Mrs Crumpet made us all a big pot of fresh tea and opened a fresh packet of biscuits just for me and Archie and told us to tuck in. I could tell she was VERY proud of us both.

Then Muv said: 'I don't really understand how that locket found its way into the pocket of that fur coat?'

'And how you connected it to Mr Badger?' said Miss Ravioli.

I'd been over this with Chief Inspector Gladys of course, but that had been in private in the library. She was ever so interested and seemed to like Charles Darwin so I expect we'll be great chums.

I swallowed a biscuit practically whole before speaking.

'Well, I knew it had been put there around the time of the murder. Then last night I was ferreting in the lining of the coat for what I thought was a stick of rock but it turned out to be a pen. Badger's lost pen, I realised. I worked out that he must have dumped it and the necklace and his coins and things in the pocket of the coat when he was hiding in the cupboard so that he didn't make a noise when he went into the study. You know how he used to jangle everywhere all the time.'

Everyone nodded. Badger hadn't jangled since Friday evening.

I continued – telling them what I'd told Gladys:

'He only remembered he'd put them there when he looked in his pocket for his pen the next morning to make notes and it wasn't there. I had to give him my pencil (which I MIGHT ADD I never got back). I think he must have realised his things were in my coat and that's why he let me get involved with the investigation – he was keeping me close waiting for a chance to get everything back. He never expected me to solve the case. And he had no chance to get everything back because I haven't taken this coat off since Friday!'

Muv looked me up and down and flared her nostrils.

'Hmm . . .' she said. 'Perhaps now you could . . . ?'

I ignored her and took another biscuit.

'Also, the pen had "G. BADGER" engraved on it in tiny letters. I'd missed that. Gladys spotted it just now so I'll give her that one. Would have saved me a bit of time if I'd noticed it!'

'Goodness,' said Aunt M, 'well, that explains that, then. But what *I'd* like to know now is where the family silver went? Did Badger steal it?'

'Oh no,' I said, simply, 'Farv pinched that.'

'EDNA!' cried Muv.

'What?' I said. 'It's true and you know it too, of course! That's what Farv was down here doing when Grandpa was murdered. He didn't have a glass of milk with him when he came back upstairs, and he wasn't murdering Grandpa, so what else could he have been doing?'

Farv sighed and hung his head in shame. 'Yes OK, it's true,' he said. Then he bristled. 'If everything was going to go to er . . . Miss Ravioli with the new will, I thought I should have **something**!'

Aunt M goggled at him.

'I was going to share the money with you both after I'd sold it all,' said Farv, sheepishly.

Uncle Roderick grinned a weaselly grin.

'You sly old thing!' he said. 'Not so different are we, you and I. *My* plan had been to pinch the housekeeping money tin and scarper. That is what I was saying to Gloria when old Big Ears heard me that night. We were both a bit worried that Giovanna was a member of the Bellissima gang who, I . . . er . . . owe a little money to. But if she's really a Ravioli, then we're all right! Well, for a bit . . .'

He flicked my earlobe in what was maybe an affectionate way.

'I told him not to,' said Gloria quietly.

Aunt M pursed her lips and flared her nostrils.

'Well, I'm ashamed of both of you,' she said, and she sent Farv to fetch the silver back right away. He'd hidden it in the old cannon where as a child he used to hide Gappy's umbrella for a lark. Aunt M stood over him with her arms folded until every piece had been put back in the cupboard, and Mrs Crumpet refused to give either Farv or Uncle Roderick pudding at dinner that night.

A few days later the snow thawed enough to make leaving Grimacres a possibility. I was walking along the corridor to my room with Charles Darwin under my arm when I saw Miss Ravioli in her room zipping up her suitcase.

'Are you going?' I said.

'I'm afraid so,' she replied. I felt a bit sad. Since she'd been able to be herself and not Miss Bellissima, she had been great fun. She'd scraped her hair back into a bun and not bothered with anything other than lipstick. We'd spent a long afternoon together roaming the house as she pointed out all the things in the Grimacres Collection that she had been looking for. All of them were here by not necessarily legal means; the Egyptian sarcophaguses, the totem poles, the samurai swords had been looted by Gristles long gone, plus there were a lot of items that had been stolen by Grandpa in his youth.

'They'll have to be returned, you know,' she'd said, gently. And I'd nodded. I understood. I loved them, of course, but they didn't really belong to us.

'I'm sorry you didn't find your grandmother's necklace,' I said. 'Are you sure we've looked everywhere?'

She nodded. 'Everywhere!' she said.

'Did you ever ask Grandpa about it?' I asked.

'Well, I had to be careful. I didn't want to give myself away,' she said, 'but when I did casually get the conversation around to it once, he just said something a bit odd: "I have so many treasures, I must have lost sight of it," or something, then he laughed. Well, cackled really so I think he was tricking me. What he meant though, I don't know!'

Well, I love a challenge so that got me thinking.

Was there a clue there?

It only took me a moment to realise that yes, yes there was.

I ran upstairs to my bedroom, dragging Miss Ravioli and Archie with me.

Then I pointed at the polar bear with the eyepatch. '*Lost sight* . . . get it?'

I got Archie to give me a leg up so I could reach the animal's head then I flipped up the creature's eyepatch. There, instead of an empty hole or a painted glass eye, something sparkled. I reached in and pulled it out. The Eye of the Storm.

I gave it to Miss Ravioli, who gasped with delight and held it to her heart. Then she gave me a lipsticky kiss on the forehead. Now, I usually don't like that sort of behaviour, but I let her off this once because she was obviously a little bit overexcited.

But the biggest surprise of all came the morning after Grandpa's funeral, from Mr Grabbit, Grandpa's solicitor.

He was a small man whose bald head and rather protruding eyes made him look like an irritated seal. He gathered us all around the dining table so that he could read the will.

'I'm very sorry about Ignatius's death,' he said in a voice like a badly played oboe, 'and I'm afraid I think you might all be in for a shock.'

He laid the envelope on the table and we all looked at it. It didn't really concern me, Charles Darwin and I just found watching everyone else rather interesting. The effect of one piece of paper on the grown-ups here was extraordinary! Indeed, Grandpa been murdered for it. Could what was written on it be so explosive?

'Now the good news for you all,' he said, 'is that *yes*, the new will he made doesn't count, because Ignatius didn't manage to get married before he was . . . well . . .'

He went a bit green around the gills as a murmur of relief went around the room.

'So *this* is the old will – although I must ask you to prepare yourselves.'

'Why?' said Muv.

Mr Grabbit pulled a face. 'I think I ought to just open it and read it,' he said.

And so he did. I'd expected a great wodge of paper to come out of it, but instead he removed a single sheet.

He cleared his throat and read:

'HA. HA. HA. None of you useless, good for nothing, horrible little skunks are getting any of my money because I've spent it all. SO THERE! Signed Ignatius Gristle.'

Everyone was shocked. I don't know why – this was Grandpa in a nutshell.

'What does this mean?' asked Aunt M.

'Well,' sighed Mr Grabbit, waving a hand around the cluttered walls of the dining room, 'it would appear that anything he couldn't steal or swindle for the Grimacres collection he bought. He spent money like it was water.'

There was silence.

'There is SOME money though,' continued Mr Grabbit, 'but what there is is mostly tied up in the Jolly BonBon business. And there is this house of course.'

Everyone breathed another sigh of relief.

'So who gets Grimacres? asked Muv. 'Bernard, I presume?'

'Well . . .' said Mr Grabbit again, looking more peevish than ever, 'this is most unusual. MOST unusual, it really is, but well . . . as you saw from Ignatius's note – he hadn't actually made a proper will at all before the new, invalid one. HOWEVER, in this circumstance there is a very ancient Grimacres tradition that deals with this exact problem. It would appear your ancestors have found themselves in this situation before . . .'

Everyone looked at him.

'Well?' said Muv.

Mr Grabbit removed another, very old piece of paper from his briefcase. It was a scroll tied up with ribbon. He unravelled it, cleared his throat again and read:

'In circumstances in which the head of the family refuses to grant an inheritance to anyone or any organisation, upon their death, Grimacres and its contents is awarded to . . .'

Everyone leant in further.

'The youngest member of the family at the time of the deceased's death.'

Silence.

411

Then, as one, everyone turned to look at me.

I could feel the blood pumping in my ears.

I felt a bit dizzy.

I didn't know what to do, so I just picked up Charles Darwin and together we slithered from my seat and lay down under the table.

THE END

ACKNOWLEDGEMENTS

I WOULD LIKE TO THANK ALL THE PEOPLE WHO HELPED ME TO TELL THIS STORY BOTH IN WORDS AND PICTURES AND TO GET IT INTO YOU (THE READER'S) HANDS. THEY ARE LISTED IN THE CREDITS OPPOSITE AND I AM HUGELY GRATEFUL TO EACH OF THEM FOR THE HARD WORK AND ENTHUSIASM THEY ALL BROUGHT TO THIS PROJECT.

I WOULD LIKE TO SAY A SPECIAL THANK YOU TO MY AGENT, TAMLYN FRANCIS AT ARENA ILLUSTRATION, FOR BEING WITH THIS STORY SINCE IT WAS A TINY LITTLE SEEDLING IN MY NOTEBOOK, AND FOR HER TIRELESS SUPPORT AND GUIDANCE. THANK YOU FOR FOREVER LIFTING ME UP WITH YOUR BRILLIANCE (AND MANAGING THE CONSTANT CHAOS THAT IS **THE SCHEDULE**™ WITH SUCH ZEN-LIKE PATIENCE!)

THANK YOU ALSO TO MY LOVELY FRIENDS MATTHEW LAND AND ELIZABETH SINGH FOR BOTH VERY KINDLY AGREEING TO BEING THE VERY FIRST VISITORS TO GRIMACRES. THEIR NOTES AND THOUGHTS ON THE TEXT WHEN IT WAS IN RAGGED BITS WERE INCREDIBLY USEFUL AND ENCOURAGING, AND I AM SO FOREVER GRATEFUL FOR THEIR KINDNESS AND FRIENDSHIP.

FINALLY, MY HEARTFELT THANKS GOES TO MY LOVELY (AND THANKFULLY NOT A BIT LIKE IGNATIUS!) GRANDFATHER, SID.

HE WAS A LIBRARIAN, A TEACHER AND A WRITER. HE WAS ALSO MY MENTOR, CHEERLEADER, INSPIRATION AND DEAREST FRIEND. HE INTRODUCED ME TO THE JOY AND THE POWER OF STORYTELLING, AS WELL AS THE MIND-BOGGLING WORLD OF WHODUNNITS AND GOLDEN-AGE CRIME FICTION. HAD HE NOT SAT ME DOWN AS A CHILD TO WATCH MY FIRST MISS MARPLE ON TV, OR SLIPPED MY VERY FIRST POIROT INTO MY HANDS — THIS BOOK WOULD NOT EXIST.

MANY YEARS AGO, I PROMISED THAT I WOULD WRITE A BOOK JUST FOR HIM, ONE FILLED WITH ALL HIS FAVOURITE THINGS — SNOW, ROARING FIRES, MYSTERY, MURDER AND SILLINESS, AND NOW I HAVE.

AND SO THIS BOOK IS FOR HIM.

CREDITS

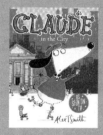

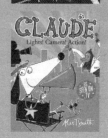

The Adventures of Mr. Penguin

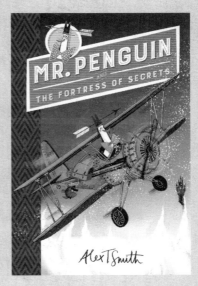
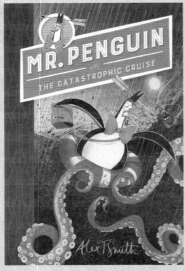
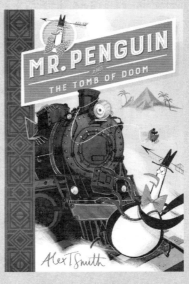

AUTHOR-ILLUSTRATOR

Alex T. Smith

IS THE AWARD-WINNING CREATOR OF THE
BESTSELLING **CLAUDE** SERIES, WHICH IS PUBLISHED
IN 20 LANGUAGES WORLDWIDE, AND IS ON TV.
HE IS ALSO THE CREATOR OF THE CRITICALLY
ACCLAIMED AND MUCH-LOVED **MR. PENGUIN.**

ALEX HAS WON THE UKLA PICTURE BOOK AWARD,
THE WORLD ILLUSTRATION CHILDREN'S BOOK AWARD
AND THE SAINSBURY'S CHILDREN'S BOOK AWARD,
AND BEEN SHORTLISTED FOR THE WATERSTONES
CHILDREN'S BOOK PRIZE. HE HAS ALSO BEEN THE
OFFICIAL WORLD BOOK DAY ILLUSTRATOR.